I0576384

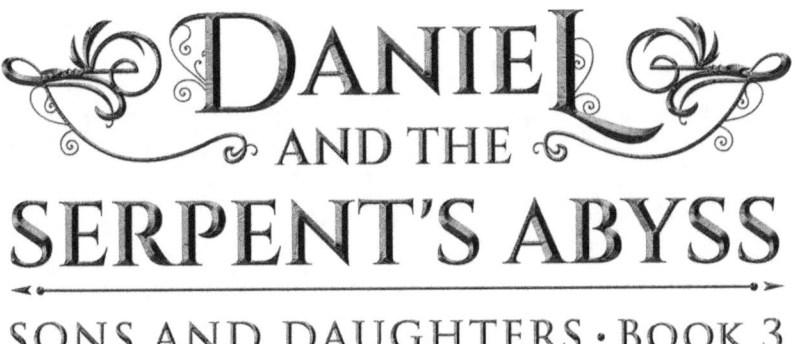

DANIEL
AND THE
SERPENT'S ABYSS

SONS AND DAUGHTERS · BOOK 3

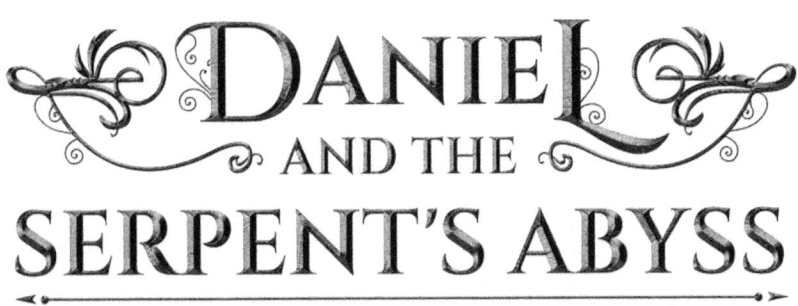

DANIEL
AND THE
SERPENT'S ABYSS

SONS AND DAUGHTERS · BOOK 3

NATHAN LUMBATIS

For other books by Nathan Lumbatis,
including Books One, Two and Four in the
Sons and Daughters series, visit:

nathanlumbatis.com.

Daniel and the Serpent's Abyss
Sons and Daughters Book 3
Published by Dove Christian Publishers
P.O. Box 611
Bladensburg, MD 20710-0611
www.dovechristianpublishers.com

Copyright © 2024 by Nathan Lumbatis

Cover Design by Donika Mishineva

All rights reserved. No part of this publication may be used or reproduced without permission of the publisher, except for brief quotes for scholarly use, reviews or articles.

This is a work of fiction. Names, characters, places, and incidents either are the product of the author's imagination or are used fictitiously. Any resemblance to actual persons, living or dead, events, or locales is entirely coincidental.

Library of Congress Control Number: 2020907201

ISBN: 978-1-7343032-9-2 (paperback)

Printed in the United States of America

For Allison, without whom none of this would be possible.

1

Targets

Seren raised her fiberglass bow and pulled the string back to the corner of her mouth. She waited a moment until the wind, hissing through the trees near Granny's house, died down. "Watch, my young students, and learn from the master."

She let the string snap forward, sending an arrow in a smooth arc straight toward the bullseye. Five wobbly concentric circles were painted in white on the side of a makeshift target made of old bales of pine straw and boxes piled six feet high.

"That's how it's done." She flipped silky, blond hair over her shoulder and sauntered past Daniel, tossing him the bow as she passed.

"That's how it's done," Daniel muttered, imitating Seren's voice. "'Master' my foot."

Seren whipped her head around and drew herself up to her full height. At eighteen, she wasn't quite as tall as Daniel, despite being three years older. Her lithe frame and piercing blue eyes nevertheless spoke of authority and fierce intelligence. "What was that, Daniel?"

"Nothing. Here goes!"

Daniel nocked an arrow and pulled the string back. As soon as he felt his hand touch his cheek, he let it snap forward. The arrow sailed through the air and hit just outside the outermost ring. He looked down at the bow. "I think there's something wrong with this stupid thing."

"There's something wrong with the archer," Seren replied flatly. "You just need to practice more."

Daniel handed the bow back to her. "Oh sure, I'll squeeze it in between sword practice, homework, chores, and saving the world. How's six Tuesdays from never sound?"

Seren ignored him and turned to Ben, who was sitting at the base of a tree reading through something on his phone. "Your turn."

Ben pushed a curl of black hair out of his eyes and stood. He slid the phone into his back pocket before taking the bow from Seren. "Daniel. Arrow, please."

Daniel trotted to the target and yanked the arrow out of a pine bale. He hurled it like a spear toward the ground in front of Ben.

Ben jumped back in surprise and immediately transformed into the Triune Shield.

Daniel doubled over in laughter. "Skittish much?" he roared between guffaws.

Ben's defensive and angry voice shouted from inside the shield where his body was outlined between the three intersecting rings. "You get shot and killed by the Bolt of Pestilence and see how skittish you are. I need my feet, in case you haven't noticed! Geez. Next time hand it to me like a normal human, you dweeb." "Duh. Practice arrows aren't sharp," Daniel replied, wiping tears from his eyes.

Ben returned to normal in the next moment and stooped down to grab the arrow. "Oh, okay. I'll just use you for target practice then. Stand still."

"Just shoot. I want to see how terrible you are."

"Bet I can at least hit inside the rings."

Daniel snorted. "It's harder than you think. But sure, give it your best shot."

"Thanks for your confidence."

"You guys are such children," Seren said, both hands on her hips. "Can you go five minutes without trying to one-up each other? Just shoot!"

"So pushy." Ben raised the bow and drew back the string in one smooth motion. Since coming back from his quest to retrieve the Triune Shield, he'd been practicing martial arts with Daniel. The activity had added muscle to his wiry, thirteen-year-old frame, but he was still lanky. He waited a moment while adjusting his aim and let the string snap forward. The arrow sank into a box just outside the bullseye.

"Hey, look at that, Daniel!" Ben dropped the bow to the ground and pointed both index fingers at the target. "Look how terrible I was. Oh, wait. That was you. I actually hit the target. Boom."

"Hey, I hit the target, too," Daniel retorted.

Seren reached down to pick up the bow and dusted it off with an irritated glance at Ben. "Outside the rings doesn't count, Daniel. Ben, can I see your phone for a minute?"

"Hear that, Daniel?" Ben cupped a hand around his ear. "Outside the rings—"

"I heard. Shut your trap."

Ben flashed Daniel a smug grin as he moonwalked toward Seren and handed her his phone. "Here. What do you need it for?"

She promptly dropped it in the dirt and kicked it around a little.

"What—what are you doing?" He dove toward the phone and grabbed it before Seren could kick it again. "What's your problem?"

"Oh, I thought we were playing the Drop-Other-People's-Belongings-In-The-Dirt Game. No? My mistake." She raised the bow and brushed off the dust toward Ben.

Ben growled something under his breath and shuffled back to the base of the tree while Seren resumed target practice with a satisfied grin.

Daniel sauntered toward Ben and heaved a contented sigh. "Ah. What goes around comes around. Right, Ben?"

Ben grunted and focused on his phone.

Daniel lay down and ran hands through bushy, brown hair before resting them behind his head. The air felt cool and crisp, and the woods were beginning to change color. The forest floor behind

Granny's house was carpeted with recently fallen leaves, making a mottled bed for Daniel as he stretched out his long legs and gazed at the sky. Glimpses of vibrant blue peeked through a net of dark gray and brown branches, dotted with the autumn oranges, reds, and yellows of leaves yet to fall.

A brisk wind blew through the trees and into the open windows of Granny's tiny, ivy-covered house. Memories came to life within the shadows of the curtains, and Daniel found himself replaying his, Ben, and Seren's time in India.

The quest had been six months ago, and that meant six months since they had seen Raylin. Daniel pictured her as she had last appeared: hair a shock of white, right arm fused with the Voidblade, flying on inky wings, desperate and driven mad by the overwhelming evil of the Enemy's spirit. He searched the sky through the branches and twigs, their dull gray reflected in his brown eyes. What was he expecting? A fiery message in the sky from the Three telling him where she was? Raylin to fall out of thin air? Granny to come flying by on her broom?

He turned over on his side, one arm tucked under his head. An empty feeling settled into his stomach. Everything around him fell quiet, and he suddenly realized it had been some time since he'd heard the sound of Seren's arrow hitting the target. He raised his head and looked down past his feet. She was standing beside the target with her hand, motionless, on an arrow stuck in one of the outer rings.

Seren was probably thinking about Raylin too. She never missed the bullseye unless she was distracted. There were few times she wasn't thinking about her sister, anyway.

Daniel tapped Ben's foot with his own and nodded toward her.

Ben looked up from his phone. He followed Daniel's gaze to Seren, still lost in thought. "I don't blame her. It's torture for her to wait," he whispered, immediately taking in Daniel's thoughts. "I don't get why the Father is waiting. Why doesn't he call for us to start the quest already?"

Seren seemed to remember herself and finally pulled the arrow free before returning to her shooting point.

Daniel turned his head to look deeper into the forest. He could just barely make out the rising slope of Pedestal Hill through the trees and half expected to see Granny waltzing down it any moment. Nothing moved but flitting birds and cautious squirrels digging in the ground for acorns. "I don't know. With all the Babylonian Seal stuff, I'm not sure why it didn't begin right away."

"It's like the Three are waiting for things to get worse," Ben said, the words ending with a sigh. "Look." He tossed his phone to Daniel.

A news feed was pulled up on the screen. It detailed conflict around the world: bombings in London, wars all over the Middle East, guerilla skirmishes in Peru, persecution of Christians in India. There was more, but Daniel skimmed over it as he scrolled down the webpage. One story caught his eye. The United States was pulling out all its troops stationed in the Middle East and pledging billions of dollars per year to support some new peacekeeping organization called Ealim Wahid. Daniel's mouth moved as he tried to silently say the words.

Must be Arabic or something.

He clicked on a photo embedded in the article. It showed the two leaders spearheading the group. A man—tall, dark-haired, olive complexion, deep-set eyes, and dressed in a perfectly tailored suit—smiled as he gestured toward a woman to his right. She was about the same height with features so similar, Daniel guessed they were twins. She wore a suit of the same color, though hers sported a tight, knee-length skirt instead of pants. Thick hair cascaded down one shoulder and all the way to her waist. Both were muscular and had a look of fierce intelligence. But something was off. They looked almost too perfect and put-together, while their dark brown eyes were dull, lifeless, and empty—almost not human.

Like a shark's eyes, Daniel thought. And then a chill went down his spine. *Or a Creep's.*

He studied the photo a minute longer. No talons, no fangs. If they were Creeps, they were hiding it well.

He read a few more lines of the article and caught details about their headquarters being in some city in Iraq called Tell Abu Shahrain. They were working out of existing government structures but were also constructing new headquarters just outside the city. A photo of the unfinished building showed a hulking tower of steel beams and cement.

Daniel slowly pronounced the city out loud. "Tell Abu Shahrain?"

"Bless you," Ben said. "Can I have my phone back now?"

"Just a sec." Daniel didn't look up but skimmed the rest of the article for any other pictures.

Seren leaned her practice bow and the quiver against the tree and joined the boys on the ground. She nodded toward the phone. "Something interesting?"

Daniel shrugged. "I don't know. Just weird random stuff happening all over the world. Seren, Babylon is modern-day Iraq, right?"

She nodded. "Yeah, and when I was working with the Enemy, we'd go there a lot. But it was strange; his plans never went particularly well." She shuddered. "I mean, don't get me wrong. I remember him doing some terrible things, but whenever we were there, his strategies would get messed up. And he could never stay long because he would get too edgy and scattered."

Ben stretched his arms above his head and yawned. "He's always seemed a little edgy. I mean, let's be real here, he IS evil incarnate. Little insane, if you ask me."

"This was different," Seren replied. "He was confused sometimes and flew off the handle for no reason."

"Do you think it was the Babylonian Seal thingy?" Ben asked lazily as he closed his eyes.

Daniel nodded matter-of-factly. "Right. That's where the Enemy lost his power, so he's trying to get it back."

"Not exactly 'lost,'" Seren said. She pulled her ponytail over one shoulder and twirled a few strands of hair. "When the Enemy first deceived the Earthborn, he claimed that land as his own. It's kind of like he marked his territory by pouring a lot of his power into the earth there."

Daniel snickered toward Ben. "Like a dog. What a weirdo!"

"Say that to his face the next time we see him. I dare you."

"Oh, man. He'd lose his mind." Daniel sat up and plopped the phone in his lap.

Seren took an exaggerated breath. "Hey, kindergartners. Focus."

"Oh, come on," Daniel pleaded. "You were thinking the same thing."

Seren stared back, unblinking.

"Eh … never mind. Please continue."

"Putting power into the land was kind of like he was building a fortress—like a king sitting behind his castle walls surrounded by his weapons. But the Enemy doesn't have limitless power like the Three."

"Wait a minute." Ben leaned forward, a look of dread on his face. "Does that mean he's going to get stronger when he's there?"

"Kind of," Seren explained. "It's more like his power is more focused. It's the difference between using a hammer on a nail versus a rock. You're still the one doing the work, all your power is just more focused on one point if you use a hammer."

Daniel narrowed his eyes as he tried to work this out. "I guess that makes sense. I wonder how that's going to change things when we have to fight him."

Seren drew a long breath and nodded, the question clearly on her mind as well. A few leaves floated down from the sparse canopy above. Seren shot out a willowy hand and caught one as it spun its way to the ground. "Well, the Father put a lot of his children in Babylon … Iraq … over the last several thousand years. Their prayers formed a barrier which kept the Enemy from getting at his power there. You could say it locked him out of his fortress. When you were searching for the Triune Shield, didn't you learn that prayer is powerful? I guess we better start praying."

"Yeah. It doesn't change the fact that it's still scary, though," Daniel said.

Ben clapped his hands. "Oh, now I get it! Babylonian Seal!" He nodded his head and leaned closer to Seren like he was sharing a special secret. "It 'sealed' the Enemy out. Not 'seal' like an Arrr!-Arrr!-Arrr!-I-want-some-fish kind of seal. It's like an 'I'm sealing this Ziploc bag,' seal."

Daniel and Seren looked at each other, then stared back at Ben.

"Sure," Daniel replied, shaking his head. "Ziploc bag."

Seren sighed in disgust. "I'm surrounded by preschoolers."

"I thought it was kindergartners?" Ben said.

Seren snapped her head toward the target and squinted her eyes.

"Something wrong?" Daniel asked, following her gaze.

"No," she said absently after a few moments. "Just a squirrel behind the target, I guess. Daniel's the kindergartner." She nodded to Ben. "You're the preschooler."

Seren leisurely scanned the woods, eventually standing to lean against the tree. "Anyway, it's different now. Most Christians are gone, and the Seal is weakening, if it hasn't vanished entirely. The Enemy has probably already moved back."

Daniel shuddered. He didn't want to think what the Enemy would be like once he was even *more* powerful. The image of the great seven-headed dragon, rearing over the plains in India, flashed through his mind. He and the other Vessels were supposed to fight him and somehow seal away his spirit. He shook his head. That still seemed impossible.

"Can I have my phone back now?" Ben repeated.

"No. You're addicted. Just hang on a sec." Daniel showed Seren the pictures on the screen. "Know these guys?"

Seren glanced at the screen and shook her head. "Should I?"

"I don't know," Daniel mumbled with a shrug. "Something's not right with them." He read to the end of the article and caught a few more details. In addition to peacekeeping between countries in the Middle East, Ealim Wahid would also work on preserving archaeological sites in the area, beginning with the oldest known Babylonian city of Eridu. A map showed the ruins of the city less than a mile from their new building. "They're talking about Babylon, too. They seem suspicious."

Seren took the phone and read the last part of the article. She nodded. "Definitely suspicious, and we're stuck here with nothing to do but twiddle our thumbs and wait."

Ben threw his hands in the air. "Is this Steal Ben's Phone Day or something? Don't you all have your own?" He pushed himself to his feet and held out his hand.

Seren pretended to hand the phone back to Ben but passed it to Daniel at the last second. "Yours, I believe."

"Correct. Kind of you to notice," Daniel replied. He slid the phone into his pocket.

Ben stuck out his jaw and growled. "I'm going to kill you both. It's like I have two annoying older siblings now. Phone!"

Daniel shied away in a look of pretend fright. "Oh, no! What are you going to do? *Shield* us to death?"

Seren broke out into laughter. "That's a good one. Congratulations, Daniel. You've graduated to middle school now."

He snorted and was about to finally surrender the phone to Ben when it vibrated. Daniel glanced at the screen and saw a text message. He slid it to the right and read:

World News Update
County Sligo, Ireland: More sightings of a large bird flying over the countryside at dusk. Creature reportedly dug a hole in Carrowmore Cemetery. Fifth sighting this week. Locals baffled and alarmed. Click here for the full story.

Daniel touched the link. The article began with a fuzzy photo of a huge, winged shape, dark against the evening sky, hovering over a field. "Thank goodness you signed up for creepy news updates, Ben. I'd hate to not know about the baffled locals of Ireland." He held up the screen so Ben could see.

Ben snatched the phone back and punched Daniel in the shoulder. "I want to know what's happening in the world," he retorted, his tone icy, "since we have to save it and all. I'm never letting you borrow my phone again. By the way, that's the fifth time this week that weird bird has appeared, and—"

"Duh. I can read."

"*And*," Ben continued, drawing out the word, "each sighting has been in an ancient ruin or some old cemetery."

Seren squatted next to Daniel, her elbows on her thighs. "You think this has something to do with the Enemy?"

"Not the Enemy." Ben tapped his screen, enlarged the photo, then turned his phone sideways. He held it out for Seren to see the blurred photo of the bird. "I think it has something to do with Raylin."

Seren eagerly studied the picture.

Daniel squinted his eyes, trying to find Raylin's features in the pixilated image.

The phone *dinged,* and a text from Mrs. Jones peeked down from the top of the screen before sliding back up.

Come home. Important.

Daniel focused back on the picture. "Could be her." He wasn't truly sure, but Seren looked so hopeful that he didn't have the heart to say it out loud.

Ben shoved the phone in his back pocket and shrugged. "Maybe. The other day I was praying to find her, and the article about the first sighting popped up on my phone. I could be reading too much into it, but I think it's a sign."

"So what if it is?" Seren stood, her mouth drawn tight. "We still have to wait on the Three. And while we wait for the Father to give the 'Okay' for the quest to begin, Raylin's out there suffering. Wandering through graveyards or something."

Daniel looked at Ben and nodded toward Seren. They both got to their feet and moved closer to her.

"Seren," Daniel began, trying to make his tone as soft and reassuring as he could, "look, we don't even know if this really is Raylin. But the Father will send us a sign when the time is right. If it is, we at least have a clue about where she is, and we know that she's okay."

Ben smiled, his dark blue eyes warm with compassion. "Trust us. We've been through two quests now, and things have always worked out."

"For you two, you mean." Seren kept her head down and glanced at Daniel and Ben from the corners of her eyes. "Me and Raylin haven't been so lucky. Both of us were enslaved to the Enemy most of our lives, remember? And now she's wandering, lost and driven out of her mind."

She opened her mouth to say more, but then stopped and took a deep breath. She stood silently as she stared, unfocused, toward the target. "Sorry. I know," she paused, "I'm supposed to trust the Three. It's just still new to me, and when I think things are going wrong, the old me pops up."

Daniel gave a dismissive wave. "I get it. It's hard to wait." Against his will, his mind drifted to Gabriela. He gave a slight shake of the head to ground himself in the matter at hand. "Just … uh … just choose to trust that the Father loves you and will work things out at the right time." He tilted his head. He actually *felt* what he was saying was true. He wasn't even faking it. "Besides, if the *old* you was popping up, Ben and I would be running."

"Right on," Ben added. "Speaking of running, we better head home."

"Hello?" a deep voice shouted from the front of the house. "Anybody home? I, uh, have some popcorn I'm selling, and it's good, or something." A loud series of knocks shook the tiny home.

Daniel and Ben looked at each other. They knew the sound of that fist anywhere.

2

Ham Fists and Family Reunions

Seren missed the boys' exchange and broke away toward the front of the house. Daniel and Ben quickly followed.

A broad, muscled figure hulked on the front porch. Her brown hair was put up in a sloppy bun on top of her head, and she stood a little over six feet tall. Daniel was normally the height of seniors in his school, but Gator still dwarfed him. She pulled back a hammy fist to pound on the door again but noticed them walking around to the front of the porch. Her eyes fell on Daniel and Ben, and her already low forehead seemed to cover her eyes entirely as they bunched together and darkened. She pursed her lips and frowned at the same time. The overall appearance made her look like some human/Shih Tzu hybrid.

As soon as Daniel's eyes fell on her, he sensed a gentle "nudge" from the Three. There was something important about Gator, or something she needed to hear. One glance at Ben told Daniel he had felt the same thing. He had a far-off look in his eyes and seemed momentarily distracted.

"I-I didn't realize you had company," Gator stammered in Seren's direction. "I'll come back another time."

Seren joined her on the porch before she could step off. Daniel stayed in the yard. He'd been in one too many tight spaces with Gator to risk being cornered now.

Ben stood on the steps and waved at her. "Hey, Gator. You back with your dad now?"

Gator blushed. "Yeah," she snapped. "You going to make fun of me or something?"

Ben took a step back. "No. I was just wondering. Honest."

Gator looked back and forth between both boys and made to dash off the porch to leave. Seren held out a hand. "Wait. You haven't shown me the popcorn yet."

"The what?" Gator seemed to remember the now wadded-up order form in her fist. "Oh. I'm … uh … selling Christmas popcorn. It's some stupid fundraiser my school is doing for our senior trip. I have to sell it, or I can't afford to …" She tossed a wary glance at Daniel. "Uh, everyone has to sell it. Here." She shoved the crumpled sheets into Seren's hand.

Seren took it and pried open the order form. "These look amazing. But—wow, they're expensive. I'm sorry, I don't have that much money. Wish I did, though."

Gator seized the form back and shoved it in her pocket as she stomped off the porch. "Knew I shouldn't have come here," she muttered. "Stupid Dad made me."

She tried to push past Daniel. "Go ahead. Have a good time laughing."

Daniel snatched the form and scanned the photos.

"Hey!" Gator protested. "What do you think you're doing? You looking for a black eye?"

"Ben. Look at these. They're smothered in chocolate! You think Mom and Dad would order some for us?"

"I said, give it—wait. What?"

Ben took the form from Daniel. "Mom's a sucker for chocolate covered anything. Gator, why don't you bring this to—" He lay a hand on her well-muscled shoulder. "Good grief! You're like a rock. How much are you working out these days?"

Gator shook off his hand and looked uncomfortable with the compliment.

"Sorry. Why don't you bring this to our house? Our mom would love to buy some."

"Yeah, Gator," Daniel chimed in. "We were just heading home now, anyway." Another nudge from the Three, this time strong and urgent. A prickly sensation trickled down his spine. "Seren, too."

Seren raised her eyebrows and looked sideways at Daniel. "I was?"

"Yes," Daniel answered emphatically. For some reason, it was very important that all four of them leave quickly. He wasn't sure if it was because they needed to be home, or just away from Granny's house. Either way, it was clear they were to go immediately. "Yes, you were. I don't know why, but you were." He gestured toward the sky with his thumbs and shrugged.

"Oh, right. Yep, I sure was. Heading that way now, actually."

Ben watched their exchange. "Did I miss something?" he whispered toward Daniel.

Daniel cleared his throat. "I'll explain later," he muttered. "But we need to hurry."

Gator stared at all three and sneered. "If this is some kind of prank, I'm going to—"

"Tie us into knots?" Daniel interrupted. He grabbed the order form from Ben and trotted toward his house. Ben fell in step behind him. "Beat us within an inch of our lives with your skull-studded belt?"

Gator ran after them. "Bring back that form! And I don't have a skull-studded belt!"

"Why not?" Ben called back. "It'd match the whole Brutal Amazon look you have going on. You should definitely get one."

Seren brought up the rear, but easily sprinted past the lumbering Gator and caught up with Daniel. Her face was lit up with excitement. "Did you hear something from the Father? Is our quest about to begin?"

"Shhh! Not so loud," Ben hissed, waving at Seren. He glanced back at Gator, but she didn't seem to notice.

"I don't want to sell your dumb family my popcorn!" she wheezed. Apparently, she didn't mix much cardio into her workout routine.

"But our mom will want to buy some. I'm sure of it!" Daniel shouted. He turned to Ben and Seren, still jogging next to him, and lowered his voice. "Look, I don't know why, but the Three wanted us to leave Granny's house. That's all I know." He paused to catch his breath. "No idea if this is the start of the quest. Did you guys not feel anything?"

The dormers of the Jones's house came into view over the trees lining the street. Daniel jumped over the curb and onto the sidewalk. He looked back to see if Gator was still following them. She was, but something else caught his eye, too. In the woods back toward Granny's house, there was a dark pulse. It was the only way he could think to describe it. It lasted only a second and was as if all the colors in the woods had temporarily faded darker before returning to normal. He didn't think any servant of the Enemy would dare attack Granny's directly.

His stomach went cold.

No *ordinary* servant of the Enemy, anyway. One of his Generals might. Or a monster as powerful as Ravana or the Pitwolf.

"I just felt something," Ben whispered. He'd gone pale.

Seren nodded. "Me, too. What was that?"

"I have no idea. But—"

"Stop bullying my daughter!" someone bellowed in a gravelly, hysterical voice.

Daniel snapped his head behind him and saw that a shaggy caveman wearing three-sizes-too-small running shorts, a skin-tight tank top, a tennis headband, and flip-flops with knee-high socks, had joined the chase. Crimson hair, like fuzzy flames, bristled out from his body in every conceivable direction. A cheap, red toupee streamed out behind his head, flopping wildly in the wind.

"Where did The Barth come from?" Ben shouted. "Seriously! Did he just jump out of a trashcan or something?"

"Dad, quit following me around the neighborhood!" Gator commanded. "I can take care of myself."

Barth fell in step behind his daughter as the entire group

reached the Jones's yard. "I have to keep an eye on you, dear." He fell to his knees and gasped for breath, the brief burst of running too much for him. "I'm not going to let that nag of a social worker Ms. Julie accuse me of being a bad parent again!" he said in loud bursts between labored breaths.

"Hello, Mr. Gurge." Ms. Julie stood up from the front porch swing, where she, Alan, and Mariah Jones were sitting. Her stormy gray eyes flashed down at Barth.

Barth's face blanched white. "Why are … you better not … aren't you a surprise … a *nice* surprise!" His voice cracked and went two octaves higher as he stuttered out the barely comprehensible statement.

Gator skidded to a halt and froze, her eyes pinned on Ms. Julie as if she were a rattlesnake ready to strike.

Daniel ran up the front porch steps and into Ms. Julie's open arms. Despite his years desperately wishing to leave the Holy Moses Home for Bleeding Heart Orphans, she had always been like a mother to him. He was taller than she was now, and when they broke away, she stepped back and reached up to tousle his hair. "Hey, Daniel. How've you been?" Her voice was calm and reassuring.

"Good!" he said. "So good. It's awesome living with Mom and Dad." He let his eyes fall on his adoptive parents, still sitting in porch chairs adjacent to the swing. They were barely smiling and kept glancing at each other. His mother craned her neck to look out over the yard, her long, black hair tucked behind one ear. After a moment, her icy-blue eyes flitted back to his and held it as though searching his mind.

"Is something wrong?" Daniel looked back at Ms. Julie and noticed for the first time that she looked much older. Worry lines wrinkled the corners of her eyes, and streaks of gray and white snaked through her once dark hair. "I don't have to leave home, do I? Am I in trouble?" Daniel felt as though his stomach was about to flip.

Ben had been hovering near the porch steps, but once he heard Daniel's question, he was immediately at his shoulder. "What? Daniel has to leave?"

Seren, expressionless, watched the exchanges from the yard. Gator and Barth hung back just behind her.

"Serves him right," Barth muttered to Gator. "After all the trouble he caused."

"Oh my, no!" Ms. Julie exclaimed. "Goodness gracious. You kids (and adults)"—she looked hard at Barth—"sure are quick to jump to conclusions!"

Barth withered under her stare and hid behind Gator, who rolled her eyes at her father's skulking.

"I came by because I have some interesting news," Ms. Julie continued. "But, perhaps, it would be better to discuss it without an audience."

The front door was flung open, and Janice stuck her head out. She rubbed the corners of her eyes and yawned. "Heavens. What's all the excitement about? Oh, hello, everyone. Look at all the company we suddenly have! Such a surprise." Her voice was a nasally barrage. "I simply *love* sitting with family on the porch and chatting." She suddenly produced her knitting bag as if it had been waiting just inside the door for her to grab in an emergency, and she stumbled out onto the porch. Her blue eyes, made giant through coke-bottle glasses, flitted back and forth until they alighted on a rocking chair on the other side of the porch. "That'll do," she muttered to herself. "I can still be a part of the conversation there. Just like the good old days. Front porches, knitting, family. How terribly grand." She plopped down in the chair, adjusted her pants, which were pulled up too high, and flung frizzy, dull red hair out of her freckled face with both hands. Her knitting needles were out in a flash, and she was busy clicking away before anyone could respond.

"Um," Ms. Julie's voice trailed off as she looked back and forth between Daniel, the Joneses, Seren, the Gurges, and Janice.

"It's okay," Daniel said. "Janice and Seren are family."

Mrs. Jones gestured toward Janice. "That's my cousin. She's living in our spare bedroom until she can find a house in the neighborhood. Seren is a neighborhood friend."

Everyone turned around and looked at the Gurges. Barth squirmed under the scrutiny.

"We're just here to sell popcorn," Gator said defiantly. "I never would've come except that little, snot-faced …"

Barth's hand flew to Gator's shoulder. He mumbled something from behind her massive back, and Gator changed her tone.

"I only came because Daniel has my order form. I need it back."

"Please," Barth intoned.

"Please." Gator growled the word and stared at the ground like she wanted to beat it up.

Daniel felt a nudge from the Three again. What was happening? They're supposed to leave Granny's because of some strange presence, and he's supposed to be nice to Gator? Between that and Ms. Julie's cryptic visit, he was thoroughly confused. "Give me a second," he said to Ms. Julie and his parents. He jumped off the front porch and walked up to Gator.

"Listen, I'm sure my mom will buy some popcorn. Just come by later. You don't even have to talk to me or Ben when you do."

Gator stared. "Why are you dweebs being so nice? This some sort of joke?"

Barth's flaming red hair poked out from behind her right shoulder. "Don't trust them, Dear." He gave his best shot at whispering, but his raspy voice grated its way across the yard. "He's just trying to look good for that witch, Ms. Julie."

"I'm still here," Ms. Julie said in a singsong voice. She waved at Barth. "And I can hear everything you're saying."

Barth threw up his hands and darted out of the yard like he'd been stung by a bee. "Run, Gator!" he screamed over his shoulder. "She's calling the judge! Meet at our ren-dez-voos spot!" His voice trailed off as he made his way further down the road toward his house. "I'll pack the bags!"

Gator gritted her teeth and silently turned on her heel to leave.

"Popcorn?" Janice looked up from her handiwork. She stood and fumbled off the front porch, still clicking her needles. Her knitting bag hung from one arm. "I hope it's that yummy, chocolate-covered kind that every kid sells before Christmas." Daniel handed her the order form, which she pinned between her thumbs and needles. Her giant eyes studied the page. "These look scrumptious. I'll walk you home ... Gator, was it? I've got my checkbook in my knitting bag. Oh my! Caramel with sea salt is my favorite."

Gator looked stunned by the onslaught of kindness and obediently marched toward her house, with Janice chattering away as though nothing interested her more than holiday popcorn.

"Well, now that there are no more—uh—distractions," Ms. Julie said, leaning against the house, "we can have a chat."

"Daniel," Mr. Jones's voice was calm but serious. "Come sit. We have something to talk to you about." His eyes were a perfect match for Ben's; his hair was closer to Daniel's brown, but normally brushed neatly to the side. Now, however, it was disheveled, as if he'd been nervously rubbing his temples.

Mrs. Jones stood. "Seren, I'm sorry, but maybe it would be best if you went home."

Ben snapped his head toward Daniel. Seren looked at both boys and raised her eyebrows. Daniel knew they were all thinking about the strange dark pulses and terrible presence they had felt at Granny's. If the Enemy had sent something to the neighborhood, they needed to stay together.

"I'd like Seren to stay," Daniel blurted out. "Because ..." he looked at Ben.

"Granny wanted her out of the house for a while," Ben said. He flashed a self-satisfied smile. "There's some kind of surprise she didn't want her seeing yet."

Daniel was impressed with Ben's quick thinking. It wasn't a lie, really. They had told his parents that Seren was Granny's relative to explain her sudden presence in the neighborhood after the last quest, which was also true. They were all a part of the Celestial Family, after all; they never said how distant of a relative she was. And Granny, wherever she might be, probably didn't want Seren at her house because of whatever monstrous problem awaited them there.

"Oh, okay," Mrs. Jones replied. "If you're sure."

Daniel nodded. "I'm sure."

"Then come have a seat. Ms. Julie has some important news to tell you."

All three kids joined the Joneses and Ms. Julie on the front porch. Mr. Jones beckoned for Daniel to sit between him and Mrs. Jones on the swing. Ben and Seren took a chair, while Ms. Julie stayed standing.

"Daniel," Ms. Julie began. "About a month ago, I received a letter from your biological mother."

Daniel's heart skipped a beat, and a surge of complex emotions flooded his body. Excitement, hope, fear, confusion—those and about a thousand thoughts deadlocked his mind at once. He sat in stunned silence, his mouth slightly agape.

His dad put a hand on his shoulder and gave it a reassuring squeeze. His mom, however, looked troubled.

Ms. Julie pulled out the letter. "She's been trying to find you for the past couple of months. Child and Family Services has certain policies in place when this happens, of course, so we couldn't just put her in touch with you right away. The first is for me to call the parent back and interview them. You understand, of course. I had to make sure she was … um … healthy."

"You talked to her?" Daniel blurted out. "What was she like?"

Ms. Julie gently laughed at Daniel's eagerness. "Very nice, and she seems stable. Both important things when parents want to reconnect with their children." Her expression softened into one of pity. "But there's more. Your father." Ms. Julie paused.

Daniel leaned forward. Was his father looking for him too? It was like a dream. Growing up in the orphanage, he constantly fantasized about his parents searching for him. Somewhere, out in the world, they were desperately trying to find him. They had never meant to leave him for so long; it had all been a misunderstanding. And one day—one day soon—they would barge into Ms. Julie's office and demand that he be allowed to come home.

As these thoughts crowded in on him, there was a check in his heart. Did he really want to leave Ben? Could he imagine a life without the Joneses? Somehow, despite the longstanding desire to be with his biological parents, his excitement changed into a complicated, bittersweet, Janice-type tangle of feelings.

"Your father died a little over a year ago, in the summer." Ms. Julie's statement broke in on his thoughts like a splash of ice-cold water. "I know that must come as a shock. You probably feel confused, and I know you were hoping to see him too. That's normal for any adoptee."

Daniel tuned out as Ms. Julie continued talking in reassuring tones, trying to comfort him with her vast knowledge about what foster children and adoptees experience in such situations. But his mind was somewhere else. Slowly, irresistibly, it was drawn to one particular memory from his quest in Peru. He stood at Intipunku, and the Father was taking his anger from him. In return, he was filled with the Father's purifying power. It was then that Daniel felt he had truly become a son.

The Father's voice filled Daniel's mind. *That day, your earthly father cried out to me and was purified of his anger and pride before he died. He came to me the same moment you accepted me as your Heavenly Father.*

Daniel realized Ms. Julie had stopped talking, and everyone was staring at him. His cheeks were wet with tears he didn't even know were falling. He looked down and wiped them away.

His dad pulled him into a side hug, searching his face with dark blue eyes, but saying nothing.

Mrs. Jones dabbed her eyes and sniffled. "I knew this would be too hard for him." She fixed Ms. Julie with a stare that was half pleading, half accusatory. "Maybe we should keep talking another day."

"No," Daniel said in a quiet voice. "I'm fine, really." How could he explain that his tears weren't just from sadness, but also from relief? He now knew he would see his biological father again. One day, at least, when he went to be with the Three in Heaven.

He looked around and found Ben and Seren watching him intently. Daniel nodded at them. "It's good. I know he's in a better place now."

Seren gave a faint smile, and Ben tapped his ears. Had they heard the Father's voice? Good. For some reason, it felt right to have them experience this with him. He turned back to Ms. Julie. "What else did my biological mom say?"

"Well, it turns out your father had a life insurance policy. He named your mother as the beneficiary, but his will indicated that he wanted you to have half. She'd like to bring the money to you and your parents if you're interested in meeting her."

"Of course! Yes!" Daniel stood abruptly, rocking the swing back so that its swing forward caught him in the back of the knees and jolted him. He didn't notice. "When is she coming? Mom, Dad?" He spun around. "Can she stay with us?" His mom suddenly looked panicked. His father's face remained a chiseled, somber mask. "What's wrong?"

"You can't leave us." It was Ben. He grabbed Daniel's arm. "Even if she is your biological mother, you're a part of *our* family now. It wouldn't be fair if you just left to live with her."

Daniel immediately saw the same fears reflected in his parents' eyes.

Ms. Julie's reassurance spilled out faster than he could respond. "Oh my, no! Is that what you all have been worried about? I should've led off with that. Adoptions can't just be undone because a biological parent shows up. No. Daniel is your son, period. Now, if all parties agree, arrangements could be made for a regular visitation plan. But that's not really what this first meeting is about."

Daniel leaned against the porch railing. "I don't want to leave anyway," he said flatly. "This is where I'm supposed to be, but I do want to meet her."

Mrs. Jones let out an audible sigh of relief and buried her face in her hands. She pulled a wad of tissue from her pocket, wiped her face, and then looked up.

"If you think it's a good idea," Mr. Jones said, scooting closer to his wife on the swing, "then we support Daniel's wishes, but I want to talk to her first. I want to know what kind of person she is, what she wants, and what kinds of things she'll say. I want to know why she gave Daniel up in the first place."

Daniel stiffened. Inti had once explained this, in the secret chamber under Coricancha. The Enemy had somehow influenced his biological father to abandon his mother. Alone with a new-born, and probably desperate, his mother was then pressured by the Enemy to give him up. What lies had he whispered into his mother's mind? Daniel felt white-hot hatred well up inside him as he imagined the Enemy manipulating his parents, all so Daniel would feel neglected and be easily drawn into his service—all for revenge against the Father.

Ms. Julie continued in her bright and cheery voice. "Of course! I have all her contact information right here." She reached into a briefcase leaning against the house and pulled out a file. "I do think it's a good idea, by the way. It's normal for Daniel to want to know about his roots, and it's healthy for adoptees to meet their biologi-cal family when the circumstances are right. As far as I can tell, his biological mother is in a good place. What's more … Daniel," she turned to face him, "she seems to be a kind person; she just had some difficult circumstances when you were born, but she never stopped loving you." She opened the file and scanned the contents before handing it to Mr. Jones.

Daniel stared back. Her words, surprising but timely, had bro-ken through his storm of anger and resentment like the afternoon sun into a prison cell. "Did she tell you that?"

"She did. From the sound of it, neither did your biological father. Now, if I'm reading you all rightly, I should get all the paperwork in order and give your mom a call. Once everything is approved, I'll give you the 'Okay' to call her. Does that sound—"

"Yeah! I mean … yes." Daniel stepped toward her and eagerly touched her arm. "Yes, please get all the paperwork done." He cleared his throat as he glanced at his parents. "I'd, uh, like to call her as soon as possible."

His mom gave a barely perceptible nod as she squeezed his dad's hand.

"Wonderful. You should hear from me by the end of next week." Ms. Julie grabbed her briefcase and turned to go.

"Thanks, Ms. Julie." Daniel embraced her in an excited hug.

"Of course! It's my job, after all. But, truthfully, I was thrilled when your mother called. I'm so happy this is working out for you. It's a thrill to see my kids get adopted, but the next best thing is when their biological parents begin investing in their lives again."

She walked toward her car, waving once more before driving away.

Daniel turned eagerly toward his parents. "Dad, can I see the papers Ms. Julie gave you?"

His dad had been briefly flipping through the pages as though making sure there was nothing bad inside. Apparently satisfied, he held them out to Daniel.

Seren finally joined them on the porch, while Ben looked over Daniel's shoulder.

The top form only had a few bits of information on it, but Daniel mainly wanted to see the names. For years he had wondered what his last name truly was. For some reason, the Holy Moses Home for Bleeding Heart Orphans had never given him one. Maybe it was an oversight. Maybe it was because he was the only orphan there who had been abandoned on the doorstep without any record of his parents. Either way, he felt a thrill when his eyes finally found what he was looking for.

```
Father: Brennan Provence
Born: September 30, 1982
Died: June 12, 2017
Last Known Address: 1521 County Road 18
Newton, Alabama
36360
Mother: Leah Medley
Born: July 16, 1981
Address: 371 Daylilly Drive
Middleton, Idaho
83644
Phone: (208)555-0154
```

Daniel read the names over and over. Provence and Medley. What sort of families did he come from? What kind of people were they? What were his grandparents, cousins, uncles, and aunts like? Did his parents ever remarry other people? Did he have other brothers and sisters in the world? These and a dozen other questions swirled around in his mind.

"Where is Middleton, Idaho?" Ben asked.

His dad cleared his throat. "About three hours from here. Just across the state line."

"That would be an easy drive, right?" Daniel asked, his voice eager. Before waiting for an answer, he continued. "That's awesome! We could visit my mother on weekends, or she can stay with us!"

Seren edged closer to Daniel to glimpse the paper. "Are you nervous about meeting her?"

"You want her to stay with us?" Ben interjected. "What about Janice? And wouldn't that be weird having her in our house?"

Daniel shrugged. "She can sleep in our room. We'll just crash in the living room while she's here. Maybe she can come for Thanksgiving and Christmas! And, of course, I'm nervous about meeting her, but that doesn't change anything."

Seren's matter-of-fact voice broke through his excitement. "I wonder how much the life insurance is for. What if you're rich?"

"I totally forgot about that! Man, this is the best day of my life! However much it is, I'm definitely going to use part of it to buy a car when I turn 16. Then I can visit her all the time."

Mrs. Jones abruptly stood up and dashed inside. Daniel thought he heard a quiet sob once the door slammed shut.

Mr. Jones was beside him, gently taking the folder back and tucking it under one arm. He put hands on both shoulders. "Daniel. Slow down. Look, I know you're excited, but we need to be cautious with this. Ms. Julie still has to file all the paperwork and make contact again before we can even talk to her on the *phone*. I don't think it's wise for you to start making grand plans when we don't really know what kind of person she is."

"But Ms. Julie said she was nice!"

"Ms. Julie also let Barth Gurge adopt you."

Ben shuddered. "Good point."

Daniel pulled back. "That's totally different. Barth is a mutant. This is my mother we're talking about. She's not going to be some weird, psychopathic baboon monster who just wants a slave."

"I'm not saying she is. But we're your parents, and before she comes here or we even visit her, we're going to get to know her first."

Another sob from inside the house.

"Look, just be sensitive to your mom's feelings. Despite what you said earlier, it's not easy for us to have your biological mother suddenly appear. We need time to adjust to this, too. Why don't you three head back to Seren's house while me and your mom talk this over?"

He stepped past them and went inside.

Daniel stood in stony silence, his mom's tears and dad's hesitance smothering his hopes of quickly seeing his biological mother. He wasn't quite sure how much time they felt they needed to "get to know her first," but he was pretty sure it was longer than he wanted.

Seren joined him, looking back toward Granny's house with an excited light in her eyes.

Ben plopped down in the porch swing. "What do you think we should do?"

"Go, of course," Seren eagerly replied.

Daniel blinked back in surprise. "Wow! I have to admit I was thinking about that, but not seriously. If we went to my mother's house, Mom and Dad would freak out. I did memorize her phone number, though. Maybe I should just try to call her. No one would have to know, except you guys, of course. But what could it hurt?"

"Daniel." Ben's voice was edged with annoyance.

"What?" Daniel glanced back and forth between him and Seren.

Seren pointed over the line of trees off toward Granny's house. "We weren't talking about your mother. We were talking about *that*."

The dark pulsation they had seen before coming home was emanating from just above the forest.

"Oh." Daniel had completely forgotten about the arrival of this new threat in all his excitement. "I guess this means you guys aren't up for a trip to Idaho, then."

3

A New Friend

All three stood in front of Granny's, staring at the scene. Beside the makeshift archery range, the air pulsed and rippled as if it were an upright pool of black liquid, radiating shadows. Every few minutes, it darkened until altogether black. Then, with a noiseless "pop," a Creep jumped out. There were about thirty men and women so far, and all had the same crazed, feral look that spoke of possession by some evil spirit. They lined up in some sort of squad formation, with more arriving every minute. Each held a weapon: spears, swords, chakrams—a few even had guns. None moved to attack, but their sinister eyes stayed locked on the trio, and their claws twitched with barely concealed eagerness to fight.

Fire spiraled out of Daniel's chest and down his arm, where it eventually took the form of the tip-less, wavy-bladed Sun Sword. The woven metal hilt floated just beyond Daniel's grasp but matched the movement of his arm perfectly. His eyes lingered over the missing point. Each time he went into battle, he was reminded that the sword held only a fraction of its potential strength. He, and the other Vessels, for that matter, couldn't achieve their full power until the tip was reunited with the rest of the blade. He shook his head. If it was so important, it sure would be nice if the Three told him where it was, but, as usual, finding it was all part of a scheme to teach him some grand, spiritual lesson. He craned his neck from side to side, trying to loosen up and focus on the impending fight.

A bright light shone from Seren's forehead, then shot down to her hands as she summoned the Celestial Bow. Radiant, graceful limbs extended from her outstretched hand and took the shape of a recurve bow. She stood at the ready but waited to draw.

Ben's skin glowed as he prepared to summon the Triune Shield. Unfortunately, he'd left his golden, razor-sharp daggers at home, so the actual fighting was up to Seren and Daniel.

Some of the Creeps were dressed in jeans, t-shirts, and shorts. A few wore dresses and suits, which was a sharp contrast to their tangled, disheveled hair and crazed, strained grimaces. Others sported more exotic garb, like the Creeps they'd faced in India and Peru. But a few had on what Daniel could only guess were traditional Middle Eastern garments—turbans, veils, and a few robed women whose eyes couldn't be seen behind their head coverings.

Two Creeps tried to start a new line close to the wall of Granny's house. One tripped on an ivy vine on her way over and grabbed the other to steady herself. As they fumbled to regain balance, their hands touched the siding of the house. A fiery circle of protection sprang up around the tiny home. The phenomenon was familiar to Daniel now. A similar barrier protected his house, and another the Transportation Pedestal. The Creeps were instantly purified and their bodies vanished. The first time he'd seen this happen, he figured they'd been killed. Now he knew better. The purifying power of the Three eradicated the evil spirits controlling the Creeps, and they were taken into the service of the Father.

The next Creep to pop out of the pulsating portal hadn't seen the fate of her comrades and headed in the same direction. A Creep dressed in what was once a slick-looking suit snapped his head in her direction. "Keep away from the house!" he barked. "It's protected."

The newcomer gave an obedient hiss, then noticed the trio for the first time. She joined a line. "I'm the last," she wheezed, her unblinking eyes now fixed on Daniel. "We are ordered to attack."

Without hesitation, the Creeps surged forward.

"Ben," Daniel said calmly.

"I'm on it," Ben replied, his form glowing and immediately expanding. The radiant blue light of the Triune Shield enveloped them in a dome thirty feet in diameter. At its peak, three interlocked circles gyrated, and at their center was the silhouette of Ben's body.

Daniel stepped closer to Seren. "The guns," he said quickly and then jumped to the side as Seren widened her stance.

She drew the luminescent string back to the corner of her mouth, and an arrow of starlight formed. As the Creeps neared the borders of the shield, she let the arrows fly in succession, each blossoming Saturn-like rings as they flew toward their targets. They easily passed through the barrier, finding their mark in the chest of every Creep with a gun. Within seconds, seven were encased in a shell of light with an eight-pointed star at the point they were struck. The other Creeps surged around their bound comrades and advanced, hammering on the shield with their weapons.

"Ben, you holding up okay?" Daniel advanced to the edge of the luminescent barrier.

"For now." Ben's voice emanated from the shield in every direction. "They're just normal weapons, so it's not too bad."

A tall, muscular Creep stepped up to the shield and raised a black, wooden mace above his head. Silver script was etched into its side, running from the handle, over the blunt head, and down the other side. He swung hard.

BOOM!

Ripples radiated from the contact point, and the shield flickered.

"Oops! I spoke too soon. That was definitely not normal. I'm going to need some—"

BOOM! BOOM! BOOM!

Another Creep, her eyes glinting black behind a heavy veil, now joined her comrade at the edge of the shield, swinging a war hammer against the barrier.

"What is with these Creeps?" Ben shouted, his voice strained with effort. "It's like those weapons are specifically designed to break through the Triune Shield!"

Seren's ringed arrows flew past Daniel and bound the assaulters. Others, some with the specialized weapons, ran to their sides to keep up the attack.

Daniel raised the Sun Sword and focused his mind on relieving Ben of the onslaught and taking the burden on himself. The sword glowed a fiery orange, while glints of a deeper red danced along the edge. With all his might, he swung the blade. The Sunstorm flew through the Triune Shield and leveled the Creeps in its path. Twenty or so lay unconscious, including all those Seren had bound earlier. With a shout of anger and alarm, the others fell back and ran into the woods.

Seren targeted two, freezing them in their tracks, but the remaining eight or nine scurried behind Granny's house or into the dense underbrush.

The shield dissipated and coalesced into Ben's panting form next to Daniel. Seren joined them.

The vanquished Creeps, having been purified all at once, vanished together in a blinding flash.

Daniel rubbed his eyes, trying to clear the white spots from his field of vision. Seren turned her face away too late and stared at the ground while blinking hard to recover from the brightness. Ben held his hands over his eyes, shielding them until certain no other Creeps would disappear.

Which is why none of them noticed the Creep break from a bush to their left and charge them until it was too late.

Daniel didn't catch many details of his appearance, only that he gripped a small, glinting dagger in his right hand. Quicker than he could respond, the Creep dashed past all three and spun around, skidding to a crouching halt on the dirt.

Pain throbbed through Daniel's left arm. He looked down to see blood dripping from a shallow gash. Seren and Ben grabbed their arms in surprise, a similar-looking cut on each.

The remaining Creeps now burst out of the underbrush and rushed the trio. Daniel lifted the Sun Sword and stabbed the ground. A Fire Strike radiated outward twenty feet, stopping the assailants in their tracks and leveling them to the ground. Seconds later, they were all taken to the Father, though this time, Daniel was ready and turned his head to avoid the blinding flash.

"You poor things. Just look at those cuts!" a man's voice said. It was cool and calming, with just a hint of an accent. "Just children, after all. Hold still."

Daniel realized he was in a daze, and with the voice's last words, could barely move. The command held power. Whoever spoke approached Ben from behind and touched his bleeding arm. He moved into Daniel's field of vision.

Tall. Well-dressed in gray slacks and a white, button-down shirt. Chiseled, dark features with just a hint of stubble on his chin. Hair slicked back. Emotionless, predatory eyes. With a deft motion, he rolled up the sleeves of his shirt and pulled a white cloth out of his pocket. After wiping Ben's cut, he moved to Seren, and then to Daniel, doing the same to each.

"You are …" Daniel fought for the words as though he was wading through a foggy dream. Each second seemed an eternity. "You are that man? From … from …" He was familiar, and yet Daniel couldn't place him exactly.

"Babylon." Seren slurred and mumbled the word as if half asleep and face down in a pillow.

Ben nodded and then fell to his knees. "My phone," he muttered.

Daniel finally made the connection. He was one of the leaders of Ealim Wahid. Somewhere in his mind were thoughts of alarm. But they were far off, and he felt so lethargic, it didn't seem to matter all that much.

The man paused as he passed Daniel and bent over to look into his eyes. He lifted up Daniel's chin, which had begun to droop on his chest. "You know me already? How flattering!" The man was taller than Daniel had thought after seeing his photo on Ben's phone. He took a step back, casting a critical, sneering look at all three Vessels. "I am Abida, Prince of Babylon and son of Nergal. And you"—his mouth slowly curved into a smile and he slapped Daniel's cheek—"must be Daniel."

He reached down and placed the cloth on his cut again, then squeezed with an impossibly strong grip.

Daniel cried out but couldn't make him stop. Whatever spell he had laid on him, it was too strong. Even the pain in his arm, now throbbing from the inhuman strength of his grip, wasn't enough to draw him out of his stupor.

Abida pulled away the cloth, splotchy with three distinct blood marks. Daniel's was the largest. "That's plenty for my master to experiment on," he said, casting an appraising, unblinking, shark-eyed gaze over the trio. He leaned in, so his face was next to Daniel's, and whispered in his ear. "But maybe I ought to bring you back with me just in case. We might need more."

Daniel felt the back of his neck tingle, and a strong wind blew the leaves forward at his feet. Gabriela suddenly appeared and rushed Abida with a raised fist.

Abida, still smiling, took a nonchalant step to the left at the last second as Gabriela punched the ground where he had stood.

The earth broke open with a dull rumble, and boulders and dirt flew in every direction. The power of the impact threw Abida to the ground and several feet backward, and his insipid grin exploded into a look of furious shock.

Without stopping to watch his response, Gabriela grabbed Daniel, Ben, and Seren, and dragged them all toward Granny's house and onto the front porch. At her touch, the spell was broken.

"Gab—Gabriela! Oof!" Daniel exclaimed as she dumped them onto the porch flooring. "What's happening?" He instantly took in her appearance: chocolate brown eyes and ponytail, jeans, black jacket zipped up over a green undershirt, and a determined gaze that spoke of the trials she had already endured at fourteen.

Ben stared at her in shock. "Holy Cow! When did you get so strong?"

"This isn't the time!" Seren shouted. She stood and summoned the Celestial Bow. In one swift motion, she loosed three arrows straight toward Abida.

Abida scrambled to his feet with a look of outrage and caught all three arrows in the air. They dissipated, and a luminescent casing began creeping up his hand and arm. He gritted his teeth and made a fist. After a moment of struggle, the casing cracked, and he flung what looked like leftover stardust to the ground.

Gabriela grabbed Daniel like a ragdoll and stood him on his feet. "The Sunstorm! Quickly!"

"Yes! Of course!" It was all Daniel could think to say. He was so stunned by Gabriela's sudden appearance, and her ridiculous strength, he was surprised he was able to string two words together.

He raised the Sun Sword and cleaved the air in front of him. The explosive power of the Sunstorm flew toward Abida.

Abida lifted his other hand, palm outward, and stopped the fireball midair. The force of the impact pushed him off balance, and he had to take two steps backward. Beyond that, he might have been playing a game of strength with a child for all the effort he showed. With a swat to the side, the Sunstorm was overpowered. It spun into the woods and exploded against several trees, blasting off their bark and shattering one of the trunks into splinters.

The tree fell with a slow, crunching noise. Abida watched Daniel and the others, his infuriatingly calm smile playing at the corner of his mouth once more. He slowly approached like a tiger hunting his prey. "I'm a little out of your league, I'd say."

Daniel was stunned by his power. Even Seren as Shakti hadn't been able to overpower the Sunstorm without a shield. Who, and what, for that matter, was this man?

"What do we do?" Ben hissed in a frantic whisper. He stepped from one foot to the other, opening and closing his hands nervously. And then he seemed to remember something. His breathing slowed. His fidgeting calmed. His eyes shut for a brief moment in prayer and stared down Abida. "Okay, guys. What's the plan?"

Daniel took a moment to pray for help as well. He still felt on edge, but his mind calmed just enough to get his bearings. He opened his eyes to study the Sun Sword, an idea slowly taking shape. "The barrier should protect us, but Seren, let's shoot at the same time. Maybe a combined attack will force him back."

Gabriela shook her head. "It won't matter. Not until the Sun Sword is whole."

Abida was in front of the porch steps. The burning circle of letters roared to life at his presence, spinning around the house and expanding a glowing barrier of light outward. It pushed against him, shoving him back toward the road.

His appearance suddenly shifted. Instead of cool, calm, well-dressed, and deceptively composed, he was much more Creep-like. His eyes were now all black, teeth elongated, hair disheveled, and each finger tipped with a sharp, jagged nail. He leaned into the barrier and dug his feet into the ground. With both hands raised, fingers splayed out, he clawed at the glowing wall like a wild animal. The barrier fizzled at his touch; cracks appeared. His berserk grin fell into a look of focused determination as he widened his stance and plunged both hands deeper into the flaming barricade.

Fire erupted from the ground all around him and surrounded his body, but he wasn't purified or destroyed. A larger crack appeared between his hands, and he broke out into a maniacal laugh. "You see?" he shouted, still straining. His voice had grown deeper, almost inhuman. "The power of the Three can be broken! He's not invincible. The Master was right. Foolish Vessels! Come and join us. Escape the power of your Father and be free!"

Gabriela's eyes were locked on Abida, her lips moving in silent prayer. Her face belied a lack of peace, however, which shocked Daniel. Since she had been taken into the Father's service, he had never seen her look worried. Especially when praying.

Daniel touched her arm to get her attention. Despite the gravity of the situation, he blushed. "Um … why isn't he being purified? Who is this guy?"

Without waiting for an answer, Seren shot two more arrows. They passed through the barrier and hit Abida in the chest. He inched backward and grunted with their impact, but shook off the arrow as he'd done before, never relenting from his clawed attack.

Gabriela glanced down at Daniel's hand, still on her arm, and then up at him.

Daniel pulled his hand back and awkwardly fidgeted with his pockets.

"He is a serious problem, that's who he is," Gabriela finally said. "Pray! Pray that the barrier holds!"

The sound of desperation in her voice shocked Daniel even more. He nodded and immediately fell into prayer to the Three.

Abida laughed. "Your prayers will do nothing against my power." He strained, and the crack in the barrier tore open even wider. He laughed in triumph. "The Father is too busy to bother with you. His worthless slaves are overrun in Babylon while he hides in Heaven from our power."

Ben sidled up next to Daniel. "I've been praying since he first attacked, but I don't hear anything from the Three."

Daniel was experiencing the same. No calming words or even cryptic guidance. But he knew that didn't mean they weren't listening, or that the prayers didn't do any good.

Seren threw up her hands. "My arrows have no power. What do we do if he breaks through?" Her voice was edged with fear, and Daniel noticed the same wild and desperate look in her eyes as when she had first been purified from the Enemy's power.

Ben cast about as if he were looking for an idea hidden somewhere on the porch. "I could … I could summon the Triune Shield inside the barrier, and that'd give us some more time, at least." Without waiting for a response, Ben's body transformed into a glowing shell of light, and then expanded outward into the encompassing spherical shape of the Triune Shield. Its borders reached out to the very edge of the glowing barrier just as Abida stuck his arm all the way through. "Daniel, if I get weak, help out with a Fire Strike."

"Gotcha!" Daniel replied and charged the Sun Sword.

The Triune Shield pushed against Abida's arm. He hissed and flinched but didn't pull back. Instead, he reached his other arm through the opening and closed his fists on the air as if gripping something invisible. Dark wisps of the Enemy's spirit, shaped like tent pegs, instantly formed in his hands. He stuck them on either side of the rift and took a step back, breathing hard. The tear in the barrier remained pinned open.

Abida's eyes glinted in triumph. "Your spiritual power is nothing to me." He tilted his head to the side and popped his neck. "If I can take on a Firstborn's barrier, what hope does the Triune Shield have?" He plunged in his claws.

"Ow!" Ben screamed. "Not good! Not good! Not good!" A hole appeared in the shield just as it had with the barrier. "Anytime, Daniel!"

"On it!" Daniel shouted, while simultaneously plunging the Sun Sword into the ground.

The Fire Strike emanated outward until it reached the Triune Shield, then rebounded back and forth within. In India, this had strengthened Ben against the crushing attack of the Enemy's barrage.

"Not helping!" Ben hissed. "Still stabbing through me! Yep. Still stabbing!"

Abida's eyes were wild with glee. He was a predator homing in on his prey, intent on playing with them before the kill. "Let me in, little maggots! I promise I won't stay long."

"Why isn't the Fire Strike helping?" Ben yelled.

Abida had both hands through now.

"Help's not coming," Gabriela muttered to herself. "Where are they? Something's gone wrong."

Daniel straightened up and cast a curious glance at her. "Gabriela? What should we—"

Before he could finish, Gabriela leaped off the front porch with her fist cocked back, a look of wild abandon on her face. She was at Abida in the next second, punching him in the stomach through the rift in the Triune Shield before he could pull away.

The violence of the impact surprised Daniel—dull, but loud as if a speeding car had crashed into a massive punching bag.

Abida's smile fell, and his eyes went blank as he flew backward through the air. Before he could hit the ground, Seren loosed two arrows in close succession, each chasing him as he flew and striking him in both shoulders.

A black portal whirled open behind Abida, and two men darted through, catching him before he hit the ground.

"Gabriela?" Ben said, his voice brimming with relief and amazement. "I think you might be the strongest person in the ..." His voice trailed off as he noticed the men.

Daniel's breath caught in his throat, and the blood drained from his face. They were the Enemy's Generals. Two of them, anyway. Where the other two were, Daniel didn't know and prayed they weren't joining the fight.

On Abida's left, a tall, muscled man with blond spiked hair and a short-cropped beard helped him regain balance. The Hammer of War was nowhere to be seen, but Daniel had a hunch he could pull it out of thin air if needed. His piercing blue eyes bore into Gabriela.

Bracing Abida on the right was an African man, slightly less bulky but still chiseled with barely concealed muscles. His stare was gray and dull, a perfect match for the Whirlwind of Famine, which was also conspicuously absent. The surrounding trees faded to a dusty brown as their bark dried up and their leaves withered. The leaves beneath his feet, instantly zapped of all water, crinkled up and crunched loudly with every movement. He scanned the Vessels on the front porch and sneered before leaning down to whisper to Abida.

The blond General lifted Abida to his feet. "Chiuta is right," his voice held the rhythmic accent of some north European country.

Maybe Norway or Sweden. "Master is angry you came alone. He wants you on the front lines immediately."

Abida shook his shoulders, and the binding power of the Seren's arrows crumbled away. He rubbed his stomach while wiping away a trickle of blood from the corner of his mouth. "Silence." He waved his hand, and both Generals fell back a step. "I'm more than enough to take on these four. The little girl just caught me unawares, but no harm was done."

Gabriela clenched her fists and reflexively stepped back from the Triune Shield.

"No harm?" Ben whispered, his voice drifting down from his figure frozen between the gyrating rings of the shield. "That punch sounded like it would've obliterated an elephant! Or Ravana even."

Daniel nodded at Ben's comment while preparing another Fire Strike. Seren, still and silent as a statue, stood with the Celestial Bow at a full draw, arrow fixed on Abida. Daniel didn't know what good either would do.

Abida broke out into a full-throated laugh. "No harm," he reiterated. "Indeed, none of you have the power to truly harm me. Or my sister, for that matter." He turned to the Generals. "Look at them quake. Like little rabbits cowering in a hutch. The Master worries needlessly." He snapped his head back around. "You four will see me again. In the meantime," he pulled the bloody rag from his pocket and held it up, letting it unfurl so all three samples were clear, "I got what I came for. It will be interesting to run the final tests on the blood of a Vessel. What will you do when we remove the Image of the Three from you? Who will you serve when you are beyond redemption and the Father turns his back on you?"

Daniel didn't quite understand what all that meant, but a feeling of dread settled into his stomach like a brick. On the plains near Khireshwar, the Enemy had threatened the same thing, but was it really possible? Could the Enemy somehow keep them permanently from the Father? "He's bluffing, right?" he whispered, his lips barely moving in hopes Abida wouldn't notice.

"Hope so," Ben replied.

Behind him, Seren's breath caught in her throat. "Just focus," she muttered.

Gabriela stepped forward, her face a picture of proud defiance. "Never. He will never turn his back on his children!"

Abida raised an eyebrow. "Tyr!" he barked. "Ready the portal."

The blond General hurriedly bowed, and then stuck his left hand, fingers splayed out, into the air to his side. With a flick of his wrist, the billowing portal swirled open. He stepped to the side and waited.

Abida smirked at Gabriela and spun on his heel, pausing for a moment as if flaunting his total lack of concern that any of them would attack again. "Where is he now? Why didn't he come to rescue you from my power? Where are the Firstborn who usually protect you? Gone!" he laughed. "Gone. Scrambling. Nursing their pride after we broke the Babylonian Seal and expelled the Three's pathetic worshipers. Trying in vain to regain their foothold."

Daniel thought he saw Gabriela blink away tears and flinch as if each word stung.

Abida casually walked toward the portal. "The age of the Three is passing. Our age has come. This was fun," he snickered and then disappeared within.

Chiuta immediately followed without so much as a backward glance.

Tyr made to follow, but paused, his foot halfway through the portal. He locked eyes with Seren. "Found your sister yet?" he asked, his eyes glinting with haughty arrogance. "You both were such wastes, really. Wastes of the Master's time and energy. Wastes of life. We know where Raylin is, of course, and we plan to take care of her soon." His half grin and icy tone made his meaning clear. "And the Master has given me the order to do it. When I see her, I'll tell her you've moved on with your life, that you no longer think of her, care for her, love her. I'll tell her the Three have forgiven you for all the atrocities you committed, but that she is beyond forgiveness. I'm sure that will infuriate her. She will die and hate you for all eternity. Should be amusing."

Daniel fired a Sunstorm before Tyr could say another word.

Two Celestial Arrows flew over his shoulder half a second later.

Tyr shrugged and walked into the portal before either attack could land.

The wind blew quietly through the trees while they all stared at the empty air where the portal had been. The next moment, Ben returned to his human form at Gabriela's side, and Daniel released the Sun Sword.

Seren stood stone-still, her teeth clenched, and the Celestial Bow still summoned. Daniel didn't need the Three's ability to read minds to know she was thinking about Raylin and probably fantasizing about pummeling Tyr. His own mind was less one-tracked and brimmed with questions. What was going on with Gabriela? She seemed worried and upset. They'd been in worse situations than Abida's attack, and she'd been so calm. Why did Abida's threats seem to unhinge her so easily? And who was Abida, exactly? And where was Granny? Obviously, the quest to save Raylin was about to begin. How come she didn't come with Gabriela to explain everything? When did Gabriela get crazy Hulk-smash powers, for that matter? Why did his parents look so upset right now?

Wait …

"You boys have a lot of explaining to do!" Mrs. Jones screamed. She and Mr. Jones stomped, wide-eyed and slack-jawed from the road in front of Granny's house toward the porch. "Someone better start spitting out answers, and I mean NOW!"

Ben, his face frozen in a look of abject horror, spun around and locked eyes with Daniel. "We're dead," he mouthed.

Daniel ran his fingers through his hair. Seven-headed dragons, monsters, demons—these he could handle. His mom? This was a fight no number of magical weapons could win.

4

An Abyss-mal Quest

Mrs. Jones's hysterical questions seemed to ground Gabriela. "You are Daniel and Ben's parents?" she extended her hands in a calming gesture. It didn't work. "I'm Gabriela. I have a lot to explain and little time. Please come and sit on the porch."

Alan and Mariah exchanged confused glances before ambling uncertainly toward her.

"Well, I want to know who that man was," Mrs. Jones sputtered. "And what's with all the magical weapons?" She cast her eyes to the sky. "I can't believe I just had to ask that. WHAT IS HAPPENING?"

"How is Ben a giant glowing bubble?" Mr. Jones interjected, his voice tinged with betrayal. "What have you boys been hiding from us?"

Ben walked backward until he was abreast of Daniel. "Should you use a Fire Strike?" he hissed. "Maybe Seren could bind them with some arrows while we run to the Transportation Pedestal."

Daniel looked askance at Ben. "They're our parents, dummy. Not demons. I mean, sure, they'll probably kill us, but we can't fight them."

Seren, still lost in her own world, released the Celestial Bow, which returned to her forehead like a shooting star before dimming and then vanishing altogether.

"See?" Mrs. Jones pointed a trembling finger at Seren, now next to Daniel and Ben. "What was that? Explain! Explain now!"

Ben, frozen in terror in the face of his mother's fury, stared back, making confused, whining noises in his throat.

The conversation didn't seem to register for Seren. She opened and closed her fists, her stare vacant and distant, and marched into her house without explanation.

Gabriela took command. "Daniel. Ben. Go get your things ready. We're about to leave for the next quest. Pack warm. It'll be cold and wet where we're going."

Daniel looked nervously at Gabriela and then at his parents.

Ben grunted unintelligibly and stayed where he was as if waiting for his parents' permission.

Gabriela noticed their reluctance out of the corner of her eye and snapped her head toward them. "Go! Raylin is being hunted by the Enemy, and we have to find her first. One of his Leaders just attacked you and took your blood. Many Firstborn are fighting the Enemy directly and cannot come to help. And the Three ..." her voice faltered. "The Three have been silent. Now hurry!" Gabriela stomped her foot, and the ground rumbled deeply.

Mrs. Jones jumped in fright.

Mr. Jones paled.

Daniel flinched and grabbed Ben's wrist. "Come on!" he said, breaking into a run while trying to skirt around his parents and avoid their gaze. "Be back in a minute. Sorry, Mom and Dad," he shouted but dared not look back. "Gabriela will explain everything as far as I know!"

He and Ben hit the pavement and bolted toward their house.

Ben shook his head and wrung his hands. "We are so going to be killed, and I don't mean by the Enemy or any of his freaks. Mom and Dad are going to lock us in our bedrooms and tie us up. They'll probably get pointers from Barth and Gator. Oh, man! I bet Gabriela's getting an earful now."

They reached their house and jumped up the porch steps before flying through the door and up the stairs.

"I don't know," Daniel replied as they burst into their room to frantically pack. "I think her superhuman strength got their attention. Maybe they'll let us go. I mean, even if they try to stop us, we have to obey the Three, right? If we're supposed to begin the quest, we can't just be like, 'Sorry, my parents won't let me.'"

"I guess so," Ben replied while pulling a sweatshirt over his head and throwing three pairs of socks into his backpack. "If that's the case, though, I sure hope some Firstborn shows up to give Mom and Dad the news. Gabriela's crazy strength is one thing, but Inti in his Surya form would definitely do the trick." He reached behind his dresser and pulled out his golden daggers.

Daniel laced up his hiking boots and threw on a warm rain jacket. "Probably won't happen, though. The way Gabriela was talking, sounds like Granny and Inti are busy. Food."

Ben nodded, and they raced downstairs to the kitchen.

"Hello, boys!" Janice sang as she shuffled through the front door, her knitting bag dangling from the crook of her arm. "That Gator is so nice, I bought four bags of caramel and chocolate popcorn. Won't come in for several weeks, though. But the wait is part of the fun! Barth is the hairiest man I've ever seen. Rivals a Sasquatch, if you ask me. Weird, too. Where are you two going? Packing for a trip? I didn't know you were traveling. Parents didn't say anything about it. Oh, look at those cuts!" She rummaged through her knitting bag and whipped out two large band-aids and a tube of antibiotic ointment, then deftly slapped them on Daniel and Ben's arms.

Daniel was grateful. He'd completely forgotten about Abida's cuts and would've dashed off on the quest without giving them a thought. "Thanks, Janice."

Ben gripped her hand in both of his. "You're a lifesaver. With my luck, I'd probably have gotten it infected."

"Don't mention it. Where did you boys say you were going again?" Janice plopped down on the living room couch and pulled out a beanie she'd been knitting.

Daniel and Ben whirled through the kitchen, grabbing granola bars, beef jerky, apples, and bottles of water.

"Camping trip," Daniel said, whipping out the bread and making the sloppiest PB&J's he'd ever seen in his life.

Ben stuffed four sleeves of chocolate chip cookies into his backpack. "Yep. Mom and Dad are up the road on a … walk. They'll be home soon. Bye, Janice!" He shouldered his bag and darted out the front door.

Daniel took another couple of minutes to finish the sandwiches. He shoved them into a freezer bag, slid them down between his clothes and water bottles, and then flung his backpack over his shoulder. "Pray for us, would you?"

Daniel wove around the kitchen countertop and made to zip out the door when the papers about his biological mother caught his eye. He snatched them up and read through it once more. The chaos from the fight with the Creeps and Abida, Gabriela's surprise appearance, and his parents finding out about everything had driven all thoughts of his mother right out of his mind. A sense of urgency pushed through all the pandemonium. After all this time, she finds him and wants to make contact, and now the third quest suddenly begins. What if he didn't survive? What if his parents contacted her while he was gone and decided she wasn't stable enough for them to talk? What if she changed her mind about seeing him because he didn't respond quickly enough? These and a dozen other questions flew through Daniel's mind in an instant.

"You look worried. Camping trip going to be a rough one?" Janice asked innocently, her magnified eyelids fluttering like butterfly wings. "Of course, I'll pray for you boys. Don't worry about a thing. God will work it all out for you. I'm sure everything will happen exactly as it's meant to." She began to nod as her narcolepsy kicked in. "Always praying," she muttered, and then was out cold.

Janice's reassurance slowly calmed Daniel's thoughts, and his fears dissipated like shadows at dawn. She was right. After everything he'd experienced over the past two years, he could say with confidence that the Father would work it all out.

"Thanks, Janice," he whispered, gently laying down the papers.

He walked out, quietly closing the door before breaking into a run to catch up with Ben.

The peace he felt rose to a sense of excitement as he turned his attention back to the quest. Sure, his parents were having their minds blown by Gabriela and learning all about their quests, but he had a hunch it would be for the best that they were now involved. Even Abida and his unstoppable power didn't seem to faze him. He wondered why? Was he just feeling optimistic because of his biological mother? Or, more likely, was it that Gabriela had shown up? He hadn't seen her in months, and fighting alongside her was amazing. Even if Abida had totally kicked their butts. And now, she had some super awesome power. Wow! He sighed. She was so cool.

Daniel shook his head. What was he thinking? The last time they were together, she admitted to liking him, but said they couldn't date until all the quests were finished and her people at Aguas Calientes were freed.

Yeah, but we're about to start the next quest, which brings us one step closer. Daniel furrowed his brows. *Why am I debating with myself?*

He grinned. Either way, he was just happy to get to see her. And, of course, he was excited to finally get the official word to go save Raylin. The quest itself would no doubt be difficult, but the Three would be watching them, and the Father always allowed things to happen for a reason. The last quests changed his life for the better; surely, this one would do the same.

His mind drifted back to his biological mother. The thought that she was on a quest, too—a quest to find him—seemed perfect. And he had a feeling that when they returned from saving Raylin, his parents would have gotten used to the idea of her being in his life again.

He skidded to a halt in front of Granny's house and saw Gabriela still talking with his parents. His mom wrung her hands while Gabriela paced back and forth, gesturing to the sky and talking quickly. His father stood with his mouth open, hands on top of his head as he clearly struggled to believe what she said. Ben cautiously hovered around the corner of the house, studying his parents' reactions as though they were about to pronounce his death sentence.

The door to the front porch opened, and Seren, dressed in jeans and a hoodie with a thicker coat worn over it, strode down the steps. Her sleeves were pushed up, and Daniel noticed her cut was also bandaged. Her backpack was so full of supplies, the zipper looked ready to bust. She spun around and watched Gabriela.

"You ready?" she asked Daniel, leaning slightly toward him and fidgeting with her hands with frantic energy. "Gabriela almost done? We need to get going. Maybe I should get a start up the hill. Where's Ben? Oh, never mind. Okay, well—"

"I think we should stay together," Daniel interjected. He put a hand on Seren's shoulder. "Look, I know this will be your first official quest with the Three, but trust me. We'll leave at the right time and find Raylin exactly when we need to."

Seren looked sideways at Daniel. "If you say so."

"I do. Don't forget Abida and his cronies, either. Who knows if they'll pop out somewhere again. I'd rather not get picked off one by one or kidnapped so he can run his freakish experiments on me in person." A chill spread down his spine. "How is the Enemy removing the Father's image from people, anyway? Can he really do that?"

Seren's face darkened, and her hand absently ran up her arm to the cut. "I'm not sure, but I think I remember watching him perform some terrible experiments. I was supposed to undergo the process once it was perfected."

"Sorry. Bad memories. I get it."

"We're supposed to just let them go risk their lives again?" Mrs. Jones's voice was a high-pitched siren of warning. Daniel and Ben locked eyes and moved closer together. She pushed past Gabriela. "I've believed in God since I was a girl—since before you were born—and I've never heard of anything like this!

"Boys!" she snapped, storming off the porch and grabbing them both by the wrists. "You're coming home with us this instant."

"Mom," Daniel pleaded. "We don't really have a—"

"Okay," Ben squeaked.

Daniel sighed in disgust. "Come on, Ben. You've faced demons. You've died, dude! Man up."

"Mariah, wait." Mr. Jones's voice, calm but firm, broke through the chaos. He remained on the porch, one hand resting on the railing.

Mrs. Jones stopped but didn't turn around.

"We just saw the boys, not to mention Seren and this young lady here," he gestured politely to Gabriela, "do unbelievable things. If they say this power is from God, we can't just outright deny it. And don't you feel …" he paused, struggling to find the right words. "Don't you feel something inside of you saying they need to go?"

Mrs. Jones lifted her head to the sky, and her shoulder fell as if his simple question had defeated her. "I don't know what I feel." She spun, yanking Ben and Daniel in a circle. "First, Daniel's real mom sends this stupid letter, and it feels like he's being taken away from me. Then some crazy man and his two lackeys attack both my boys and disappear. Into another dimension, I might add! And, I discover they've got super-powered weapons, one of which turns Ben into a bubble."

"Shield, actually," Ben mumbled.

"Don't interrupt!" Mrs. Jones's eyes flickered like fire.

"Now we're supposed to let them go risk their lives, even when they went gallivanting all over the world twice before and never told us a thing! Or asked permission! They could've been killed. Ben WAS killed!"

"Would you have let them go if they had asked?" Mr. Jones's voice remained steady and even.

"Of course not! I would've locked them in their bedrooms."

"Me too. Which is probably why we were kept from knowing. But now, I feel we're supposed to let them go. I feel it more strongly than anything I've ever felt before. It's like … it's like God is speaking directly to me. I can't get it out of my mind. And I feel at peace."

"So, I'm just supposed to let my boys go face death again and do nothing about it?"

"No," Gabriela interrupted. "There is something we need you to do. Follow me," she commanded, striding around Granny's house and toward Pedestal Hill.

Seren followed immediately; Ben and Daniel tried, but Mrs. Jones hesitated.

Mr. Jones stepped off the porch and took her hands off the boys. He held them tightly. "Boys, go. We're right behind you."

Mrs. Jones's face was a tempest of confusion and fear. "But, but ... Alan, wait!"

"Come on, Mariah. Don't you want to see how you can help your boys?" He led her forward, trying to catch up with Gabriela, who was already deep within the trees.

Daniel broke away from Ben, who, like a well-trained dog faced with defying its master, plodded uncertainly up the path, struggling with every step against the psychological power of his mother's commands to stay. Daniel jogged forward until he was next to Gabriela. "Hey. So, nice to see you again. Since when did you become Supergirl?"

Gabriela glanced at Daniel, then immediately let her gaze fall back to the forest floor. She picked her way over a rotten log before answering. "A while now. I just haven't needed to use it. The Three gave me other abilities, too, which we'll need on the quest." She fell silent.

Daniel nodded and smiled, trying to encourage her to continue. More silence.

"What's the plan?" Seren asked, pushing past him to get closer to Gabriela. Her words were short and clipped, like a soldier requesting commands from a superior officer.

Gabriela paused and craned her neck until she caught sight of the straggling Joneses. When they were within hearing distance, she set off again. "We're traveling to Ireland, Wales, and England to track down Raylin. To stop her. We need her to follow us to the Abyssal Staff so she can be purified."

"The Abyssal Staff," Seren said. The blood drained out of her face, and she paused for a moment.

"Is that a surprise?" Daniel asked. "I thought we knew her weapon was the Abyssal Staff already. Is there something wrong?"

Seren took a slow breath and paused at a giant oak tree, her hand lingering on the rough bark. "Not a surprise. It's just … the staff rests in the Abyss. It's a scary place, that's all."

"Oh, well. We've been to some pretty scary places. Don't worry about it; the Three will help us through."

She nodded, her eyes distracted by a spider scurrying along the forest floor. It found its web-covered hole in the ground and disappeared into the dark tunnel.

Just then, Mrs. Jones broke free from her husband's grip and ran forward toward Gabriela. "Raylin? Didn't she used to live in this neighborhood?"

Daniel left Seren at the tree and ran to catch up.

"I remember her," Mr. Jones joined in. "She disappeared a couple years ago. Right around the time we adopted Daniel. What happened?"

Seren, still looking distracted, picked back up the trail, jogging until she was just behind Gabriela.

"It's kind of a long story," Daniel said. He wondered how much he should say about her possession. Too much detail and Mrs. Jones may lose it again.

Gabriela jumped over two small boulders and headed uphill. "Raylin is Seren's sister and is also a Vessel. She was a double agent for the Enemy during Daniel's quest for the Sun Sword but betrayed him to help us. Unfortunately, she's now enslaved to evil spirits through one of the Enemy's weapons—a Dark Blade."

Apparently, Gabriela wasn't going to hold anything back.

"Alan! Did you hear her? Dark spirits. How can you be so casual about this?"

Right on cue.

Alan sighed. "Mariah, how is that any worse than facing the

Enemy? Or Ben dying? At least they're not the ones who got possessed."

Seren froze and snapped her head back to look sharply at Mr. Jones, and then stomped past Gabriela to speedwalk ahead of the group.

"Uh, oh. Was that insensitive? Sorry," Mr. Jones muttered, and then shouted, "Sorry!"

Seren disappeared through a dense spinney of mountain laurel without acknowledging the apology.

Gabriela continued. "Raylin is now totally controlled by the Voidblade and its lust for more dark power. She's wandering through old ruins and graveyards, enslaving the dark spirits possessing those places. She now has no drive other than to gain more power and will attack anyone and anything that approaches her."

The images of Raylin, her dark wings stretched out as she flew through the Chamber of the Moon, and the blurry photo of the strange terror haunting the graves in Ireland, combined in Daniel's mind. There was no doubt that it was her.

"Ben," was all he had to say.

Ben was by his side in an instant. "I know."

Everyone followed Gabriela through the laurel and came up alongside the gully, cut through the forest floor by years of rainwater running down the hillside. A few new trees had been claimed by the erosion.

Ben searched the area until he located Seren, a hundred yards ahead of them and sitting on a fallen log. He ran past the group to catch up with her, holding up his phone and explaining about Raylin.

The Joneses had paused to catch their breath.

Gabriela was just beyond them, leaning against a boulder lining the lip of the gully. Daniel walked up to her as casually as he could. He was suddenly uncertain of what he should do with his hands and ended up putting them awkwardly behind his head and leaning his elbow against the tree next to Gabriela. "How are we supposed to get Raylin to the Abyss, by the way? If she's attacking everything and anything, won't she go berserk on us, too?"

"Yes, um …" Gabriela pushed up from the rock, seemingly distracted by Daniel's nearness, and took two steps away to randomly look into the ravine.

Perfect. More awkwardness. Just what the quest needed.

"She will attack," she said, "but I think she can be bound by the Celestial Bow. We'll have to be careful. She's incredibly powerful—as powerful as several fallen Firstborn put together." Her gaze scanned the forest and then lingered on Seren, now standing on the log and tapping her foot impatiently. "More powerful than Shakti."

Something about the way Gabriela spoke about the plan struck Daniel as odd. "You *think* it'll bind her? Did the Three not give specific instructions?"

Gabriela flashed him an annoyed look. "No, they didn't. What do you want me to do about it?" She spun around and struck the path again, heading toward Seren and Ben. The Joneses resumed the hike and rejoined the conversation.

Daniel, taken aback by her response, decided it was best to avoid any similar questions at the moment. He hurriedly followed.

"Didn't Shakti—Seren—kill Ben?" Mrs. Jones asked, her hands on her hips. "Raylin is more powerful than her? I wonder how many of my kids are going to die on this quest?" She leveled her gaze at her husband.

"Mariah," Mr. Jones sighed, his head tilted in frustration.

Daniel cleared his throat. "Can the Sun Sword purify her when she still has the Voidblade?"

"Temporarily, at least," Gabriela explained. "Like with Seren, whatever darkness you purify will immediately try to repossess her because she willingly wields the Voidblade."

They reached the fallen tree. Ben stood just beyond, leaning against a thin pine while scrolling through his phone. Seren still stood on the trunk, looking down at them. She turned and jumped back onto the path. "The Abyssal Staff will have to seal away the evil once it's forced out of her body," she chimed in.

"Sounds dreadful," Daniel said nonchalantly, climbing over the trunk and then turning to offer Gabriela a hand. "Like all our other quests. Nothing we can't handle, right?"

Gabriela flashed an awkward smile and reached down to grab the trunk with one hand. With a quick toss, she upended it and tossed it into the gully. It slammed into the ground with a dull thud, teetered for a moment, and then fell over with a crash.

Daniel slowly dropped his hand. Well, at least she'd smiled.

"Seal away the evil into the Serpent," Seren called over her shoulder. "*The* Serpent."

Daniel felt a lump forming in his throat. "Oh," he muttered. The Enemy's true form. The great, seven-headed serpent—all horns and teeth and evil aura so powerful it made his Supai form seem like a baby bunny by comparison. It had taken weeks to get the image out of his head, though he still had nightmares every now and again.

Ben looked up as they all passed by and fell into step next to Daniel. "You mean we'll have to see the Enemy like that again?"

"We'll fight the Serpent," Gabriela said quietly, and then disappeared through thick foliage.

"Whoa, whoa, whoa!" Daniel objected, winding quickly between the branches of two close-growing cedars. "I thought we didn't have to fight him until we had all the Weapons of Power! You're telling me we'll have to battle him without Raylin's help? While we're trying to save her at the same time?"

Gabriela pushed past Seren and lead them at a fast pace up the sharp incline toward the ridge of Pedestal Hill. "We're not going there to seal away the Spirit of the Age, but we will have to defend ourselves. It can't be helped."

The Joneses were hot on Daniel's heels.

"The Serpent?" Mr. Jones asked, his voice tinged with confusion and concern, drawing up beside him. "Could someone explain, please?"

Daniel filled them in on the unhappy news.

Mrs. Jones looked angrier than ever but plodded along in uncharacteristic silence.

Mr. Jones just nodded, breathing hard with the exertion of keeping up with Gabriela.

"I don't get it though," Ben said. He'd slipped his phone back in his pocket and was going up the hill on all fours. "If we can bind her with the Celestial Bow and somehow get her to the Abyssal Staff, how will we use it? All of us have a Weapon of Power already."

"Yeah," Daniel interjected. "Can we wield two at the same time?"

"Not exactly," Gabriela answered. "But you can temporarily use the staff if all three of you are touching it at the same time. You won't be as powerful as its true Vessel, though. It's going to be tough to pull off," she continued. "So, I'll be with you on the whole quest."

"You will?" Daniel asked, sounding a little too excited even to his own ears. He cleared his throat. "I mean. Cool. Yeah. Because Granny hasn't shown up or anything, and we can use all the help we can get."

His dad looked at him sideways.

His mother rolled her eyes.

"I will," Gabriela said flatly. She reached the ridge of the hill and turned to look down at them. "The Three decided my training was done and decreed I should go on the quest."

While Daniel's heart was skipping like a deer through a meadow, he quickly realized that Gabriela looked sad, even worried.

Seren reached the top and immediately slid down to the ledge on the other side. "Great. Can we hurry up and leave now?" She shoved her way through the ivy vines hiding the entrance to the cave and disappeared within. "I assume the pedestal is keyed to my hand this time?" she shouted from inside, her voice muted from the interior of the chamber.

Gabriela cupped her hands to her mouth and yelled back, "It is! But you'll have to wait until everyone is next to you." She bounded down the ledge and darted inside.

Daniel and Ben gripped their mother's hands and helped her up the last of the incline. Mr. Jones waited at the bottom of the ledge with his hands outstretched. She hesitated.

Daniel gently nudged her. "Mom, we need to hurry."

Ben scuffled down, nearly losing his balance several times, and waited next to his dad.

Mrs. Jones sat down and awkwardly skidded down the slope in a seated position. "Now wait just a minute!" she objected, every other word punctuated by a bump over a rock. "There's no hurrying. I haven't agreed to either of you going yet, so don't think you can just run off."

Daniel joined them on the ledge while Mr. Jones helped her up. He held the ivy vines aside while Ben led his parents inside.

"Where exactly is this Abyss?" his mom demanded. "And you said there was something we could help with. I assume you mean for us to come along to make sure you *kids* don't get into any trouble."

Both Joneses spread out and began inspecting the cave, eyeing every nook and cranny as though each held some unknown supernatural danger. They quickly zeroed in on the pedestal.

"With us?" Ben hissed to Daniel, the look of wild panic returning to his eyes.

"No," Gabriela said, holding out her hands in an apologetic gesture. "You'd be in too much danger."

"Because we don't have a Weapon of Power," Mr. Jones said, his voice steady and matter-of-fact.

"Not only that. You're not used to outright spiritual warfare. It would be too much for both of you, and, honestly, you'd be a liability."

Mr. Jones nodded, putting his hands on Daniel and Ben's shoulders.

"So, what, then?" Mrs. Jones snapped, taking two steps forward and gripping the pedestal as if she were about to rip it out of the cave floor. "What do we do? Go back to the house and knit socks with Janice? Clean? Cook? Carry on like my boys (and you too, Seren—I'm sure you'll be in danger too, but … you understand)

aren't risking their lives against monsters and giant dragons and everything else unholy in this world?"

Seren sighed impatiently and hiked up her backpack. She cast an exasperated glance to Daniel.

"What?" he mouthed, slipping out from his father's grip and edging closer to her. "Like I can control them."

Gabriela gave a reassuring laugh that didn't reach her eyes. "No. But there is something very important we need from you." She stepped forward and took Mrs. Jones's hands in her own, folding them together while leading her away from the pedestal. "We need you to pray."

Before Mrs. Jones could protest the simplicity of her job, Gabriela continued. "The entrance to the Abyss is at Stonehenge, but we'll be transported somewhere in Ireland first to find Raylin."

"You mean to that place she was sighted last," Ben said, pulling out his phone. "Wasn't it in County Limbo or something?"

"Probably not County Limbo, Ben," Daniel snickered.

Seren tapped her foot impatiently. "Sligo," she corrected and then fell into a stony silence.

Gabriela stared at Ben, her brows knitted in confusion. "Sligo? If she was there, she's moved on. We'll be taken to a different location." She turned back to the Joneses. "Prayer is powerful. It weakens the power of the Enemy and protects the Father's children. It brings peace and—"

"I know about praying, Young Lady!" Mrs. Jones raised a hand in the air, one finger pointed to the ceiling and gesturing menacingly. "I pray for my boys all the time. Every day. But if you think sticking me on the prayer chain is going to make me feel better about letting them go, you've got another thing coming." Mrs. Jones had lapsed into her lecture voice.

"Oh no," Ben hissed right in Daniel's ear.

Daniel jumped. "What the heck, man? Not so close."

Ben continued without acknowledging Daniel's start. "Gabriela's about to get grounded big time. She'll probably get assigned to slave labor doing chores in our house until she turns a hundred. Mom's serious now."

"This is taking so long I'm a hundred," Seren groaned. "Look," she said more loudly, "I know you're both worried about Daniel and Ben. But my sister's life is in danger *right now*. And every moment we wait is another moment she suffers. Let's go."

Mrs. Jones was momentarily shocked into a red-faced silence by Seren's defiant outburst.

Gabriela took advantage of the moment's reprieve. "There's something more to your task, though." She backed toward Daniel and Ben and turned. "Don't move," she commanded, holding out her palms and covering both their eyes. She muttered something under her breath. Daniel blushed, and he felt his cheeks grow warm at her touch. Too quickly, she had finished and went to do the same to Seren. Finally, she held her hands over her own eyes, then folded them in front of her chest. "When we are in need, you will know our need. You will see our need," she said, her tone like a recitation of poetry or a long-rehearsed speech. Her palms opened and Daniel saw a clear sphere appear in her hands. She breathed on it, then held it out.

Mr. and Mrs. Jones eyed it with evident distrust.

"This is an Orb of Seeing. When we need help, this will allow you to see through our eyes to better know how ..."

The crystal sphere flared bright gold. The light coalesced into an image showing the back of Daniel's head, Gabriela's left shoulder, and the Joneses holding the ball.

Daniel turned around to find Ben standing behind him and Gabriela. "Uh, Ben. Are you in need of something?"

Ben glanced up at Daniel and the others, the image in the sphere changing in real-time to reflect everything he saw. He shrugged. "I need to go to the bathroom."

"I need to go to the bathroom," Ben's voice parroted from the orb.

"You'll be able to hear some things, too," Gabriela said, putting her hands on her hips and tilting her head to the side while study-ing the orb. "Its setting is awfully sensitive, though."

Seren groaned angrily and slapped a hand to her forehead.

Daniel laughed, "I'd say. I don't think Mom and Dad want a first-row seat to every time Ben needs to … uh … you get the picture."

"Let me see it back for a moment." Gabriela snatched the orb from the Joneses and cupped it in her hands again. After a sec-ond of silence and concentrated grimacing, she handed it back. The sphere was now dark, save for a slowly pulsating light in the center.

"When we're in *true* need," she said, casting an annoyed look at Ben.

"What? It's not like I did something wrong."

"You'll be able to see how to pray specifically, and how the Three answer your prayers."

Mrs. Jones still looked uncertain.

Daniel summoned the Sun Sword and let it float horizontally in front of him. "During the last quest, when you all were in the Cay-man Islands, I learned about how powerful prayer was—more pow-erful than the Sun Sword or any other weapon. I always thought it was kind of pointless, saying the same things over and over. Just tradition, or ritual, or something. But, Mom, the Father will answer your prayers, and he'll send the help we need at the right time. Even if it doesn't seem that way. Trust me."

"And now," Gabriela said, grabbing Daniel and Ben's hands and pulling them back closer toward the pedestal, "we are pushed to the limit." A backpack had been stowed at the base of the pedestal next to Seren's feet. Gabriela grabbed it and hoisted it onto her shoul-ders. "Goodbye, Mr. and Mrs. Jones."

Even Mr. Jones was caught off guard by Gabriela's sudden tran-sition. "Daniel. Ben. You be careful." He tried unsuccessfully to look severe and commanding.

Mrs. Jones flew into a state of hysterics. "Wait!" she shouted. "What about food? Where will you sleep? When will you be back? I need answers!"

"Good grief!" Seren's voice was steely and beyond impatient. She lunged forward and shoved her hand into the handprint on the pedestal.

Maybe it was her sense of urgency and lack of hesitation. Maybe it was a mercy from the Three. Either way, Daniel had never experienced the Transportation Pedestal fire up and transport them out of the cave so quickly. No hovering. No gradual spinning of the room. The barrier roared to life in front of them, and they hurtled through a nauseating vortex of light and blurry, squirming images.

5

Newgrange

Seren drew back her hand from the stone. The handprint, along with the entire stone, emanated a gentle white light that barely illuminated the immediate area. It slowly faded, and Daniel's eyes grew accustomed to the silvery gleam of a bright, half-moon shining over the landscape. They weren't in a cave this time but in the open air. Instead of a pedestal, they'd been transported to a stone about eight feet tall and cut in irregular angles with ancient, weatherworn swirls carved into the surface. The ground was strewn with gravel, but beyond that, a vast field of grass dotted with other imposing standing stones stretched toward the horizon in every direction. The sky was clear and filled with fiery stars. Even in Oregon, Daniel had never seen them burn so brightly.

A dark, rounded structure loomed ominously in the distance. One light shone from the ground in front of it, barely casting back the dark shadows it draped over the ground like a fallen cloak. The light was enough for Daniel to make out a square doorway, black against the feeble glow like some giant's mouth, stretched open in an eternal yawn. A lazy wind blew over the landscape, drawing a moan from the opening. He shivered and turned to his companions.

"Does transporting always feel like that?" Gabriela gasped, leaning against the stone, a hand to her forehead.

"Yes," Ben said flatly. "Orbs of Passage are just as bad. Maybe worse, but you probably remember that from India. Speaking of bad things," he turned to Daniel, "I somehow don't think everything will be hunky-dory when we get home."

Daniel snorted. "Mom will probably blame us for transporting before she had a chance to lecture us thoroughly. It's the death sentence for sure." He thought for a moment. On the other hand, maybe his parents finding out about his secret life battling evil could help his cause with his biological mother.

Father, please make sure that whatever Mom and Dad see of our quest helps them realize I'm mature enough to handle bringing my mother into my life.

He didn't hear a reply, but that didn't surprise him.

Seren stood motionless, oblivious to the others around her. Her eyes were locked on the structure in the distance. "I've been here before," she muttered.

"This is Newgrange," Gabriela said, scanning the sky.

"Is that supposed to mean something?" Ben asked. He surveyed the area with a look of distrust. "Let me guess: it's full of demons and bad guys, right?"

Seren seemed lost in her own world and plodded in the direction of the dome as if drawn toward the open doorway. "This was the resting place for the Celestial Bow," she finally said. She shut her eyes and turned back to the group. "Why are we here?"

"Since Raylin is our quest," Gabriela answered, "we transport to where she is. She is either in the area or soon will be."

The wind picked up and blew in waves across the undulating sea of moonlit grass. Daniel zipped up his jacket. "I thought she was looking for evil spirits to suck into the Voidblade or something. Wouldn't this be, I don't know, some kind of holy place?"

"It *was*. But anywhere the Three are moving and working, the Enemy seeks to corrupt." Gabriela put her hands on her hips and nodded toward the dome. "It's been many years since the Celestial Bow was here, who knows what sort of evil spirits have moved in once Seren took it. Raylin is probably after them."

"Uh, guys?" Ben had taken a few steps away from the group and stared at something in the darkness. He pointed toward a large standing stone rooted in the ground to the right of the dome. "What's that?"

Everyone was at his side in an instant.

A gigantic bird roosted atop the monolith. Its solid gray feathers gave off a faint shimmer, except for a crown of black plumage cresting its head. The bill was flat and rounded—like a goose. The creature's entire shape was that of a goose, in fact, though Daniel could never remember one looking so beautiful. Its eyes, deep blue and glowing, suddenly focused on the group.

Daniel felt his entire body gripped by some unseen force as if some giant had taken him gently in hand. It was mesmerizing. "Is it evil?" he asked the others. He tried to turn his head to see if they were experiencing the same thing but found he couldn't look away from the bird.

"It doesn't feel evil," Seren said, her voice monotone and subdued. She stepped forward. "It's kind of peaceful."

"Yeah," Ben agreed. "Like it's staring right through me. It makes me feel naked. I don't know why that would be peaceful, but it is. Am I wearing pants?"

Daniel could hear the faint patter of Ben slapping his thighs.

"Yep. Pants."

"Dude. You're sounding crazy. Stop talking."

Gabriela had fallen silent since they'd noticed the bird.

"Gabriela?"

Before she could answer, the sensation of peace shattered, replaced by a nauseating wave of dread.

The goose craned its neck toward the sky.

Daniel followed its gaze. Raylin, sporting Garuda's inky black wings, flew across the moon directly above Newgrange. She sported a pair of torn jeans, bare feet, and a dirty gray t-shirt riddled with holes. Her hair, white as snow, was a wild mass of tangles and snarls.

She spotted the goose and paused in flight, beating the air to keep herself suspended. With a shudder, she raised her right arm. The Voidblade, black as pitch and still grafted to her right hand, sucked the surrounding moonlight into its hellish depths, blurring and warping the air. A blood-red fireball burst into flame at the tip, then grew to an immense size. With a shriek, Raylin swung the sword, flinging the fireball toward the bird.

Daniel wanted to cry out a warning as the roaring flames neared the goose, but his concern wasn't needed. The bird lifted its head, took a breath, and exhaled. The fire flickered out like a candle flame before a gale.

The bird spread its wings; the undersides were adorned with intricate lines of luminescent blue. With one flap, it was beside Raylin in the sky.

She screamed in fright and swung the Voidblade wildly to keep the giant bird at bay.

"Careful, Mr. Goose!" Ben shouted. "Daniel, shoot a Sunstorm!"

But even if Daniel had done so, it would've been too late. The jagged blade, razor-sharp and honed down to a needle's point at its tip, struck the bird's outstretched head.

Sparks like fireworks burst outward with sizzling pops, streaking toward the dome below. Wisps of dark spirits exploded out of the sword; eight-pointed stars flamed to life on each before they were sucked into small portals of white light opening beneath them. The bird, however, seemed completely unaffected.

Raylin pumped her wings and flew backward, sending two more fireballs at the bird. The goose extinguished them as easily as it had the first, and it quickly flanked her. Her back was now turned to the Vessels.

Two flares to Daniel's right brought him spinning around. Seren had fired a round of arrows straight toward Raylin and was readying another one on the luminescent string. It followed its predecessors in the blink of an eye.

Raylin spun toward them as if sensing their presence. Immediately before they struck, she barrel-rolled to the left and came up facing the companions. With a shriek of rage like some angry hawk, she dove toward Seren.

Daniel summoned the Sun Sword and fired a Sunstorm as quickly as he could. Raylin's breakneck speed made her a difficult target, but the arc of fire was at least enough to make her veer off course and buy them a few more seconds. "Ben! We—"

The Triune Shield was already expanding outward from where Ben stood to Daniel's left. Raylin swung the Voidblade wildly toward Seren. Inches from her neck, it met the expanding borders of the shield.

Raylin shrieked and crashed into the barrier, hammering it with the Voidblade. Her eyes, small pinpoints of inhuman red, glowed fiercely in the darkness outside the shield. They were fixed on Seren.

"Raylin!" Seren shouted. "We're here to save you. Don't fight us!" Seren fired two more arrows, but Raylin easily dodged them and continued her assault.

Daniel channeled all his energy into the Sun Sword. "Ben, you need a Fire Strike?"

"I'm good," Ben replied, his voice calm and unharried. "Compared to that Abida dork, this is easy."

"Raylin!" Ben said, turning his focus to her. "We're your friends, Raylin. Don't you remember us?"

But there was no recognition in Raylin's eyes. Only burning hatred and rage.

Daniel fired another Sunstorm, but she evaded it easily.

The gray bird closed in, obscuring the night sky behind Raylin. It spread its wings to cut off her escape, but at the last second, she folded hers and fell like a stone to the ground. She crashed into the grass with a thud and then scurried on all fours out from under her assailant. A split second later, she took to the air and tore through the darkness toward the gaping doorway of Newgrange.

The giant bird flapped its wings to change directions. A few pinions flicked the Triune Shield. The second they made contact, Ben cried out in surprise, and something happened so jarring to Daniel's senses he could hardly process the experience. The Triune Shield enlarged and lifted off the ground. Daniel felt himself filled with the presence of the Three; his body hovered in the air, and a pure white flame burned above his head. He remembered something similar when Granny had given him and Ben the Gift of Tongues before the last quest, but this felt different. It was more like the Father's Blessing at Intipuncu, though not quite as powerful. He didn't have time to look over at Seren, but he knew she experienced the same. He could feel her, Ben, and Gabriela. In that fleeting moment of peace and power, all were connected—one in mind; one in spirit. For a brief moment, his attention shifted to Gabriela, and Daniel sensed a sadness. Not depression or despair, but a feeling of loss. Grief. Somewhere deep inside her. Before he had time to consider its source, the giant goose flew skyward, and the feathers broke away from the shield. The moment passed. Their bodies were normal again, and the Triune Shield regained its usual size.

"What just happened?" Ben gasped, his voice giddy with excitement.

Seren, breathless but beaming with joy, replied, "I … I don't know. But we still need … we still …"

"Focus on Raylin," Gabriela said flatly. She pointed toward Newgrange. "She flew into the ruins and is probably searching for dark spirits. We need to stop her before she grows more powerful."

Daniel stayed quiet. He searched the starry sky for more signs of the goose. After a moment, he spotted its faintly glowing feathers and iridescent sapphire eyes hovering over Newgrange. Its head hung low as if in contemplation of the ruins below it, and then it shimmered and simply faded away. His mind raced. What was it? Some unusual Firstborn come to their aid? Why didn't it communicate with them and give any direction? It couldn't have been an emissary of the Enemy sent to destroy Raylin. Its power was clearly holy.

Ben returned to his human form next to Daniel. "What's with Gabriela?" He whispered. "It felt like she was upset about something."

Daniel nodded. "I sensed it, too. No idea."

Seren pushed past them and charged off toward Newgrange. "You heard Gabriela. Let's get a move on."

Gabriela took off after her.

"Seren, wait a minute," Daniel called as he and Ben hustled to keep up. "Listen. I know you're anxious to save Raylin, but we've got to be a team here. Ben barely had time to use the shield after you shot at Raylin. Give us a little warning when you're about to engage an enemy so we can all be prepared. We need to have a plan."

"You want to have a plan, Mr. Fly-By-The-Seat-Of-Your-Pants?"

"Hey, I learned stuff on the past two quests. And I also know that Raylin is like, crazy powerful."

"Look. She was open, and I had to take the shot," Seren retorted. "If the arrows had hit—"

"*If* they had hit. But they didn't, and she attacked so fast you were nearly cut with the Voidblade."

Seren fell into a stony silence as they approached the domed structure.

The building was massive. One light shone on the entrance, illuminating the structure but penetrating no more than a few feet into the pitch-black doorway. Thin-cut stones lined the opening, standing upright to form the side jambs of the door. A similarly slender stone, rough-hewn and slightly beveled, formed the head jamb, which framed the bottom of a rectangular window positioned directly above the entry. Thousands of square, gray blocks stacked on each other like stone-age bricks formed the imposing walls immediately surrounding the doorway. Beyond this, white stones stretched around the circular structure, studded at precise intervals by dark, rounded rocks. Enormous blocks of granite lay on their side, collaring the circumference of the ruins. A thick thatch of grass grew upon the earthen roof, which curved into the starry night like the surface of some planet, lost in the depths of space. Directly in front of the ruins, a wooden fence forced would-be visitors to take one of two sets of steps—one to the right and the other to the left of the entrance.

Voices, muffled and angry, echoed from the darkness of the interior. The companions cautiously took the left set of stairs, which bridged huge stones laid on their side in front of the doorway. The center stone, carved deeply with patterns of swirls and diamonds, sat between two slightly larger rough-hewn rectangular blocks. They paused to the side of the doorway.

"Just communicate, okay?" Daniel whispered to Seren.

"Sure," she said flatly.

Daniel wasn't an expert on girls, but he was sure this meant the exact opposite of what he was going for.

Ben and Gabriela darted across the opening to stand on the other side.

"Elephant in the room here," Daniel said. "Does anybody know what the giant bird was? Is it a Firstborn that'll help us? Because if so, I wish it would've stayed."

They all looked at Gabriela, who seemed irritated with the attention.

"Not sure," she replied, keeping her eyes fixed on the doorway. "Can we maybe talk about it a different time?"

Ben persisted. "But you spent all that time with the Three. If it was a Firstborn, you would've met it, right? I thought you knew all about the spirit world."

"Well, I don't," she snapped. "Now focus. Something's happening!"

Gabriela was right. The voices were louder now, and one had begun shouting.

Daniel summoned the Sun Sword, but Gabriela frantically waved for him to release it.

"The light will give us away!" she hissed.

Daniel immediately let the sword return to his chest and held up his hands. "Sorry. How are we going to see?"

"There's a light from inside. It's just dim."

Daniel rubbed his eyes and peered inside the passage. She was right. A faint glow, brownish-blue, reflected off some of the interior rocks.

Gabriela made a move to go in, then hesitated.

"Something wrong?" Daniel asked.

Gabriela shrugged. "No. I'm fine. It's just that, I'm not sure who's in there with Raylin."

Seren tapped her foot. "Isn't that the point? I need to bind her before she absorbs any other demons."

"It's a pretty tight area," Gabriela said, chewing her bottom lip. "We might get trapped. Maybe we should wait and ambush her when she comes out."

Daniel studied Gabriela. Something was different from when she had joined them in India. She seemed more … nervous. More uncertain. He fell into prayer.

Father, what do we do? Should we wait for Raylin to come to us? And what's up with Gabriela? Why is she so afraid?

For the first time on the quest, an answer came, and immediately.

Follow after Raylin. Quickly.

Okay, so he was just going to ignore the question about Gabriela.

"The Father says we should go in and fast," Daniel said.

Gabriela snapped her head toward him. "He answered you?"

Daniel nodded, perplexed by her tone. He couldn't tell if she was relieved or irritated with him. "Yeah. But we need to act fast, apparently."

Gabriela took a deep breath. "Okay. Follow me." She ducked her head and silently melted into the gloom of the ruins.

Seren pushed past Daniel to follow, and he and Ben fell into step behind them.

"What was that about?" Ben whispered.

"No idea," Daniel replied. "None at all."

Following Gabriela's lead, all four kept close to the right wall of the corridor, flattening themselves as much as possible to use the periodic jutting stones in the passageway as cover for whatever awaited them inside. Every few feet, they had to duck under a low-hanging stone spanning the path. They crept along like this for about fifteen yards, the voices growing louder and angrier the further they went. Ahead, the passageway took a slight turn and opened into a chamber. Gabriela paused at the last jutting rock and peered around. Daniel crouched down and did the same, happy for an excuse to be so near her. Ben and Seren peeked around their shoulders.

The entire chamber was only about seventeen feet long and twenty feet wide. Above them, great slabs of stone were stacked in an ever-narrowing pattern until they reached chimney height, where a wide slab of mottled gray granite capped them off.

Raylin stood with her back to the passageway, wings folded as she waved the Voidblade back and forth. Three beings, each standing in an alcove situated to the north, west, and east points in the chamber, glared out from their recesses, some object or weapon brandished before them to ward off Raylin's inevitable attack.

"Afraid to move against us, are you?" the being in the center taunted. She spoke quickly and with a thick Irish accent. Her hair, grey-green and long, flowed around her like a sea of weedy water. Her pale brown dress complimented her skin, which glowed with an unhealthy shade of gray. She held a silver ewer in both hands, the spout pointed toward Raylin as if it was some dangerous weapon. "Did not realize we would be ready for you now, did you? Eh? Eh?"

Raylin stared silently back and inched forward.

"Quit wasting our time talking to the girl, Boann." This from the creature on the left. His voice was scratchy and deep and similarly accented. Goat horns curved out of his head, and a great shaggy beard grew down to his stomach, covering his bare chest. He brandished a staff toward Raylin in one hand and cradled a harp in the other. He reminded Daniel of Greek stories of fauns, though his legs were human, except for wicked looking claws sprouting from his toes like daggers. His beady, red eyes and sharp teeth added to the deeply sinister look. No gentle, mischievous faun here. "She is not going to talk. Let us kill her and be done with it. Then Master will reward us! He will send those simple-minded druids with more sacrifices."

He made a quick move toward Raylin, and the Voidblade was suddenly screaming toward him in a wild black arc. He flew backward, growling and waving his staff wildly in the air to deflect the blow. It missed his chest by inches but sliced the lower half of his beard clean off. The hair transformed into dark spirit and was sucked into the Voidblade.

Raylin shuddered and her breathing quickened.

"Daghdha, you fool!" Boann nagged from her center alcove, her murky eyes never moving from Raylin. "You made her stronger. Idiot. That is what happens when you rush into things. Aengus," she snapped, whipping her head toward the man in the right alcove for a brief second. "You and Daghdha attack at the same time, and I will try to drive her out. It will be safer to fight once we have pushed her outside."

Aengus, tall with dark features, stepped out of his recess in the wall. He wore a kilt of some animal skin with a cape draped over his shoulders. His chest, too, was bare, except for twin tattoos of swans. Instead of a beard, his face was youthful and clean-shaven. Dark shadows under his eyes gave him a tragic, forlorn look. If Daniel didn't know he was really some evil spirit taken form, he would've mistaken this guy for some teen heartthrob. A straight, double-edged sword flashed out from the folds of his cape, and he advanced toward Raylin.

Quicker than Daniel's eyes could follow, Aengus slashed at Raylin. Her free hand shot out in a blur and caught the blade in an iron grip and snapped it in two. She shifted her weight and tried to stab him with the Voidblade. He dove under the attack and retreated to Boann's alcove. "Do something!" he shouted, looking around her dress toward Daghdha. "You were supposed to attack at the same time!" His voice did not match his looks. It held the same inflection as Boann's, but instead of suave and crooning, it was harsh, demanding—like a toddler's.

"I answer to no one! I am the Daghdha, and I am your leader! You two attack at the same time. I will back YOU up."

Boann rolled her eyes. "Always were a bunch of sniveling little cowards, you were. The both of you." She lifted her ewer toward Raylin, and a powerful spout of muddy water blasted out of its mouth.

Raylin lifted the Voidblade defensively, but it had no effect. The water simply flowed around the sword and crashed into her body, driving her backward toward the corridor where Daniel and the others were hiding.

Daghdha, emboldened by Boann's attack, strummed his harp furiously. The sound vibrated through the ruin. Two small slabs of stone broke from their resting place in the side of the wall and wheeled through the air, smashing into Raylin from either side and pinning her arms to her body.

She growled, writhing back and forth in an effort to break free.

Aengus smiled from behind Boann and stepped out with a confident air as if he hadn't just been cowering in the corner. He sauntered toward Raylin, the broken sword hilt still in his hand. He raised it to his left; the broken blade, fallen to the ground somewhere out of sight, flew to the hilt and reattached itself. "We are the Tuatha Dé Danann!"

Raylin hissed at Aengus as he approached.

Boann and Daghdha, both still focusing their powers on keeping her bound, smiled cruelly.

"We need to attack," Seren muttered from behind Daniel. "They're going to kill her!"

Daniel nodded. "Ben, put the shield around Raylin, while Seren binds her. I'll—"

Seren was already standing and drawing the Celestial Bow back to her cheek. Its light, holy and radiant, flooded the chamber. She loosed the arrow, which sped past Raylin and hit Aengus straight in the chest.

The shell of blue light encased him in seconds, and the eight-pointed star blossomed on his chest. He promptly fell over, a look of surprise and cowardice frozen on his face.

Boann gritted her teeth. "The Vessels are here too!" She flung her arm up before Seren could shoot another arrow. Vines burst out of the ground at her feet and shot into the narrow passageway, snaking around Seren, then Gabriela, and finally Daniel and Ben. They bound their arms and legs behind their bodies and flung them to the ground.

"We are going to have a serious talk about your impulsivity, Seren!" Daniel shouted. He summoned the Sun Sword, which extended straight down from his pinned arm. The vines around his legs were immediately severed. Now slack, those around his chest and arms fell off as he jumped to his feet to help the others.

He ran to Gabriela first, but with one fluid motion, she snapped the vines like spider webs and scrambled into a crouch. "I'm fine. Go help Ben. I'll get Seren."

"Oh, right. Forgot you were Wonder Woman." He dashed to Ben's side and drew the Sun Sword along the vines, then darted toward Raylin, the Sun Sword raised above his head and charging with a Fire Strike. He stabbed the ground.

Raylin, neck craned at the sound of Daniel's approach, gathered her strength and flung herself into the air and away from the purifying shockwave. Aengus was quickly purified. His dark spirit burst into the air, and his sword, now rusted and covered in what looked like ancient red blood stains, clattered to the ground.

With a shout of effort, Raylin jumped into the air and spun so fast her face blurred, then strained her arms and wings.

Aengus's purification and Raylin's sudden movement evidently caught Boann and Daghdha off guard. The strength of the water jet momentarily slackened, and Daghdha faltered in his song.

It was all Raylin needed. Her wings burst her bonds, flinging the imprisoning stones to crash back into the walls. She flew toward Aengus's enraged spirit, which still haunted the highest point of the ceiling. The Voidblade made quick work of him.

Seeing her partner vanquished, Boann shrieked again.

Daniel darted into the room toward her. "Stop screaming! What are you? Three years old?"

Boann pressed herself further back into her alcove. "A Vessel working with the traitor?" Her eyes darted back and forth between Raylin and Daniel. "She will kill you, too!"

Daniel sensed an oppressive wave of anger. Instinctively, he flung himself to the ground just as Raylin swooped over his head, sweeping the Voidblade in a wild arc.

Seren ran into the chamber, shooting two arrows at her back.

Raylin folded her wings and fell to the ground; the arrows struck the chamber ceiling and then disappeared. Her descent brought her down nearly on top of Daghdha.

He skittered backward until his back was pressed against his alcove wall, furiously strumming his harp again. At the end of each discordant chord, he flung his hand toward Raylin. The music, like an invisible fist, pounded into Raylin's chest, pushing her backward with each cacophonous barrage.

Gabriela and Ben shuffled into the crowded chamber, keeping their backs against the wall, and sidling up next to Daniel.

Boann's beady eyes glowered from the dimness of her alcove, flitting back and forth between the companions and Raylin.

Seren, now feet from Raylin, drew the Celestial Bow and fired.

Raylin dropped to her knees.

Daghdha's last attack flew overhead and slammed into Seren even as her arrow, unfazed by his musical power, nailed him in the stomach. He froze as the binding light encased his body while Seren, sailing backward, crashed onto the ground where she lay gasping for air.

In a blindingly fast movement, Raylin caught Daghdha with an upward thrust of the Voidblade, the momentum of which carried her into the air. With his dark spirit still trailing in the wake of the sword, she immediately changed directions to bring the blade down in a stabbing motion toward Seren. Only Daghdha's staff and harp remained behind.

Ben ran toward Seren, summoning the Triune Shield even as he skidded to a stop beside her. The Voidblade clanged loudly against the barrier. The border of the shield momentarily shrunk before bouncing back to its original size. Raylin's eyes glowed red and her white hair snaked around her as if the absorption of the two demons had pushed her over the edge to another level of power. In a blur of attacks, she alternated between stabbing and slashing the shield, each point of contact causing the shield to grow smaller and smaller.

"A little help here!" Ben shouted. "She's grown a heck of a lot stronger!"

Daniel ran forward, Sun Sword charging for a Fire Strike. Boann's river of water curved around the Triune Shield and knocked him against the opposite wall.

"Oh, let the traitor kill them!" she hissed. "We have no need for so many Vessels running around. One would be quite sufficient for the Master's experiments, in my opinion."

The unceasing spray of water covered Daniel's face, making it hard to breathe or see, much less intervene to help Ben. Mustering all his strength, he raised the Sun Sword into the stream of water, hoping its purifying power would extend to water. It worked. Where the murky stream met the blade, the barrage slackened and succumbed to gravity, falling to the ground like rain.

His vision now clear, Daniel caught sight of Gabriela leaping over the Triune Shield and punching Raylin in the jaw. The force of the blow flattened her to the ground, but only for a second.

Raylin threw her legs above her head and flexed her wings, turning a backward somersault that landed her next to Boann. She spun, bringing the Voidblade screaming toward the demon.

Boann instantly melted into a puddle of water before the strike landed. Raylin paused in surprise by the sudden transformation. In that moment, Boann erupted into the air, her form still that of a woman, but wholly liquid. Raylin rocketed toward her to play a game of cat and mouse around the chamber ceiling.

Ben resumed his human form, and Gabriela ran to help Seren to her feet. The movement was enough to get Raylin's attention. She changed targets and dove, Voidblade first, toward Seren.

Daniel flung himself to the center of the chamber on his back and fired a Sunstorm upward.

Raylin swerved at the last second, and the blast crashed into the ceiling.

Huge stone slabs fell to the ground with a crash, followed by dirt and smaller debris. A rock, about the size of a basketball, fell on Daniel's left leg. The Sun Sword immediately disappeared back into his chest as a blinding pain shot through his shin.

Gabriela, with Seren and Ben caught up in her arms, ran toward the corridor for cover. Moonlight spilled into the chamber from the gaping hole in the roof. Boann flew out of the opening with one last shrill scream. Raylin followed close behind, crashing through the hole and knocking more stones to the floor as she burst out of Newgrange.

Despite the constant rain of rubble all around Daniel, he couldn't move. He dimly heard Gabriela giving orders to Seren and Ben and then felt himself yanked into the air by her powerful arms as she ran with him through the passageway and into the night air. Despite being jostled around like a sack of potatoes, he caught sight of Ben and Seren running down the wooden steps and onto the lawn before the ruins.

The awkwardness of being carried by the girl he liked made Daniel momentarily forget the pain in his leg. But that all changed when she set him back on his feet.

He cried out and promptly collapsed to the grass, grabbing his left leg. He was vaguely aware of Gabriela raising her hands and a bright, softball-sized ball of white light floating into the air.

"Another one of your special powers?" Ben asked.

Gabriela gingerly rolled up Daniel's pants leg. "Yeah," she muttered, distracted as she scanned Daniel's leg. Her eyes grew wider. "Oh, no."

"Oh, no?" Daniel looked down. His shin was purple, and the part of his leg below that was turned at a slight angle. "Oh, no! Why is my leg crooked? Shouldn't it be straight?"

Ben dropped to his knees in concern, his eyes widening as he studied Daniel's leg. "I think it's broken."

Seren sucked air through her teeth in a pained expression. "Definitely broken."

Daniel let his head fall back onto the grass. Perfect. He finally has a quest with Gabriela, and he turns into an invalid.

In the distance, Boann let out an obnoxiously blood-curdling scream.

I couldn't have said it better myself.

6

The Mist

"How can it be broken?" Seren asked, her voice rising. She paced back and forth, hands on her head.

"You see," Daniel said through gritted teeth, "you rushed in to attack without listening to the plan. And then, everything got super crazy, and a giant rock fell on my leg! Make sense?"

Ben sat on the ground next to him, his eyes closed in prayer. Gabriela walked around in the light, ignoring their conversation while she searched the ground for something.

"There's no guarantee that your plan would've worked out better," Seren snapped. "Raylin was about to be killed. There wasn't time for talk; I had to act. But that's not what I meant. Why did the Three let your leg get broken at the start of a quest? What possible good can come of it? How are we going to travel around and fight enemies, find Raylin again and keep her from killing us, make her follow us or bind her or whatever, AND reach the Serpent's Abyss if your leg is broken? It's impossible!" She stabbed her finger toward the globe of light. "And isn't this going to draw unwanted attention?"

Gabriela didn't look up from whatever she was searching for. "The light's invisible to enemies."

"That's cool," Ben said. "But, uh, what *are* we supposed to do about Daniel's leg?"

"I don't have answers for all your questions, Seren," Gabriela replied. "And Ben, right now, I'm looking for sticks to make a splint. But there's nothing here." She put her hands on her hips and sighed. "We'll have to go search for them."

"You going to carry him?" Ben asked.

Daniel shut his eyes and groaned. "Perfect. More humiliation." And then a little louder, "You know, Seren, just because the Three *allowed* this to happen doesn't mean it *had* to happen. If we had followed my plan, it would've been safer. Next time, act like you're part of the team instead of a one-woman show. Work with us."

"Lay off me, okay? My sister was about to be killed."

"You both need to chill out," Ben said, his voice quiet but commanding.

Daniel looked at him sideways. Seren, too, seemed surprised.

"The first priority is Daniel's leg, not deciding who to blame." He leaned back into a sitting position. "Even with Gabriela carrying him, traveling is going to be slow with Daniel like this. And we don't even know where Raylin's headed or how far away it is. Do you think we should look for a car or train or something?"

Gabriela shook her head. "No. We'll be traveling in a different way."

"Please tell me it's someway peaceful and not by Orb or Galactic Toilet?"

"Galactic Toilet?" Seren asked, still pacing and searching the sky for any sign of Raylin.

"It's a Chamber of the Moon thing," Daniel said between deep breaths. The pain in his leg now radiated from his shin up to his thigh. "Look, can we talk about this after we've splinted up my leg or something? And did anyone pack any medicine? Ibuprofen? Tylenol? Anyone? Anyone?"

Everyone stared blankly back.

"Perfect."

"It's closer to cloud," Gabriela said. "But Daniel's right. Splint first."

Ben stood. "Wait, we're traveling by cloud? Oh, awesome! We've done that before; it's super relaxing. I'll go look for a few sticks."

Gabriela shook her head. "It's not like—never mind. You'll see in a minute."

"Again: what are we going to do after that?" Seren interjected. She finally stopped pacing and crouched down next to Daniel. "Daniel can't fight. Anyone heard from the Three? Cause they're not giving me any direction when I pray."

They all looked at Gabriela.

"I'm not sure. I haven't prayed about it yet," she replied.

Ben held up his pinky and thumb to his ear like a phone. "What happened? You used to have like a 24/7 direct open line to the Father."

Gabriela flashed him an irritated look and glanced toward the ground. "That was when I was in training with Granny. Now, I have to pray and wait for an answer just like everyone else."

"Guys," Daniel gasped, the pain reaching a crescendo. "Somebody do something please!" He closed his eyes and fell into prayer but could do little more than repeat "Help!" over and over in his mind.

Seren stood again. "Sorry, Daniel," she muttered. "Sorry for everything. And, uh, I'm praying for you." She went back to searching the sky.

Gabriela nodded to Ben. "I'll try to reset the bone. You need a light?"

"Nah," Ben replied. "You're not the only one with some new tricks. I've been working on something." He drew out his golden daggers and closed his eyes; the blades began to glow with the same light as the Triune Shield. "I figured out that if I'm touching something small, I can cast a shield over it as long as I'm in contact with it. It should be enough light to find a few sticks with."

"Cool," Daniel said, his voice quiet and strained. "What's this about resetting the bone?" he asked Gabriela. His voice had gone up an octave.

Gabriela flashed a fake smile, then turned to Ben. "There are some trees at the edge of the field." She pointed behind them where the light of the moon now streamed through the branches of a thin line of large trees growing like sentinels around the edge of the Newgrange compound. "Why don't you and Seren go get us two sticks about an arm's length. Hurry, but be careful."

Ben tapped Seren, and they jogged out of the light of Gabriela's globe.

Daniel changed positions and winced. He was finally alone with Gabriela, and he had a broken leg. Just his luck.

She knelt down beside him and gently ran her hands over his shin. Despite the pain, he felt a little thrill at the thought of being alone with her. "How is Aguas Calientes these days?" he asked, trying to breathe through the pain. "Had a chance to check in on your parents?"

Gabriela momentarily paused in her examination, then resumed with a look of grim determination. "I'm not sure. The Three have given me assurance they're alive, but beyond that ..." she shrugged. "As far as I know, they're still in darkness. Okay, one, two—"

"What's with the counting—AH! Why are you squeezing my leg?" A searing pain shot through Daniel's shin and into his thigh. His vision went black for a second and a wave of nausea churned through his stomach.

Gabriela held up her hands apologetically. "Sorry! Sorry! I had to reset the bone. It'll help it heal better."

Daniel repositioned himself and another sharp pain wracked his body. "Where did you learn that?" He grimaced. "Spirit-world medical school?"

Gabriela smiled for the first time since beginning the quest. It was almost enough to make Daniel momentarily forget about his pain. Almost.

"More or less," she finally replied. "Granny taught me some basic survival and first aid skills. Someone's got to keep you all safe."

"That's good to hear." Daniel smiled back and laid his head down. His thoughts were immediately drawn into prayer. A calm spread through his mind, and his racing thoughts slowed. Despite the gravity of the situation, he felt reassured that even his broken leg was a part of the Father's plan. And, somehow, he was at peace with this. Maybe it was all the times he had witnessed the Three taking even the worst situations and turning them into something amazing. Whatever the reason, in the midst of his pain, he felt close to the Father. He also felt it was time they moved on.

He opened his eyes and found Gabriela staring at him. She blushed and quickly looked away.

"Did the Three speak to you?" she asked, easing down into a sitting position.

"No, but they helped me feel okay about all this." He gestured to his leg.

Daniel summoned the Sun Sword and let it hover in the air. After a moment of wavering, it fixed its direction to the southeast. "And I think we're supposed to move on soon."

Gabriela nodded. "As soon as we bind up your leg." She pointed behind him.

He couldn't see what she was pointing at, but soon heard two sets of crunching footsteps approaching. He gathered by her calm exterior that Ben and Seren had returned rather than some new enemy.

"Is this going to hurt, too?" Daniel asked.

It was a mumbled whimper of a question, but Gabriela took in the meaning.

"Shouldn't much," she said matter-of-factly.

Ben and Seren gave Gabriela the two sticks they'd cut. Reaching into her backpack, she pulled out an extra sweatshirt, which she quickly tore apart. After wrapping Daniel's leg with some to act as padding, she set to work tying the splints in place with six or seven strips of cloth. She ran her hands over them once more, making sure everything was positioned correctly, then tightened each one.

Daniel winced from the pressure but tried to breathe through the discomfort.

"Can you stand?" Seren asked once Gabriela was done.

He nodded and took a deep breath. Taking Ben's offered hand, he pulled himself into an awkward standing position. Each movement brought more pain, but it was bearable. "As long as I don't put any pressure on my bad leg, I think I can manage. Not sure what to do about walking, though."

"I cut you these," Ben said, hurriedly grabbing two chest-high sticks lying in the grass. They were crooked but looked strong—each about the width of a stout walking stick. Both had two short, wrist-thick branches shooting off in opposite directions at their top, padded with strips of fabric torn from Gabriela's sweatshirt.

"Crutches! Ow. Ow. Ow," Daniel said, hobbling toward him. "Thanks!"

He tried them out and was able to walk around. Each swing of his leg made the break throb, but he tried to hide the pain. "Now that's finished, we need to go." He summoned the Sun Sword to show Seren and Ben their intended direction. "Gabriela, where's the cloud?"

Gabriela watched him silently for a moment, then dusted off her knees as she stood. She shook her head. "We're not riding on a cloud like you did in India. We're traveling through the Mists," she explained.

"Sounds wet," Ben replied, looking a little disappointed. He grabbed his backpack and walked at Daniel's pace toward Gabriela. "That's fine, I guess. As long as I'm not being dissolved into a raging fire or flushed into the icy cosmos, I'm good."

Seren stood quietly next to Gabriela, her face quizzical. "Mists?"

"It's how I showed up at Granny's without anyone noticing." Gabriela lifted her hands in front of her and made a circle with her fingers. The air before her turned gray and misty.

The change was so gradual, it seemed as if the Mist had always been there, hidden in plain sight.

In one swift motion, Gabriela flatted her hands, palms outward, and spread them apart. An opening appeared in the gray curtain, like a circular portal into a world of fog and shadows. "Follow me. And stay close." She stepped through the swirling gray door and was immediately obscured by wisps of cloud.

Daniel and the others hastily obeyed. Once through, he stared at the world around him in awe. The portal world he'd seen the servants of the Enemy use so many times was nothing like this. Theirs had been a gateway into a drab world of lifelessness. This was a world brimming with secrets, burning stars, and dreams. They walked through a forest, dark and dripping with dew. A constant breeze blew through the branches, swirling the Mists through the canopy like magical thread through a giant forest loom. The trees swayed back and forth, their edges blurred against the night sky. Thick grass, soft and swishing, carpeted the forest. In the distance, the faint sound of singing, now growing louder, slowly made its way to where they stood like an ocean wave. Rising to a quiet crescendo, it passed by, falling back to a hushed chorus of beautiful whispers. Daniel was immediately reminded of the Father's Mountain. He wasn't sure why; the places were completely different. No, on second thought, not completely. Visually, maybe. But there was something about the air—it felt permeated with the Father's Spirit. Another wave of song washed over them. The back of Daniel's neck prickled, and he knew the eyes of the Three were on him. He hobbled after Ben and Seren and soon found Gabriela waiting for them beneath the eaves of a shadowy tree, bathed in a mixture of starlight and shifting drizzle.

"What is this place?" Ben asked, his mouth agape with wonder.

Seren, too, seemed affected. Her tense exterior had changed in an instant to one of tranquility and patience. "It's beautiful."

"We're in a space between spaces," Gabriela explained. "Distances are different here, so we can walk to wherever Raylin flies—even if it's over the ocean—and get there quicker."

"If you could do this," Daniel said, shuffling out from behind Ben, "why didn't we escape from Abida into here?"

Ben folded his arms. "Or use this instead of the Transportation Pedestal?"

Gabriela pulled out her hair tie and redid her ponytail. She was so beautiful. Daniel caught himself staring.

"Well," she began, "the Transportation Pedestal is still significantly quicker. As far as Abida goes, though, he's powerful enough to break through and follow us in. It wouldn't have done any good. The safest place was behind Granny's barrier."

"And even that wasn't strong enough," Ben snorted. "Man, that guy's trouble. Um, I'm sure you'll probably just give me some cryptic answer that doesn't make sense. You did train under Firstborn, after all, but: care to explain how space is different here?"

Gabriela took a moment to collect her thoughts. "Granny told me it was like a river. Imagine you're in a channel, constantly moving forward with the flow. To get from one place to another, you just have to keep moving forward. Ahead, there's a bend in the river that loops it back almost parallel with itself. But, instead of staying in the current, you climb out on the banks, walk over the land, and then jump back in further upstream. You would have been outside of normal space for a short while and arrived at the destination much quicker than someone who just floated all the way around."

Ben reached up to touch a branch of the tree, swayed by a fresh breeze that had just passed by along with another wave of singing. The bark faintly glowed with each touch of his finger, as though the tree itself was excited to be noticed. He giggled awkwardly, then seemed to remember himself. He cleared his throat once he noticed everyone was watching him and said in a deeper voice. "That was kind of cool. I guess."

Seren watched the strange reaction, but her thoughts seemed elsewhere. "We'll *definitely* get to Raylin's next destination first, or we'll *probably* get there first?"

Gabriela shrugged. "If we keep moving, we'll beat her. But time doesn't stand still for the outside world while we're in here, so we can't wait around for long."

"Okay, guys. You heard her." The peaceful, relaxed Seren was gone. "Let's get a move on."

"Drill Sergeant Seren has returned," Ben muttered under his breath.

Daniel rolled his eyes and sighed. "For real," he said through gritted teeth as the pain in his leg grew. "Okay. Let's get moving, then."

Gabriela held up a hand of warning. "We all need to stay together, though. Space in the Mist is bent. If you get separated from me, there's no telling where you'll end up. I can sense directions to most places in the outside world, but not to people."

"So, don't get crazy and run off," Ben offered.

"Bingo. Daniel? Can you guide us to Raylin?"

Daniel shifted clumsily and summoned the Sun Sword for direction. After wavering a moment, it settled on a direction to their right.

With a nod, Gabriela struck off at a leisurely pace.

An hour passed, and each movement was agony for Daniel. Despite the Spirit-filled peace of his surroundings and the beauty of the music that bathed the landscape, his pain continued to grow. Just when he thought he could go no further, two things happened.

"Heads up. We've got company," Seren said, pointing to the sky.

A large dog, as gray as the goose they'd seen at Newgrange, but far larger, bound across the sky. Like the bird, its eyes shone like illuminated sapphires, and a subtle web of iridescent blue fur gleamed amidst the solid gray. Its presence brought a feeling of peace, but it was fleeting. With a shimmer of swirling cloud, it disappeared directly overhead.

Simultaneously, the Sun Sword arose and pointed down. "Guys, I think we're here," Daniel grunted through the pain. "Any idea what that was?"

Ben and Seren still searched the sky for any other sign of the dog.

Gabriela motioned for Daniel to move aside. She didn't answer his question, though Daniel sensed there was an edge to her silence. Did she know, but didn't want to answer? Had he said something wrong?

Seemingly unaware of his inner confusion, Gabriela used the same hand gestures as before. The Mists parted exactly where the Sun Sword had indicated they should stop, and all four stepped out of tranquility and into the cacophonous roar of wind and ocean.

7

A Giantess and a Brawl

A bright moon illuminated the landscape with silvery light, though it had set in the west considerably. Its beams reflected in a glistening, rocking trail over the ocean, stretching from sheer cliffs toward the horizon. Daniel craned his neck from side to side to take in their surroundings without walking around. They seemed to be on a small peninsula, though there was no beach to speak of, only cliffs falling down some unknown distance to a rocky coastline below. To their left, a stretch of land jutted out to sea, while to the right, the shore fell away behind them in a dim line of frothy wave and jagged rock.

An earthen dome, significantly smaller than Newgrange, stood a hundred yards in front of them. The position of the moon behind the structure made it hard to catch any features, and there were no lights to give away the details. A sudden gust of wind whistled over the cliff's edge and blew over the peninsula. Daniel felt himself lose balance. In an awkward, uncertain moment, he got one crutch behind him for support, but the other he somehow managed to entangle in some vines. He promptly collapsed backward onto the ground with a yelp of surprise. After the initial shock and pain, though, he was grateful for the rest.

Ben and Gabriela rushed to his side.

"Are you okay?" Ben shouted over the wind. His hand brushed Daniel's forehead. "Oh, man. You've got a fever."

"I do?" Daniel asked, feeling the side of his cheeks. "That's why I feel like death."

"Yeah. You look it, too. I mean, like, awful. If I didn't know better, I would've thought Seren had taken up her old ways and shot you with the Bolt of Pestilence or something."

Seren walked by just at that moment and smacked Ben on the back of the head. "Not funny."

"Ow! Don't be such a hater. It was just a joke. And geez! Keep your hands to yourself."

"Not a time for jokes," Seren snapped. She wandered a small distance away and began searching the sky.

Gabriela placed a palm on Daniel's forehead and nodded. "Let's get you further away from whatever that place is." She nodded toward the structure.

"Good idea," Ben agreed. "It's giving off a weird vibe, like it's alive or something. I get the feeling we're being watched."

Gabriela slid her arms under Daniel's shoulders and legs and lifted him without any sign of strain.

Daniel was glad for the darkness because, despite the fever, he was pretty sure he was blushing from embarrassment.

Gabriela continued, "I think places like these were usually old tombs. Let's set up camp away from it so we don't risk cueing any evil spirits to our presence. Hopefully, our arrival was quiet enough to avoid being noticed.

"I'm not sure how far we are from Newgrange, so there's no telling when Raylin will get here," she said, walking away from the structure.

Seren followed close behind. "What about that dog-spirit we saw? Do you think it was connected with the goose somehow? They looked kind of similar." She turned and walked backward, keeping her eyes on the tomb. "Both gray, anyway. But if Raylin shows up, it might attack her again."

Ben scanned the sky. "It did disappear from the Mist world the same time the Sun Sword told us to stop. It could be hiding anywhere around here." His eyes fell to the surrounding rocks and dimpled hillside as if each one housed the spirit. "Not that I wouldn't mind seeing it again. I mean, sure, I kind of felt naked when it looked at me, but it was peaceful at the same time. It must be from the Three."

"If it's here, then it's here," Gabriela said flatly. "Nothing we can do about it."

Daniel tried to avoid staring at Gabriel's face, but he couldn't keep from stealing periodic glances, especially with her being so near. While talking about the spirit, she seemed troubled again. It was the same look she'd had at Newgrange when the goose showed up. What was it? Irritation? Frustration? Shame? But why?

They were now in the middle of a large field, the tomb far enough away that it was only a faint rise in the land, outlined by the moon setting behind it. Gabriela gently laid Daniel in the grass, then turned to summon her globe of light.

Daniel winced. "Thanks. Oh, that feels better." His entire body ached with a wretched blend of pain and weariness. "What's the plan?" He leveled his gaze at Seren, hoping she was paying attention.

Ben rummaged through Daniel's backpack and pulled out his sleeping bag. While he was busy trying to arrange it so Daniel could get in, Gabriela straightened up and locked her eyes on the tomb in the distance.

"I think I should scout out the place. Find out where we are and what Raylin might be after."

"And once she gets here?" Seren asked. She gestured to Daniel. "He's not too mobile right now, so what if we have to give chase?"

Gabriela shook her head. "If Raylin flees, then we'll have to travel through the Mist again and simply lie in wait like we're doing now. She's too fast, anyway. Besides, it would hurt Daniel too much for me to carry him on a bumpy chase over the countryside."

Daniel tried to grin, but the expression was only a pained grimace. "Guys, I'm right here. Do you have to talk about me like I'm not around?"

Seren shrugged. "Sorry."

Gabriela was too deep in thought to respond. "Maybe we should have Ben summon the shield when we see her approaching. It'll draw her straight to us. Seren and Daniel: you can be ready to fire when she comes to attack."

Ben zipped up Daniel's sleeping bag and stood. "What's to stop her from just dodging the attacks like she did before? She's too fast when she knows we're going to attack. Besides, if she sees the shield, she'll immediately go on the defensive. Why don't we hide, and Seren can shoot her when she tries to enter the tomb? There's only one entrance as far as I can tell, so we know where she'll go in. When her back's turned …" he fired an imaginary arrow in the air, "*boom*—she's bound and ready for purification." He looked down at Daniel. "Or is it more of a *zap*? *Zing*?"

"Definitely *zing*," Daniel replied.

Seren watched them, expressionless. "Fine. That plan works for me."

Gabriela nodded. "Good thinking, Ben. Okay, I'm off to check the place out," she stepped over Daniel and strode toward the tomb. "You all stay here and rest, but be ready. If Raylin shows up while I'm gone, you'll have to help Daniel get to the tomb, and quietly."

"Where do we rendezvous?" Ben asked.

Gabriela looked past him to Seren. "How close do you need to be to get a good shot?"

Seren put her hands on her hips and narrowed her eyes at the ruins. "I'm pretty decent at sixty yards for a target her size. Any farther and I might miss, or she'll sense it coming."

"Sixty yards in front of the tomb, then," Gabriela said and moved silently away. Her globe followed her, floating overhead like a magical searchlight.

Daniel watched her disappear, then turned his head to stare at the stars overhead. He wasn't sure what time it would be in Oregon, but between the warmth of the sleeping bag and the relief he felt from finally resting his leg, he could feel himself already on the borders of sleep. His mind replayed the last several hours. He'd gone from leader to dependent invalid, but it surprised him that he didn't seem to mind. The Three must have done some serious work on his attitude, because the thought of not being in control of the group would've driven him bananas in India. Even depending on others to take care of him was something that used to irk him. Growing up as an orphan, he'd learned to take care of himself. If you needed help, then you were weak. But now? He felt fine letting Ben and Gabriela take care of him. Sure, being carried by the girl he liked was an embarrassment he could do without, but at least he got to be near her.

He heard Seren and Ben talking in low voices a little distance away. It was obvious that the Father had been at work in Ben's heart too. He seemed much more confident in himself. Heck, he was even coming up with strategic ideas that were actually really good. That didn't surprise Daniel, though. Since the quest for the Triune Shield, Ben had matured in a lot of areas. Having to sacrifice your life has that effect on you.

Seren, on the other hand, still seemed stuck. Where she'd been anxious to start the quest before, now she was edgy and irritable. And, instead of trying to keep that in check, she acted as if her attitude were justified. He thought back to her reaction when his leg was broken. She certainly didn't act sorry, much less acknowledge the part she'd played in all that.

She's bossing everyone around like she's the leader or something. Like this whole mess isn't her fault. Shoot, if it hadn't been for her, Raylin wouldn't be in the mess in the first place! Yeah, that's right. She's the one who sold Raylin into slavery. If she hadn't done that, Raylin might not have been so obsessed with revenge and would've listened to Granny's advice to get rid of the Voidblade to begin with.

A quick twinge in his conscience suddenly brought him out of his head. He rubbed his eyes, surprised by his resentment. Maybe he wasn't so at peace with not leading after all, and obviously he was angrier with Seren for his leg than he'd realized. But she deserved it, right?

Another prodding in his conscience, clearly from the Three. Okay, so it wasn't okay for him to dwell on his anger, and maybe he could be a little more understanding. Fine.

Seren said something to Ben as she stood, pointing toward the tomb where the glow of Gabriela's globe cast her elongated, dancing shadow onto the field around her. Seren let out an audible sigh of frustration and stuck her hands back on her hips. The transition from Shakti to Seren, and her confession in India, helped to draw out some of her darkest sins, and that creepy Shadow. But she was still struggling with something. Daniel knew enough about her past that she had to still feel guilt and fear—fear, especially. For Raylin. For herself. Of the Enemy. Of his terrifying plan to somehow remove the Image of the Three. That was probably why she seemed so tense since the quest started. Honestly, Daniel couldn't blame her. Every thought of Raylin's continuing enslavement would naturally remind Seren of her sin and shame, and that couldn't be fun.

Father, please help Seren to find peace so she'll chill out a little. And Raylin—free her from the Enemy's grip. While you're at it, some healing for my leg would be awesome because it's killing me!

He took several deep breaths to try to relax his body. Despite his present pain, his thoughts drifted back to Gabriela. She had apparently been more bothered by the Three's silence than she wanted to let on. She acted distracted, to say the least. The peaceful, serene Gabriela now seemed like any other girl. Daniel said a prayer for her, too, before the pain in his leg began throbbing again.

What he wouldn't give to be at home in his bed, with his mom caring for him. His mom *and* his biological mother. That would be a dream come true. He let himself indulge in the fantasy until sleep took him.

***

He awoke to the sound of Gabriela's voice, and to the growing awareness that his leg was hurting more now than ever. He gingerly sat up and reached down to feel his leg. A large, swollen bump had formed on his shin, and each touch from his own gentle examination brought a wince to his face. The pain radiated up into his thigh. He hoped his parents were seeing his need and praying. Hard. But, at the same time, maybe if they didn't know every detail, it wouldn't be so bad. So far, this quest was not sizing up to be the proof of independence and maturity he'd hoped they would see. Forget going to see his biological mother; his parents were likely plotting how they could keep him locked in his room until eighteen.

Ben was quickly by his side. "You okay?" He unzipped the bag and helped Daniel stand.

Daniel stifled a cry. The change in blood flow brought a momentary but searing pain to the broken bone. He almost passed out but clung to Ben's outstretched arms, his eyes tightly shut until the wave of pain passed. The remaining ache, terrible as it was, was welcome in comparison.

"Not really, but I'll survive," Daniel finally gasped. He took his crutches from Ben and tottered over to Seren and Gabriela.

"What's the news?" he asked, trying to seem like it wasn't taking everything he had to stand.

Gabriela cast an appraising look over him. "I found a sign near the tomb. We're at a place called Barclodiad y Gawres. In Wales."

"Am I supposed to know where that is?"

"It's in the UK," Ben added with an air of knowing. He plopped down next to Seren on the ground. "West of England. And it has nothing to do with large sea mammals."

"Don't act like you already knew that. You probably had to ask Gabriela."

"Uh, some of us listen in Geography class. And you're welcome for not calling you some name like 'dork' or 'airhead.' I'm trying to be nice since you're injured."

Daniel smacked Ben's shoulder with one of his crutches. The pain that shot through his leg was worth it. "Not so injured that I can't take you on."

"Ooo. Big, bad, broken Daniel. What are you going to do? Limp me to death?"

"Would you two shut it?" Seren snapped. "Gabriela was *trying* to explain what she found."

Gabriela leaned back on Daniel's backpack. "Like we thought, it's another tomb. But I didn't hear or see any demons when I scouted out the place. I can only assume that either there's nothing here, or it's hiding."

"But if Raylin's coming," Seren added, "there's got to be something powerful she hopes to absorb. She wouldn't fly all the way here if it was just an empty pile of stones."

Gabriela shrugged. "We'll find out when she arrives."

Daniel noticed a movement in the sky. A dark shape flew across the moon, which had begun to set below the ocean horizon. "Guys. Something's coming."

The others quickly stood and searched the sky.

Within seconds, it became clearer. It was the gray dog, running through the air as naturally as if it had been through a field. It was reminiscent of a German Shepherd—if a Shepherd were the size of a Clydesdale, gray with glowing tufts of blue, and could fly. Wisps of cloud clung to its feet as it descended toward the tomb, silently alighting on the grass to the right of the earthen dome. As at Newgrange, it turned its unblinking sapphire eyes on the group, unfazed by their presence.

Daniel immediately felt the pain in his leg lessen, and he breathed a surprised sigh of relief. No one else seemed to notice because their attention was locked on the dog.

Gabriela's brow furrowed as though she were troubled. Seren and Ben stood, trancelike, with arms limp by their sides. Daniel noticed all this in an instant, until the dog turned its eyes upward and the moment passed, replaced by a feeling of dread trickling down Daniel's back. He shivered as he followed the dog's gaze up and over the neck of land jutting out to sea. Raylin, enshrouded by a darkness so deep it was evident against the night sky, and born up by her ebony wings, tore through the air like a furious missile.

The gray dog took to the sky again, padding through the air on its cloudy footholds straight toward Raylin. She slung the Void-blade in a wide arc; water exploded from the sword and careened into the dog. Apparently, Boann had met her fate at the edge of the Voidblade after all. Daniel expected the gray spirit to be knocked to the side or to struggle with the current. But the sword's power seemed incapable of harming it. It advanced as though the raging river were nothing more than a light shower. Raylin immediately switched tactics and with a backswing, let loose a sonic blast filled with faint, clanging harp music. The noisy barrage passed by the dog and crashed into the ground below it, tearing up rocks and dirt and flinging them into the sky back toward the spirit. The gray spirit took a deep breath and blew toward the Voidblade. The noise immediately stopped; the boulders and dirt fell to the ground with a dull thud, and Raylin was blown higher into the sky. With teeth bared, the dog lunged. It crunched down on the jagged edge of the Voidblade. As before, shrieking spirits streamed into the air from the sword. Each made it only a few feet before an eight-pointed star blazed to life somewhere on their amorphous bodies. Seconds later, they were sucked into the blazing white portals.

Raylin spun wildly, wrenching the Voidblade free of the dog's teeth before diving through the yawning mouth of the tomb.

The gray spirit watched her momentarily, standing as still as a statue. Then, slowly, he turned and ambled away in the opposite direction. The air in front of him grew misty, and he disappeared into a curtain of fog.

"Something's happening!" Ben said, alarmed. He gestured wild-ly at the tomb.

Raylin had just hurtled out of the opening and landed flat on her back as though she'd been thrown out. The tomb crumbled into itself and then regurgitated the boulders and rough-cut stones out of the entrance.

"It's turning inside out," Daniel said, perplexed. "What's going on?" He summoned the Sun Sword.

Seren already held the Celestial Bow in her hands, and Ben's stomach glowed as he prepared to summon the Triune Shield.

Raylin, still on her back, was suddenly dwarfed by the materials of the tomb, which were self-organizing into the shape of a giant woman. The last stones and rocks clicked into place where the giant's face would be, forming her eyes and mouth. Stiff sheets of grass formed her hair, which grew upside down from the crown of her head and bristled straight down her back. Links of dark spirit showed between the chinks of earth and rock, knitting the giant together.

"Arrogant girl!" The giant's voice, gravelly and thickly accented, was hard to understand.

"What did she just say?" Ben said to Daniel, digging in his ear with his pinky finger. "What's an Arrrrrgant gaaarrrrl? Oh. Now I get it. It's easier to understand if you say it yourself."

The giant continued booming. "Did you really think you could enter my home and steal my power so easily?"

Raylin, still lying on her back, flipped her legs over her head to vault herself backward onto her feet. She returned the giant's question with a fireball.

The giant didn't even bother batting the blast away. It crashed into her face while she simultaneously punched the ground where Raylin had been standing with an earth-shattering fist. "The Master warned me you would come."

Raylin had taken to the sky and now circled the giant.

"You," the giant turned her carved eyes onto Daniel and the others, "and the rest of the Vessels." She smiled. Or tried to. It looked more like a bunch of rocks jerking themselves into a jagged, vaguely half-moon shape on her face. "Now I can kill two birds with one stone!"

Seren snapped her head toward Daniel. "I feel like she's talking to us, but I'm not following a single word. What's a 'burdwitwonstune'?"

Daniel shrugged. "I'm as lost as you, but she seems kind of happy to see us."

"If she's so happy," Ben said, his voice rising in alarm even as he summoned the Triune Shield, "then why is she hurling a boulder at us?"

The boulder crashed against the shield and bounced off to slam into the ground. Raylin continued circling overhead and began raining down alternating blasts of water, fire, and a mixture of what sounded like Garuda and Daghdha's noise attacks.

"Master will reward me when I destroy you!" the giant bellowed to Raylin. "But for you three," she turned back to Daniel and the others, "he has something special planned. Something new!" Her mouth hung open in a look of hideous excitement.

"Ugh," Ben groaned in disgust. "Doesn't he always?"

"What is she saying?" Seren snapped. "What in the world does 'hawssoomthunspeshaplooned' mean? And how can you understand her?"

Another giant boulder bounced off the Triune Shield. "Ow! It's not worth repeating," Ben replied. "Just the usual threats. And I've no idea how I caught what she said. You kind of have to let your mind go blank for a second and then keep repeating—"

"I didn't actually want an explanation," Seren said, her tone flat and annoyed. "What's the plan now?"

Gabriela's head swiveled back and forth between Raylin's lightning-fast attacks and the giant's lumbering responses. She balled up her fist. "So much for the element of surprise. I don't see that we can do much against Raylin with the giant hurling boulders at us."

As if to punctuate Gabriela's remark, a slab of granite slammed into the Triune Shield and slid down the side.

"I'm doing okay, by the way," Ben tossed in. "It's easy to deflect boulders, so you guys take your time."

Daniel's mind raced. If they didn't do something quickly, Ben would run out of energy, and they'd really be in a desperate situation: trapped between the raging power of the Voidblade and a barrage of boulders. "Seren," Daniel hobbled closer to her, "aim for any spirits that come out of the giant if I'm able to hit her."

She nodded and drew the Celestial Bow back to her the corner of her mouth.

Daniel paused, clearing his mind to focus on Ben, and fired three Sunstorms toward the giant. He figured she'd take them on the chin just as she'd done with Raylin's fireballs, but the giant had another idea. Moving with a speed Daniel didn't think was possible, all the rocks and stones making up her body suddenly disassembled and spread apart to let the blasts harmlessly fly through and out to sea.

"Did you think I was a fool?" the giant roared.

"She asks if you think she's a fool!" Ben shouted.

"I don't care," Daniel yelled back. "Seren, shoot at the same time!"

Seren fired two arrows in succession, even as Daniel fired off another two Sunstorms.

The giant, preoccupied with Raylin for the moment, had her back to the attack, but opened up like stony Swiss cheese at exactly the moment of impact, letting each blast fly through and into the sky.

"Your attacks are nothing to me!" The ground shook at the sound of her voice. She swatted at Raylin and nicked her leg.

Raylin spun down toward the seashore and disappeared from view.

"And now it is your turn," the giant laughed.

"What's she saying?" Gabriela asked.

"Just that she's attacking us again," Ben shot back.

Swirling around, the giant drew back her fist and threw all her weight into a punch.

If it made contact, Daniel knew the shield would shatter, and they (him especially) would be sitting ducks. He raised the Sun Sword and stabbed it into the ground, sending a Fire Strike shockwave to strengthen Ben. Then, without waiting, he fired a Sunstorm straight at the giant's fist at the same moment that it made contact with the shield.

Ben groaned under the strain of the impact, but only for a moment until the Fire Strike took full effect.

The speed and nearness of Daniel's attack were enough. The Sunstorm blasted the giant's fist and arm apart up to her elbow, peppering the landscape with rocky shrapnel. The giant howled in anger as she fell back, crashing to the ground with a crunching, thudding noise. Individual tendrils of dark spirit snaked into the air from the part of her arm Daniel had targeted. They rose for a moment, then quickly descended toward the ground, each moving independently of the other, and so fast Seren couldn't hit any.

Daniel paused. He'd first thought that one spirit was controlling the giant, as with previous demons they'd faced. But maybe the giant was made of numerous evil spirits acting in tandem with each other. If so, that would mean she wasn't down for the count yet, and defeating her for good would require more than one blast.

Darkness streaked through the air, and Raylin was amid the spirits, her back turned while swinging the Voidblade back and forth, mowing them down like wheat before a scythe.

Gabriela pointed toward her. "Seren!" she hissed. "Now!"

Seren fired off five arrows—one straight for the center of Raylin's back, and the others several feet around her in each direction to catch her off guard in case she dodged it.

As in Newgrange, some sixth sense seemed to warn Raylin that the arrows were approaching. She spun around and, with inhuman speed, caught the arrow aimed directly at her with the flat of the Voidblade. She calmly let the other four pass by within inches of her body. The blade was encased with a shell of light, and the eight-pointed star blossomed where the arrow had struck the sword. Raylin's eyes glowed red. With a scream of wild rage, she punched the Voidblade with her other fist. The blow was so powerful that the sword rang like a bell struck with a hammer. The binding light shattered, and Raylin darted toward Seren to attack the portion of the shield directly in front of her.

The giant jumped to her feet behind Raylin, blotting out what little light was left from the moon, and hurled a boulder toward her. She was suddenly crushed against the shield. Her eyes fluttered closed as she crumbled to the ground, unconscious.

Ben groaned with the impact and lost his shield form, returning to his normal body with a bright flash.

"Ben! The shield!" Seren ordered, even as she nailed Raylin with three arrows. Her body, wings and all, were quickly encased by light. "Before the giant attacks again!"

Daniel raised the Sun Sword, trying to simultaneously prepare for either a Fire Strike or a Sunstorm, not knowing which he would need first.

"I'm trying!" Ben gasped, "but I can't summon it. I'm too exhausted!"

The giant lumbered forward, a huge slab of stone held lightly in her hand. "I am going to squash you all into jelly!" she bawled

"Ben, just do it!" Seren yelled.

The pain in his leg growing with each moment that passed, Daniel balanced on his good leg with the help of his crutches and switched to full Sunstorm mode. He raised his sword to fling the arc of purifying power toward the giant when he felt himself knocked forward to the ground and dragged backward. He screamed in agony, his captors not caring whether his broken leg was jolted against half-buried rocks in the grass. Despite the darkness, the wheezing breath and the claws digging into his arms told him he'd been attacked by Creeps. They seemed to be dressed in long robes, and their faces were obscured by hoods. His sword arm was held in the iron grips of at least two, while two more held his other arm and good leg. He struggled to get movement with the Sun Sword, hoping to fire off at least a weakened form of the Sunstorm, but he couldn't budge in the slightest.

"Help!" he shouted. "Creeps!"

Just then, he caught sight of Gabriela leaping into the air to punch a hole in the giant's chest and using her momentum to vault back toward the others.

The giant stumbled backward, but, regaining her balance, immediately flung the huge rock in her hand straight at the companions.

Seren and Ben grabbed Raylin to drag her away from the skirmish. They weren't going to make it in time; the enormous slab of jagged stone whistled through the air, its crushing weight bearing down on them like a heat-seeking missile. Gabriela stood in its path like a lone soldier facing the onslaught of an entire army. She raised both hands, spread apart her legs to brace herself for the impact, and caught the boulder.

The giant followed close behind, jumping on top of it and piling all her bulk onto Gabriela at once.

Daniel's blood ran cold. Ben and Seren had gotten Raylin out from under the attack, but only barely. They broke into a panicked run. The look of horror in Ben's eyes as he craned his neck to search the pile of demonic rubble for Gabriela was certain to mirror Daniel's.

"Ben!" Daniel shouted, putting all his strength into squirming against the Creeps. He ignored the screaming pain in his leg; he had to do something, or all of them were going to be crushed.

Just like …

He couldn't even finish the thought. "Help me, Ben!"

"No one will help you now," one Creep hissed into his ear.

The other three gave dry, wheezing laughs.

"Our lady has crushed your friend, and you four will be bound and taken to the Master."

"He discovered it, you know," a female Creep gushed. "The way to remove the Image of the Three from humans. He and the two Leaders want to practice on you all."

Daniel didn't care what they were threatening him with. His entire focus was on searching the pile of stone for any sign of movement.

The giant lurched forward and pushed herself back into a standing position. But there was no sign of life beneath her. She lumbered toward Seren, Ben, and Raylin.

A third Creep wheezed, "They offer you a life of your own making."

"With no control from the Three. Beyond their short-sighted redemption," the fourth chimed in. "Beyond their power or punishment. Free from judgment. The master of your destiny!"

The giant burst into a booming laugh. "Yes! The life you want to live, and then after—oblivion. No ridiculous eternal anything. Just oblivion! It is what we all want, is it not?"

Between his own pain, the rasping chuckles of the Creeps, and the giant's thick accent, Daniel couldn't catch half of what she said. And he didn't care. Seren and Ben were muttering to themselves, and Daniel tried to focus on being ready for whatever they planned to get out of this situation.

He was sure his parents were watching, and hopefully, they were praying for them. He was too shocked by the giant's attack on Gabriela to be praying for himself.

Please let her be okay! Please, Father! Let her be alive! was all he could say. It ran like a broken record track, stuck on a frenzied repeat over and over in his mind.

Ben suddenly charged the Creeps.

At that same moment, the Creep holding down Daniel's right leg broke away and prepared for the attack, and Raylin burst free from her bindings with a flash of red fire and the sound of shattering glass.

"No!' Seren screamed, firing arrows at her in rapid succession.

Her freedom, however, did distract the giant away from Daniel and the others. Like a hornet, Raylin zigzagged through the air, slicing at any exposed spirits in the chinks between the giant's rocks.

With a dull, metallic thud, Ben's Creep fell to the ground. He drew back his daggers and rushed the other three.

One of the Creeps holding Daniel's left arm had no choice but to relinquish his hold and defend himself against Ben's attack. Without waiting for the remaining Creeps to readjust their grip, Daniel used that moment to struggle with all his might. He got some movement with his sword arm, and an enormous Sunstorm, powered by his complete desire to take Gabriela's place—wherever she was—fired off the Sun Sword. Both Creeps were immediately purified in the blast. Their possessing spirits tore through the air toward the giant, but Raylin caught them on the Voidblade in a passing sweep. In seconds, their bodies had each disappeared.

"My slaves!" The giant stomped in anger, swatting furiously in the air to bat Raylin to the ground.

Raylin was too quick, though, and simply dropped like a stone in the air below the attack, slicing at the giant's knee where sinewy spirits held the joint together. The rocks below the cut crumbled to the ground, leaving the giant hopping on one leg and fighting with one arm.

Seren alternated shots at Raylin and the giant, but it didn't seem to do much good. Each arrow that found its mark in the giant simply bound individual rocks; unless Seren could hit the dark spirits inside her, she couldn't restrict her movement in the slightest. And Raylin, still zooming around in the darkness, easily avoided the brilliant approach of any arrows shot her way.

Ben and the remaining Creep were squared off, eyeing each other and looking for an opening. Daniel, still reeling from the pain of being attacked and pinned to the ground, charged a Fire Strike and awkwardly stabbed it into the ground.

The bright flash brought the Creep spinning around. With inhuman strength, he jumped into the air, hissing loudly as he sailed over Daniel, and landed outside the shockwave's reach.

Dark shapes appeared out of the darkness and surrounded Daniel and Ben. There must have been at least forty more Creeps, each in long, hooded robes that hid their snarling features.

Ben dove toward Daniel and summoned the Triune Shield. It was small, big enough for two people max, and flickered wearily.

Daniel, exhausted himself, summoned another feeble Fire Strike to strengthen Ben. The borders of the Triune Shield glowed brighter momentarily, then gradually shrank back; Ben couldn't last much longer. Daniel's mind raced from their predicament to Seren and Raylin's, to Gabriela's. The giant had moved away from the stone she'd used to attack Gabriela, but there was still no movement. He had to believe she was simply stuck beneath it, but otherwise okay—her superhuman strength saving her from being crushed. It was the only way he could keep going.

"Seren!" Daniel shouted. "Help us!"

He saw her turn and instantly take in their plight, but at that moment, Raylin had enough of the skirmish. She dodged one last wild punch from the giant and flew off to the left, following the coastline south.

Seren screamed her name, and ran after her, firing arrows wildly into the sky.

Several of the Creeps pulled out black weapons, each etched with silver script that shimmered with a cold glow. They approached the shield and unleashed a barrage of attacks. The blows rang loudly inside the barrier.

"I'm about done!" Ben gasped.

With the last of his strength, Daniel fired a Sunstorm to the area where the Creeps seemed the most densely packed. The blast passed through the shield and exploded against the attackers, flinging them into the air. Their purified bodies disappeared with bright flashes before they hit the ground.

The giant turned in a rage and glowered down at Daniel and Ben. "Those are MY slaves! No matter the Master's plan. I am going to crush you both!"

With lumbering leaps, the giant hopped toward them on her one good leg.

"Seren!" the boys shouted in unison.

The giant now towered over them and jumped onto the Tri-une Shield. Ben gasped like he'd been punched in the gut, and the shield failed, returning to Ben's body even as he fell on top of Daniel's outstretched arms. The crushing weight of the boulders bore down on them, squashing them into the ground.

And back out again into the Mists.

8

Lost

Gabriela stood over them, her face clouded with frustration. She reached out a hand to Daniel. "Are you okay?"

Daniel didn't quite understand his position. A second earlier, he'd been knocked onto his back in the outer world, with stony tons of rock bearing down on him. In the next moment, he'd felt as though he'd been squished through the ground and come up on the other side.

He took Gabriela's hand and allowed her to pull him to his feet, crutches and all. When she let go, he grabbed her by the shoulders and pulled her into a hug. At first, her body was rigid with surprise, but Daniel didn't care and held on in silence. She warmed to his touch and wrapped her arms around him.

"I thought you were dead," he said, blinking back tears. "What happened?"

Gabriela gently pushed Daniel away. "In a minute."

She walked a few yards away with her hands held palms out. With one quick motion, she parted the mists, and Seren stumbled backward through the portal, the giant's screams of anger and the angry din of the Creep mob following her through.

Gabriela waved her right hand, and the portal shut, abruptly cutting off the raucous noise.

Even in the dim light of the Mists, Seren's face was clearly wan with fright. She gawked at Gabriela and then found Daniel and Ben.

"I thought … I thought," Seren sputtered. "I thought you all had died! I thought I was going to die."

Gabriela gestured for her to join the boys. "When the giant jumped on me, I was pushed into the ground. Like a nail driven by a hammer into a board. The weight of the giant was too much for me to push off, so I was stuck. Once she stepped off, though, I knocked some of the dirt away from me and got my hands free enough to open the mists."

Daniel kept his eyes glued to Gabriela; he couldn't look away for fear of losing her again. He knew it didn't make sense, but he didn't care. "Well, me and Ben were almost pancakes. Your timing for saving us was perfect."

"Same." Seren shrugged off her backpack and took a deep breath. She wiped sweat from her forehead. "Once the giant thought you both were finished, she and all her Creeps turned on me. They had me surrounded; I was so exhausted from trying to bind Raylin that I could barely shoot another arrow. And then with the thought of you all being dead. I was all alone."

Gabriela pointed to the ground. "Sit. We need to—"

"Isn't that what you wanted?" Ben stepped past Daniel and Gabriela and threw his hands in the air. "You've been acting on your own pretty much this whole night. First, you break Daniel's leg—"

"I didn't break his leg!" Seren jumped to her feet. "Daniel's the one that fired the Sunstorm into the ceiling at Newgrange."

"To save you!" Ben pointed an accusatory finger at Seren. "Because you attacked Raylin on your own and were in danger. And just now, you could've come to help us when we were surrounded by Creeps. But no. You were acting on your own again. Chasing down Raylin no matter the cost to anyone else."

"The giant hadn't attacked you yet. It was just some Creeps. I figured you both could handle them."

"Normally, yeah. But this is our third fight today. And, news-flash: haven't gotten much sleep tonight. Kind of feeling tired. It was all I could do to keep a small barrier around Daniel. Whose leg is still broken, by the way! And he's wiped out, too. We could've used your support."

Daniel tottered between Ben and Seren, his leg throbbing. "Ben's right, Seren. You're not the only one who cares about Raylin. We all want her saved. But you've got to be a part of the team!"

"A team, huh? Well, I seem to be the only one on this *team* who really understands the situation. While you lecture me, my sister is still a slave to who knows how many evil spirits, and each moment that goes by is torture. Who knows when the Enemy will capture her? Or whether she'll actually become so far gone that she can never be normal again? Do you know what it's like to live with that kind of fear? No. You don't. So, instead of acting like things are okay, maybe you all need to understand why I'm risking everything to save my sister."

Gabriela stepped between them all. "You all need to stop. We're wasting time."

Ben completely ignored the interruption. "You think we don't care about Raylin?" he shouted, tossing his hands into the air. "Really? I gave up my life to save her, Seren! From *you*, if you recall. I literally died! That's great that you love her … *now. A*nd that you want to save her … *now.* Maybe if you had done those things before selling her into slavery when she was five, we wouldn't be in this mess!"

Daniel's mouth fell open; he stared at Ben. "What is wrong with you?" he whispered.

Gabriela sighed and rubbed her temples.

Ben's mouth moved, but no sounds came out. He looked scared, as if his own words surprised him. "I … I, uh …"

Seren's head hung low. Her fists, balled up tightly, shook along with her arms and shoulders. Her breathing had grown shallow and fast. Daniel knew she was crying or trying not to.

"I didn't mean …" Ben sputtered. "I didn't mean it. I'm sorry, Seren. I was just—"

"No. You're right. This *is* all my fault. Raylin wouldn't be enslaved if I hadn't done all those horrible things." She picked up her bag and slung it over her shoulders. "And I can make it right. I've begged the Three for forgiveness; I think they've given it. But you don't forgive me, do you, Ben?" She put a hand on a nearby tree, steadying herself through another round of silent sobs. "Well, that makes two of us."

Before Ben could respond, Seren bolted into the Mist. The swirling fog swallowed her running form within seconds, and the dripping of the trees and swelling waves of singing drowned out any noise of her flight.

Daniel stared at the spot she'd been standing like she was still there. Her flight had been so sudden, he wasn't sure what to do, but Gabriela sprang into action almost immediately.

"Seren!" she shouted, cupping her hands and darting forward. "Seren, come back! You'll get lost. You can't get out of the Mist unless I open it for you. Seren!"

There was no response.

Gabriela's urgency spread to Ben. He sprang into action at her side, shouting Seren's name and searching the shifting fog for any sign of movement.

"Let's just run after her," Daniel said, trying to speed up his hobbling despite another wave of pain and exhaustion.

Gabriela grabbed his backpack to prevent him from moving. "It's not that simple. Remember: space in the Mist is constantly changing. Even if we ran in the same direction as Seren, we wouldn't necessarily end up in the same place."

Ben spun around. "What do we do, then?" His eyes brimmed with panic. "We can't just stand here. I mean, how big is this place, anyway?"

Gabriela cast a sidelong glance in Ben's direction. "Any idea how big the entire universe is?"

"You're kidding," Daniel muttered.

"Nope."

Ben's shoulders dropped in obvious defeat. He turned to stare into the sheets of fog that hung like curtains through the forest. "This is all my fault."

Daniel leaned against the closest tree and slid into a sitting position, the bark scintillating at his touch. He didn't know what to do and was so distracted by pain and weariness that he could hardly think. Without Seren, there was no way they could capture Raylin and get her to the Abyssal Staff for purification. Of course, the Three had orchestrated each quest to help them all grow. Maybe Seren running off was something she needed to do. Truthfully, he almost didn't care at the moment; it was all he could do to simply breathe.

Father. I can't go on like this. Please heal my leg.

He waited in silence, focusing on relaxing his body. A sense of calm spread over him, but the pain remained. Well, that was something, at least.

"Maybe the Sun Sword would point toward her," Ben suggested.

Gabriela considered this for a moment. "It's possible. Daniel, summon the …" She cast an appraising look over Daniel. "Okay. I'm thinking we need to stop for the night."

Ben left his post and crouched down next to Daniel. "Is it that bad?"

Daniel gritted his teeth. "I think it's feeling better the longer I lay down. I just haven't given it much of a rest, so the pain is catching up with me."

Gabriela raised her hands. The globe of soft, white light floated gently into the air until it was above the canopy of trees. She knelt next to the boys. "I'll leave the light out for Seren. Maybe she'll see it if she wanders back in this direction. In the meantime, I think we should all get some sleep."

"What time is it?" Daniel whispered.

Ben pulled up his sleeve and looked at his watch. "Almost 4:00 AM, Greenwich Mean Time. 9:00 PM Pacific Time."

"You're such a nerd," Daniel muttered and lay down between the roots of the tree. Thankfully, the ground was soft and spongy, and, despite the permeating Mist, they didn't seem to be getting wet. "I'm just going to take a short nap," he whispered.

Darkness took him.

***

Daniel drifted through a series of unpleasant dreams where Gator and her portly aunt, Barf, took turns working over his leg. Gator was having fun punching him in the shin, then wandered off out of sight to eat a protein bar. That was apparently the signal for Barf, dressed in a purple Hippopotamus costume, to use his leg as a chair while she scarfed down twenty-seven pizzas. Toward the end, she took a break to knit a gargantuan pair of hippo underwear, and then somehow turned into Janice.

"You poor boy. We're all praying for you, you know. Constantly. I pray while I knit. I like to think my prayers are woven into the yarn of the things I make. Isn't that nice? I'll give you a pair of prayer underwear when you get back. How fun! Tell Ben I said …"

She passed out before she could finish her message, and Daniel awoke to the sound of another swell of music passing through the forest. He blinked to clear his vision and rubbed his head. Reality slowly drifted back to him. He was still in the Mist with the dark woods, deep grass, gentle breezes, and broken leg. One of the Three's magical dreams would've been nice, but so far, little of this quest had been what he'd expected. Ben lay curled up next to him and was snoring softly. Daniel reached down and pushed the light button on his watch. 7:30 AM. So that meant, in the time zone he was used to, it would be somewhere around the middle of the night.

He yawned and surveyed the woods. Gabriela dozed against a tree a couple feet from his head. She was sitting up, as though attempting to keep watch, but her head nodded against her chest, and her breathing was deep and slow. Hair, pulled back into a hasty and disheveled ponytail, fell prettily over one shoulder. Her eyes moved rapidly below heavy lids, and she muttered something unintelligible in her sleep.

Daniel watched her until the dream passed. With a sharp intake of breath, her eyes fluttered open, and she was suddenly staring back at him.

He averted his eyes to the branches above, hoping it wasn't obvious he had been studying her.

"How are you feeling? You in pain?" She scooted next to him and spoke in a whisper.

Okay, maybe she hadn't realized he'd been watching.

"Better than earlier." He shifted his leg, and the dull ache that had settled in quickly shifted to a sharp stabbing. "Nope, nope, nope! Not better at all."

Gabriela gently palpated his shin. "The swelling seems just as bad." She sighed, and the same troubled expression haunting her features since the quest began settled back into her face. "I don't know what we're supposed to do. Nothing's going right!" She cast an irritated glance at her globe, still hovering above the trees, and searched the woods as if hoping Seren would come stumbling out from behind a tree. "Abida shows up. Your leg gets broken. Seren's arrows can't hold Raylin for longer than five minutes, and she runs away. Oh, and did I mention that the Three are being awfully silent lately?"

"Yeah, you did mention something like—"

"It's like they don't want us to succeed! Like they're trying to make things as hard as possible." She punched the ground, sending a deep rumbling noise echoing through the woods.

Ben stirred in his sleep and gave one rousing snore. "Creeps and Creeps and Creeps," he mumbled, his words slurred with sleep. "Get your hands off my popcorn, you weirdos."

Daniel ignored his pain and pushed himself into a sitting position. "I know it can feel like that sometimes. Trust me. But, my broken leg aside, things really aren't much more difficult than in previous quests."

Gabriela drew her knees up to her chest and drew in an irritated breath. "I guess. But why won't they respond when I talk to them? What possible reason does that serve? For a year, I was with them constantly, or at least on some mission with Granny. But I could always feel them like they were right next to me. I was never alone. But now … now I can't feel them, I can't hear them, I can't see them. It's like they've abandoned me!" She wiped tears onto her knees and kept her head down, talking to her stomach. "I feel afraid, Daniel. For the first time since leaving with Granny, I'm terrified. I can't stop thinking about my family in Aguas Calientes, or wherever they are now. When I was with the Three, I felt at peace waiting. Now? Now I can't draw a breath without worrying about them. I don't know what I've done. Do you think I did something wrong? Do you think I'm being punished?"

Daniel felt a nudge in his heart. There were no words thrust into his mind, no burning message, but he knew he was supposed to somehow reassure Gabriela. He didn't need the Father to prod him, though. Seeing Gabriela distressed drew out every protective instinct within him.

"They haven't abandoned you. And I'm sure you haven't … well, I don't know if you've done something wrong or not. But when I disobey, I know it. There's usually not a whole lot of guessing." Daniel paused for a moment, thinking back on his life since adoption into the Celestial Family. "When Ben and I were on our quests, everything that happened—even all the bad things—the Three allowed those so we would get stronger. Or closer to the Three. Or to show us if we'd done something wrong. But I can't remember them pulling away to punish us." He paused, weighing his words. "I'm sure that everything that's happening is to help you grow, even though it stinks."

Gabriela peered out from behind her legs. "I guess so." She didn't sound convinced. "But, there's more."

Daniel stayed quiet; he nodded to urge her on.

"The gray spirit isn't some Firstborn." She grabbed her ponytail and absently braided it down the side of her shoulder. Once done, she flopped it over her back and rocked back and forth as if trying to avoid talking about this subject. "He's THE Spirit. The Blessing. One of the Three."

Daniel nodded slowly, trying to take this in while understanding why Gabriela would be acting so embarrassed about it. "Okay. That's really great."

"No, it's not." She stuck her feet out and plopped backward into the soft grass. "I spent more time with the Spirit than with any other Person of the Three. And he's God, just like the Son and the Father are God. It was amazing being with him. More than amazing."

Daniel remembered his time with the Son. It was life-changing. Mind-blowing. The memories of that conversation still seemed so real and vivid, more so even than his conversation with Gabriela. He still didn't follow why she was upset, though.

"And then he shows up at Newgrange and doesn't even acknowledge me! He barely looked at me and didn't say anything. It's like the person you love the most in the world sees you at a party and pretends you don't exist." She gave an exasperated sigh. "That doesn't even come close to how this feels. It's like he's rejected me, and I have no idea why."

Ben stirred and slowly pushed himself into a sitting position. "What's all the hubbub?"

Daniel wasn't sure if he should explain, but luckily didn't have to.

"Nothing," Gabriela replied. "Just talking about the quest. We should probably get a move on." She got to her feet and slung her backpack over her shoulder.

Daniel leaned back for a moment, trying to savor the last few minutes of rest before getting back on his broken leg. He could understand why Gabriela was frustrated, on the one hand. On the other, it had to be some sort of lesson the Three knew she needed to learn; it was for her own good. But telling her that point-blank seemed like a bad idea. He'd probably end up smacked. Or worse: ignored.

"Oh," he said aloud, Gabriela's feelings now making more sense. *Yeah, being totally snubbed would be pretty bad. Father, help Gabriela*

understand what's happening, because I don't, and I've got no idea what to say.

Ben grabbed Daniel's outstretched hand and pulled him to his feet. He sucked a breath through his teeth as he put pressure back on his leg. *Me, too, by the way. Not sure why my leg had to get broken, or what to do about it. Pretty sure we can't help Raylin with me like this. So …*

No response.

"Daniel," Gabriela said, her voice still sad and distracted. "Summon the Sun Sword. Let's see which sister it points us to."

9

Rhiannon

Gabriela and Ben alternated calling for Seren as they walked. Daniel fumbled along in silence, trying to focus on keeping the sword summoned while not succumbing to the tugging motion of the blade, which had nearly pulled him over several times. Between the constant focus he needed to keep from face-planting and his pain, he knew he couldn't go on for long. He half-expected to be walking for hours, but after fifteen minutes, the sword stood up on its end, pointing to the ground.

Lifting her hands over her head, Gabriela summoned another globe of light and sent it floating high above the canopy of trees. She and Ben resumed shouting for Seren but gave up after several more minutes and joined Daniel where he was cradled between the roots of a towering tree.

"The sword must not be taking us to Seren," Daniel said to Ben, who was pacing back and forth in front of him.

Gabriela had her hands on her head, watching Ben like a cat watching a ping-pong game.

Daniel continued, "So what does this mean? We just leave the Mists and hope to find Seren later?"

Gabriela shook her head and gave an exasperated sigh. "I don't know. I don't know anything."

"What good would facing Raylin do right now, anyway?" Ben blurted out. "Without Seren to bind her, all we could do is purify her for a second before she was re-possessed. Not that Seren's arrows could hold her for long."

Daniel slowly nodded and passed on the question to Gabriela.

She threw her hands in the air and parted the Mist with a quick, irritated gesture. "Let's at least see where we are."

The landscape beyond looked just as foggy. They looked, as through a window, onto a broad lawn leading up to a ruined castle. The stone walls were lit by dim, yellow lights situated somewhere at the base of the fortress. It was nestled up to a thick band of trees on its right side, and an open field dotted with sparse shrubs that fell away to its left. Compared to the two tombs Daniel had seen throughout the night, the ruined stronghold looked cheery and inviting.

"Any idea where we are?" Ben asked, following Gabriela as she stepped up to the portal and looked about.

She shrugged her shoulders and muttered something about leaving the Mist open and waiting for the time being.

Daniel breathed a sigh of relief. Hopefully, that meant he could rest a little longer. He shut his eyes and leaned back, listening to the next wave of song wash over the forest. It grew louder, but then stopped as if stuck somewhere nearby. Daniel opened one eye and realized they were not alone. A group of people, tall and shimmering, approached through the trees. They were a good three hundred yards away, but Daniel could see them as clearly as if they'd been by his side. The Mist appeared to honor them by parting as they plodded through. At their head, a woman riding a white horse played a golden harp and sang in a beautiful, high voice. A sword of matching gold, studded with gems, hung on her back. Her long, white hair cascaded over one shoulder and draped over the side of her steed. Her gossamer silver dress was partially concealed by a glistening gray cape that seemed to be part of the Mist itself. Her eyes shone golden in the dim lighting of the forest.

The men and women who followed in her train were similarly dressed, each with a long dress or robe, cloaked by the magical gray shrouds. They all held bright spears or glinting swords in one hand, and brilliantly polished, silver shields in the other. There must have been at least a hundred of them, and each one took up the chorus behind their leader. The very forest itself joined the song with swaying branches and whispering grass.

"Uh, guys?" Daniel said in a hushed voice. "I think some Firstborn are coming."

Gabriela and Ben were still talking in low tones, standing just beyond the portal to study the castle and its surroundings. Neither noticed the nearness of the music now.

"We've got company," Daniel said, this time a little louder. Still no response. He picked up a nearby stick and threw it at Ben's back.

"Ow! What was that for? Tired of being the only one in pain and decided to—Oh." The surprised and irritated look on Ben's face instantly changed as his eyes fell on their guests.

Gabriela's own look of surprise quickly faded into one of relief. "Rhiannon!" She left the portal opening and ran toward the woman on the horse who was now directly in front of Daniel. "The Sons of Don are with you!" Her eyes swept over the bright figures of Firstborn trailing back into the woods. "And the Children of Llyr. Why are so many of you together?"

Rhiannon smiled down at Gabriela and gracefully slid out of her saddle to the ground. Even then, she was still at least seven feet tall. She wrapped Gabriela in a strong embrace. "We march to war," she explained.

"To Babylon," Gabriela said. Tears welled up in her eyes. "What's happening? We've barely heard from the Three this entire quest. Abida attacked us before we left. Did you know that? And the Spirit keeps showing up, but he won't speak to me!" She was now openly weeping. "Daniel also broke his leg, but we haven't had any help. Raylin's too powerful for us to bind, and Seren has run away in the Mist, and we can't find her! Why won't the Three help? We can't save Raylin if they're not with us."

Rhiannon held Gabriela out at arm's length and brushed a few stray strands of hair out of her face. "Still. Still, my friend. Be at peace. The Spirit goes where he pleases, and no one can tell where he comes from, or where he goes. He is with you always, even if you do not feel him. Do not doubt his purposes. All will be made clear."

Daniel cocked his head. It sounded like Rhiannon was quoting something he'd heard before, but he couldn't place it. He wasn't quite sure what it meant, either. Gabriela, at least, seemed to understand. She took a deep breath, and her body relaxed. Rhiannon gestured for her to sit next to Daniel.

Ben trotted up and plopped down beside them.

Rhiannon cast a brilliant smile in his direction; he blushed a deep crimson and waved.

"We cannot linger long and can only offer a little help. Here." She raised a finger and one other Firstborn, as tall and regal as Rhiannon, broke from the ranks behind her and approached. One by one, he took horseshoe braids of twisted gold and silver out of a bag at his side and hung them around Gabriela, Ben, and Daniel's necks.

Its touch was soothing to Daniel—cold and heavy, but comforting.

"We have placed a blessing on these torques. Once, and only once, they will be able to hide you from the eyes of the Enemy and his slaves. You will need this soon."

Daniel and Ben exchanged glances.

"Sounds like we're about to have some fun," Daniel whispered.

Ben shook his head and sighed. "Just what I was hoping."

"Can't you stay to help us?" Gabriela asked, her tone both pleading and hopeful.

"No, my friend. We are going to Babylon." She knelt so she didn't tower over them quite so high. "You know the Babylonian Seal was weakened, and the Enemy has gone back to take up his old power. He has also experimented with the Image of the Three and seeks to remove it from mankind."

Daniel's hand automatically went to the torque around his neck.

"So we've heard. That Abida freak took some of our blood."

"Don't remind me," Ben grunted. "Talk about disturbed. That guy gives me the chills." He shuddered. "Should we be concerned about that, by the way?"

Rhiannon glanced at the brilliant host of Firstborn now spreading around them through the forest. Some strode up to the Mist portal to study the castle beyond. "We heard what Abida did. He is extremely dangerous, and you should avoid him until you are ready."

"We didn't have much choice," Gabriela interjected. She wiped the last stray tears from her cheeks. "He showed up at Granny's and broke through her barrier. Her barrier AND the Triune Shield."

Rhiannon held up a hand defensively. "Yes, we know. You could not have avoided that battle, Gabriela, and you acted well. I do not mean to blame you, only to warn the boys."

Ben snorted. "Consider us warned. I won't go within a mile of that guy ever again."

"That will not be possible." Rhiannon fixed Ben with a curious mixture of pity and amusement.

"Come again?"

"Do you know who Abida and Amira really are?"

"Uh, beyond meeting Abida and having him stick his claws through the Triune Shield, no. And this Amira person is completely new to me. Should I know him?"

Gabriela cleared her throat. "I haven't told them about the twins, or their connection with the Enemy."

Rhiannon nodded. "I see. Amira is a *she* and the twin sister of Abida. They are Vessels too, but Vessels of the Enemy. More powerful than his Generals, more powerful than many of his Firstborn servants. They are integral to his plan for moving mankind beyond the reach of redemption."

Daniel tapped the phone bulging from Ben's pocket. "She must've been the woman standing next to Abida in the photo."

"Oh, right," Ben said. His brows knit together in worry. "But that's not possible, right? The 'beyond redemption' thing."

"If left unchecked, yes. If opposed by the Three, no."

Ben scratched his head. "But they *are* fighting it? I mean, we don't need to be worried about losing our connection with the Father just because Abida took our blood, do we?"

Rhiannon's bright, golden eyes flickered with mirth. "You are a Vessel. Your very position was created to take part in that opposition."

"Oh, right. I knew that, of course. Just wanted to make sure." Ben glanced away from her piercing gaze and began twirling grass blades around his finger.

"The Image of the Three cannot be removed from you. You have all been sealed with the Spirit. Nothing can undo that."

Daniel felt a sense of relief and relaxed back against the tree. At least that was one less thing he had to worry about on this or any other quest.

Rhiannon continued matter-of-factly, "If the Enemy did try to remove it, it would be excruciating for both your soul and your body. You would eventually die, but not before an agonizing ordeal."

And there went the relief. "Oh," Daniel muttered. "Yeah, I'm going to opt for not letting them practice on me."

"Same," Ben said, his face ashen white. "I've done the whole agonizing death thing. Kind of over it."

Gabriela cleared her throat. "The twins willingly gave up the Image of the Three—gave up their humanity—to become complete and perfect Vessels for the Enemy. It's the first time in history anyone has been able to bear more than a temporary possession by the Enemy's spirit."

"True," Rhiannon frowned. "Seren and Garuda only ever temporarily housed the Enemy's own spirit. His Generals still do at times, but that will likely change, and soon. No doubt he intends the same existence for them as the twins: the permanent indwelling of his spirit."

"And the rest of the world?" Daniel asked. "For them, too?"

Rhiannon stared through the portal. "That is his intention. For all humanity to be his Vessels and to willingly turn from redemption and abandon themselves to him—hardening their hearts so that no shred of humanity remains. What would there be left to save? Beings devoid of humanity. Shells. Monsters. He hopes the Three will abandon judgment if all mankind is lost, or that, in the very least, judgment will be impossible, and all living things, once dead, will pass into oblivion." She reached over her shoulder and pulled her sword out of its sheath. The blade was a polished mirror of silver, razor-sharp and slender, with a slight curve. She held it up and studied it a moment, her eyes flitting back and forth as if watching some scene unfold in its silvery depths. "Then he could rule, unopposed, over the universe, and escape judgment himself. *If* he were to succeed, it would be a tragedy of cosmic proportions. But we will not allow that. The Three will not allow it. All who seek the Three will find them. They who the Three call will come. The Enemy has found nothing but a means of removing the ears of those who are already deaf. If a stone falls from a mountain, and he hastens its descent, has he done anything new?"

Rhiannon fixed her smoldering gaze on Daniel and Ben.

Ben squirmed. "Are we supposed to answer that? What was the question again? Daniel, I think it was directed toward you."

Gabriela smacked Ben's shoulder. "Hush."

Rhiannon slid the sword back into its scabbard. "He has done nothing new."

Her voice was edged, but Daniel knew her feelings weren't directed toward their inability to answer her question. She seemed focused totally on the Enemy.

Rhiannon suddenly stood, and all the surrounding Firstborn tensed as if ready to blast off into the sky for a fight with the Enemy. "We will hold back his power until he is allowed to have his day, but it will be short." She clenched her teeth. "Very short."

Ben heaved himself to his feet. "Wait. What's this about the Enemy having his day?"

Rhiannon strode to her horse and jumped back into the saddle.

"The Time of the Enemy. It is explained in detail in the Three's book. Read it. Understand. But his Time has not yet come. The Three will see to that; that is why you are Vessels, is it not?"

She swung her horse around and grabbed a golden horn from somewhere in the folds of her cloak. Raising it to her lips, she gave a blast, bright and resounding. "To Babylon! To war!"

The host of Firstborn glowed brighter and answered the echoing fanfare with a shout. Without further warning, they raced off through the trees, growing faster with each stride until they were beams of light radiating off through the Mist.

Ben nudged Daniel. "They didn't heal your leg."

Daniel tried to stand abruptly but only succeeded in getting his one good leg under him before crumbling onto his back. "Hey!" He waved a crutch wildly in the air. "What about my leg? Ms. Rhiannon! Broken leg, remember? Ms. Rhiannon!"

"They're gone," Gabriela said, peering through the trees. "Probably a hundred miles away by now."

Even their song no longer wafted through the Mist.

Daniel let the crutch fall back to the ground. "Perfect. What else could go wrong?"

Through the portal, a deep drumbeat boomed over the countryside and echoed off the walls of the castle. Daniel turned onto his stomach and stared through the portal. A foreboding clamor of dogs howling and baying mournfully mixed in with the drums.

"You just *had* to ask, didn't you?" Ben grumbled. He jumped to his feet. "Gabriela?"

She walked to the portal and stared out. "Whatever's coming doesn't sound good."

"Can we just hide in the Mist until it goes away?" Ben asked. "Or just leave the portal open and watch what happens?"

"Whoever it is may not be able to see us because of these torques," Gabriela touched the glinting collar around her neck. "But they could see the open portal just as easily as we can. We'll need to go hide somewhere. Besides, what if this is all something to do with Raylin? We'll need to be ready to ambush her. Though I'm not sure what good it will do. Still, we have to try."

Daniel eventually got to his feet and tottered toward the portal. He summoned the Sun Sword and let it hover in the air until its direction was clear. "Toward the castle, then," he sighed. "What about Seren?"

Gabriela popped her knuckles as though preparing for a schoolyard brawl. "We can't worry about that now. Come on."

She led the way out of the Mist, which closed as soon as Ben had passed the borders of the portal. Despite the concealing power of the torques, they plunged into the surrounding trees rather than strike out across the open field stretching up to the castle walls. This slowed their approach considerably, as Daniel had to negotiate rather awkwardly through the underbrush and vines. They were about twenty feet from the far-right corner of the castle when the baying of hounds broke out again.

Ben gripped Daniel's shoulder and pointed across the lawn.

Spectral hounds, large as bulls and ghastly with yellow teeth and orange flames licking their black, phantom fur, loped toward the castle. Their tongues lolled out, and their red eyes scanned the area like searchlights. Behind them, astride a ghostly horse of bones, rode a mammoth figure draped in robes of gray. He wore a deer skull mask, its antlers spreading at least twenty feet. His eyes burned like pinpricks of candlelight through the mask's eye sockets. Each breath came with an exhalation of dark spirits, which drifted around him like a noxious fume. His hands were encased in gauntlets of leather with barbed blades lining the knuckles. Instead of hair, a mane of polished bones bushed out from beneath the mask, cascading down his back like some grotesque trophy of war. The same weight of dread Daniel had experienced whenever in the presence of the Enemy settled onto his chest and drove him painfully to the ground. Ben and Gabriela gasped as if the wind had been knocked out of their lungs and fell to their knees as well.

The golden torque around Daniel's neck warmed to the touch,

infusing a little energy back into his body. He breathed easier and shifted onto his stomach.

The Enemy drew up beside the castle and stopped. His hounds, still scanning the area with their lamplight eyes, settled onto their haunches as their master jumped down from the huge, skeletal horse and lifted his right hand.

Three portals whirled open before him. Tyr—the blond General with the Hammer of War—sauntered through. He had the hammer casually tossed over his shoulder. It radiated a dark, sickening energy that Daniel could feel even from his distance. Abida and Amira joined him through the other two portals, which all closed as soon as the twins passed through.

The Enemy turned his masked face toward the castle. "Come and bow before your master!" he boomed, his voice gravelly and sinister.

No sooner had the words left his mouth than a wailing erupted from within the castle. The wind picked up, blowing through the trees with a fury so sudden that branches fell all around Daniel and the others, and tree trunks groaned as they twisted and danced in the gale.

A haggard woman, tall, transparent, and draped in white rags that matched her stringy hair, materialized on the tallest parapet. She stepped into the air and floated down to the lawn before the Enemy and his entourage. "My Lord Arawn!" she moaned with a thick, British accent, finding the ground and immediately prostrating herself before the towering Enemy. "The White Lady is at your service. What brings you, your Leaders, *and* a General to my haunt?" The spirit drifted up to her feet.

Amira stepped forward and slapped the spirit in the face. Despite her ephemeral appearance, the slap landed and seemed to hurt the ghost. "That was for not immediately appearing before Lord Arawn. Speak out of turn again, and you'll spend a month in the Abyss."

The White Lady held her face and cowered, but her eyes glinted with hatred. "Yes, my lady," she muttered obediently, her voice hard and bitter. She fell to her knees before Arawn and waited in silence for him to speak.

"The traitor comes this way," he said darkly. "She seeks your power. It does not suit my purposes for her to grow in strength any longer." Each word triggered a chorus of moaning whispers all around the Enemy as if a retinue of invisible, echoing ghosts trailed beyond him into the shadows. "I am too close to victory in this age; I will not risk my forces being further weakened. Every move against the Three must be calculated, balanced, exact."

"He's talking about Raylin," Ben whispered.

Daniel nodded, shivering. Supai. Shiva, Brahma, and Vishnu. Now Arawn? Was each incarnation of the Enemy getting more grotesque and dreadful than the one before? No, that wasn't possible. Each was the epitome of terrible in its own way. Only the Enemy's true form—the great Serpent—eclipsed any of his disguises.

Arawn turned his antlered, bone-clacking head toward their hiding place and squinted his eyes. His hounds jumped to their feet, hackles raised.

"What is it, my lord?" Abida asked, craning his neck to look into the trees.

With a chop of his enormous hand, Arawn sent his hounds toward Daniel and the others. Gabriela got both boys' attention and tapped the torque at her neck. She held her finger to her lips. The message was clear. Don't move. Don't talk.

The hounds were upon them within seconds. They sniffed around the woods, their spectral feet passing through Daniel and the others in a true, ghostly fashion. Each touch was like ice sliding down his back. He kept his eyes on the hound directly over him, wanting to be ready if the torques' power failed for some reason. A hound passed through Ben; he screwed up his face in a look of supreme discomfort and struggled to remain motionless. Two passed through Gabriela. The touch was an obvious shock. She shut her eyes and kept her breathing silent but deep.

The hounds whined in confusion. They could obviously sense that something was wrong but couldn't discover the reason. His eyes still fixed on where they hid, Arawn glided toward the woods, the grass withering under his ominous presence. The General and two Leaders followed in his wake. The White Lady, however, stayed where she knelt, her icy stare boring holes in Amira's back. This was it. If Rhiannon's power didn't work to conceal them, Gabriela would have to draw them into the Mist, and fast. Hopefully, the Enemy wouldn't notice and follow them, because fighting wasn't an option.

Daniel locked eyes with Gabriela. She nodded as if reading his thoughts.

The torques warmed to the touch, and their heat spread through Daniel's body.

With one last bout of sniffing, the hounds loped out of the trees back to their master, snapping at each other and whining apologetically.

Arawn hesitated.

"My lord?" Amira asked.

"I sensed the Three, but it is gone now." He slowly pivoted on an unseen foot and glided back toward his skeletal horse.

Abida and Amira walked at his side, while the General trailed in his wake.

Abida cast another glance back at the trees. "A spy?"

Arawn paused with one hand on the shoulder bone of his steed. "It changes nothing. The Three are locked in combat with me even now." His voice grew strained as he spoke, and his entire presence— the antlered figure, the horse, even the hounds—blurred and altered, momentarily replaced by an equally large, centaur-like figure of a half-man, half-lion with wings. A great, curly black beard fell over his chest. The likeness of men, women, and animals squirmed within the hair, entangled in the giant snarls. Raking claws of burnished steel dug deep furrows into the ground as he reared on his hind legs. His cat-like eyes, green and luminous, glared down at his servants, while his lion tail flicked wildly against the castle, knocking stones loose to fly through the air. He raised his muscled arms in the air and spread them out. Each finger was tipped with scythe-like talons. "But I will prevail!" his voice boomed over the country-side. "All will be remade into my image, and the Three will, at last, be forced out of my world!"

Despite the power of terror bound up in his words, Daniel felt there was a tone of doubt as if the Enemy were trying to assure himself of his victory.

The Enemy's image suddenly shifted back to Arawn, astride his horse, and surrounded by his monstrous hounds. The General and Leaders, along with the White Lady, seemed unfazed by his transi-tion. They watched, unmoved, through the entire display.

The White Lady lifted her head and looked at Amira, who mo-tioned for her to speak. "My lord, how am I to triumph over the traitor if she defeated so many of my brethren?"

Spinning, concentric rings of black inscription appeared over the White Lady. Daniel immediately recognized it; the Enemy had used something similar to fill Seren and Garuda with his spirit when they fought in the Chamber of the Moon. From the center, a red chain, each chink thick as Daniel's thigh, snaked out of the por-tal and fell into a humming coil of malevolent energy. The White Lady hastily floated back.

"This chain will bind her, no matter how many Firstborn she has absorbed." The Enemy turned to leave. "I leave Tyr to help you." The blond General stepped to the White Lady's side and smiled. He patted his hammer. "Bind Raylin and bring her to the Abyss."

The White Lady trembled. "To the … Abyss," she repeated, as though hoping the Enemy's declaration was some mistake.

A glare from Arawn's deep-set eyes commanded obedience.

"Yes, my lord." She ventured another question. "What of the Vessels? If they appear, do I bring them too?"

"No!" Abida snapped. "We want them alive, but they must not enter the Abyss. Bind them with the chain if they appear; they take precedence over the traitor. Tyr will bring them to Babylon."

Amira folded her arms and studied the chain for a moment. "But, the Three will probably lead them to the Abyss." She looked up at the Enemy's towering, horned visage. "Lord Arawn, dispatch Abida and myself to Stonehenge. Allow us to protect the entrance and bind the children when they come."

Fire trickled out of Arawn's eye sockets and engulfed the mask, licking upward to dance on the antlers like some hideous candle flame. Amira was immediately crushed belly-first onto the ground by some unseen force.

The White Lady, still cowering from the coil of chain, smiled cruelly as she watched Amira grovel under the pressure of the Enemy's power.

"I do not need your counsel." Arawn swung into his saddle. "Before the thought had entered your mind, I dispatched three Generals, as well as Morrigan, Belatucadrus, and Agrona to the entrance. They are more than enough."

The power holding Amira dissipated, and she painfully stood.

Abida shot her a look of derision before turning to see the Enemy off.

Unseen drums beat deeply over the countryside as Arawn's horse pounded across the lawn, his ghastly demon hounds in hot pursuit. Just as the night sky began to lighten with the dawn, the long shadows of the surrounding trees, spread darkly across the field, leaped up and engulfed him, retinue and all.

"Always ready with unwanted advice," Abida snickered over his shoulder. "You're lucky that's all he did."

Amira smiled sweetly. "At least I wasn't beaten until I cried like a baby. Oh, wait. That was you, wasn't it? When the Master found the picture of Mother in your pocket? Pathetic."

Abida's cruel smile fell into a look of abject hatred. With a flick of his wrist, a portal opened, and he plodded through.

Amira, apparently satisfied that she'd won the contest of cruelty, flicked her hair over one shoulder and focused on the White Lady. "Succeed, or I will personally see to your punishment."

She looked to Tyr. Her face softened, though her eyes still looked predatory. "Defeat the traitor and quickly return to my side."

Tyr flashed her a cocky smile and puffed out his chest. "She won't stand a chance against my power. I'll bind her and return to Babylon within a day."

Amira strode up to him confidently and pulled him into a kiss.

Daniel and Ben looked at one another and rolled their eyes simultaneously.

Ben opened his mouth to say something but found Gabriela's hand on his neck. A quick squeeze rid him of any notion of making a sound. He silently nodded his head, and she let go.

"Do not fail me," Amira said, and then followed her brother through the portal, which lazily swirled shut after she passed through.

The second she was gone, Daniel felt the warm energy from the torque fizzle out until it was nothing more than cold metal. He fingered the twisted gold while eyeing Tyr nervously.

The General steadily watched the point of Amira's portal as though waiting for her return. Then, seemingly accepting her departure, he hefted his club back over his shoulder and approached the pile of chain. "White Lady!" he snapped. The spirit bowed her head with a sneer and glided toward him. "I sense the traitor approaching. Stand in the open and draw her toward the castle. I'll do the rest."

Daniel found Gabriela's eyes. "What do we do?" he mouthed, still nervous to even whisper after the Enemy had almost sniffed them out.

A shriek split the gray dawn. All three jumped in fright. Raylin skimmed the treetops above them and swooped down on the White Lady.

10

A Spirit Party

The White Lady spun around, her ghostly visage awash with terror and surprise. She attempted to fly toward the safety of the castle but was pinned to the ground like a mouse under a hawk before she could make it three feet.

Raylin stabbed downward with the Voidblade. Tyr was by her side in an instant, the Hammer of War turning aside the sword at the last minute. The weapons ground against each other, whining and furiously spitting out black sparks.

Raylin didn't look surprised. She didn't look at all. Keeping her eyes on the White Lady, she gripped Tyr by the arm and flung him into the wall of the castle like a doll.

If it hurt, he didn't show it. Flipping before he hit the stones, he planted his feet on the wall and rocketed himself back at Raylin before she had time to react.

The hammer pounded her square in the chest, knocking her back at least fifty feet from the White Lady. Daniel was sure the blow would've crushed a normal human. Raylin made no expression of pain, and the hammer might've landed a blow on a solid piece of steel for all the damage it seemed to do.

Raylin took to the sky above the castle, circling while looking for an opening. The White Lady floated up and tried to flee back toward the castle. A sharp word from Tyr froze her in her place, however.

"Get the chain and stay where you are!" he barked. "The castle is no shelter for you. She'd corner you there, and there's no room for me to fight. The chain!"

The White Lady stooped down and picked up the red chain from where it still lay coiled behind her. Her hands shook, either from fright or pain—or maybe both.

Gabriela ventured to rise from her hiding place. Daniel and Ben followed suit.

"What's the plan?" Daniel asked. Raylin circled directly overhead, still skimming the treetops. "Sunstorm up through the trees? Try to take her off guard?"

"Maybe these torques hide our presence from *her*, too, so she wouldn't sense it coming," Ben suggested.

Gabriela shook her head. "They've already lost their power."

"Aww," Ben complained quietly, looking down at the metal collar with a pouty look.

"Don't be such a baby," Daniel hissed.

"Your face looks like a baby."

"Boys!" Gabriela snapped. "Zip it! Listen, we can't jump in the middle of the fight. We'd be up against Raylin, Tyr, and the White Lady at the same. And besides, how are we going to handle Raylin without the Celestial Bow?"

Daniel shifted into a sitting position. She was right. There was no way they could take on all three at once as long as his leg was broken. Even if it wasn't, they'd probably have to end up fleeing into the Mist. "Raylin would just fly away if she had to deal with Tyr and us. So what? Pray?"

Gabriela shrugged.

Raylin dove toward the White Lady again, but Tyr leaped into the air from beneath her, the Hammer of War raised above his head. Raylin changed her momentum into a front flip, allowing the Voidblade to lead so that it knocked away the hammer while her subsequent kick nailed Tyr in the face.

He hurtled toward the ground, slamming into the turf with a dull thud.

Raylin pulled out of her flip and made a beeline for the White Lady.

At the last second, the terrified spirit flung the chain into the air before throwing herself to the ground and wailing as she covered her head.

Raylin tried to bat the chain away with the Voidblade, but it suddenly took on a life of its own. The second it touched the sword's ebony edge, it snaked around it like a python. Raylin's sword arm fell limp to her side. In the next instant, the chain slithered up her arm and quickly constricted itself around her entire body. Raylin went rigid and fell to the ground like a stone.

The White Lady's look of abject terror melted into a wicked grin. "Did you really think you could defeat a Firstborn just because you stole a Dark Blade from the Master?" She screwed up her face into a look of haughty triumph. "Stupid mortal! I am the White Lady! I cower before no one!"

Tyr sauntered up behind her. "Shut it," he said, shoving the White Lady roughly aside. He glared down at Raylin, who returned his gaze with an unblinking stare. "You're mine, you traitor! The Master will reward me richly for your capture." He flashed a smug smile at the hammer.

The White Lady looked angry. "I was the one who captured her," she whined, hovering around Tyr's shoulder. "I should get the credit."

"You did exactly as I told you to do." Tyr scowled down at her. "Had it been left to you, you would be cornered in the castle and fodder for the Voidblade."

The White Lady turned a bitter look onto Raylin. "And … do we take her to the Abyss?"

"Yes. Ready yourself," Tyr said, his voice edged as though he, too, had to steel himself to go.

Daniel kept his eyes on the battle. They were out of time. Raylin was bound and about to be delivered to the Enemy. Gabriela and Ben had their eyes closed in prayer; he hastily joined them. *Father, can you please tell us what we're supposed to do? And quick? Raylin's*

captured! Everything is falling apart. My leg still feels awful, and there's no way we could face Tyr and the White Lady. And Seren is MIA. Kind of feeling like this whole quest is a waste, actually. And I know you're busy fighting the Enemy and all that, but this is really …

Daniel's prayers were interrupted when the Mist opened directly above them. A radiant figure of a woman astride a gray deer bound out of the open portal. The deer stood nearly eight feet at its shoulders and had the same sapphire eyes as the gray spirit; tendrils of iridescent blue wisped off the antlers and formed subtle webs of azure under its fur.

The roar of wind that accompanied their unexpected appearance blew Daniel flat on his back.

Ben dove for cover. "What the—?! Was that a flying cow?"

Gabriela jumped to her feet, her mouth slightly open as the newcomers bore down on the battle before the castle lawn.

"It's the Spirit!" she shouted, almost in disbelief. "The Three answered our prayer!"

Daniel swatted at Ben. "Help me up!" he exclaimed; apparently, the new arrivals were enough to make Gabriela not worry about discovery, so he figured he'd throw caution to the wind as well.

Ben grabbed his hands to hoist him to his feet, then paused. "Someone's riding on the Spirit. Is that …?"

He absentmindedly let go, and Daniel fell awkwardly onto his back.

"Ow! Ben!" Daniel smacked Ben's calf with a crutch. "I've fallen, and I can't get up. Mind the invalid, Ben!"

Ben, still studying the figure riding the Spirit, blindly felt for Daniel's hand to pull him up. "Is that Seren?"

Daniel, finally steady on his feet, studied the woman. A small tongue of fire burned over her hair, and a gentle glow emanated from her body. A starburst suddenly shone on her forehead, then shot out to her outstretched hand. There, it formed into an enormous bow that was longer than her own body.

"It must be!" he murmured. "But what's happening? The Celestial Bow is huge. How is she so super-powered?"

"Because the Spirit's touching her," Gabriela said off-handedly. "Just like when the feathers brushed us at Newgrange." She added with more excitement, "The Spirit is finally here to help us!"

Seren drew back on the invisible string, and an arrow of light, the size of a spear, formed. Almost instantly, she let the arrow fly. Once off the string, it streaked through the air like a meteor, rings of light radiating into the air around its comet-like tail.

Tyr swung the Hammer of War to deflect the arrow, but he might as well have tried deflecting a bomb. The arrow exploded in a shower of light that encased the hammer and his entire body before slamming him to the ground. A bright circlet of fire appeared around his head.

His face turned purple with rage, and he furiously shouted in his native tongue. Daniel wasn't sure which Scandinavian country Tyr was from, but he was glad he couldn't speak the language. Whatever he said was probably best left untranslated.

Seren and the Spirit turned toward the White Lady, who looked like a cornered cat.

The White Lady's hair bristled in fear, her fingers splayed out like claws, and she hissed and sputtered her way back toward the castle wall.

The deer leaped into the air and landed in front of her, cutting off any hope she had of escape.

"I know who you are!" the White Lady shrieked. "But I will not leave! This castle is *mine*. This castle is—" The White Lady paused mid-sentence as her voice unexpectedly changed from one, to a host. It was like the voices of a thousand fallen spirits suddenly spoke out of her mouth. "OURS!" they screamed. Spirits, haggard and ghostly pale like the White Lady herself, streamed out of her body—a hundred a second—until the entire lawn and the air around the castle swarmed with wailing, moaning spirits. "We are many! We are a multitude! We are Legion!" They howled in unison and flew to attack the Spirit and its rider all at once.

Without missing a beat, Seren fired one more huge arrow.

Like a needle and thread flying at lightning's pace, the arrow and its comet tail passed through the nearest spirit, towing it along on the arrow's way to the next target until the myriad of spirits were bound by a constricting web of binding light. The thread tightened, pulling the legion of ghosts back into the form of the White Lady. Bound, she promptly fell to the ground, a circlet of fire around her forehead. Unlike Tyr, she opted for obnoxious moans rather than furiously raging against her bonds.

Raylin watched, expressionless, as Seren and the Spirit now descended to her side.

Daniel nudged Ben with his crutch. "I think it's safe for us to go out now." He slowly hobbled out of the trees, with Ben beside him.

Gabriela rushed forward, straight for the Spirit. Once by his side, she reached up and touched his fur. A tongue of fire appeared over her head, and she immediately relaxed as a soft glow of light emanated from her body.

Each step Daniel took, the urge to do the same grew, and the pain in his leg lessened. He finally tottered up next to the giant gray deer and ran his hands through its fur. Each strand brimmed with a vibrating power. It brought comfort, peace, and hope, but there was something else to it: a thinly veiled fire that Daniel sensed could overcome the Enemy at a moment's whim. It was more subtle than the Son's earth-shattering, mind-blowing power, and more familiar than the cosmic force Daniel experienced when the Father had parried with the Enemy from his mountain, but just as potent and filled with love as both. Like an electric cord, he felt the power radiating through him.

Daniel's leg immediately felt better, and all doubts, fears, frustrations, and weariness left him. Just as at Newgrange, he was reminded of the Father's Blessing—the raw, unfettered power of the Spirit, coursing through his body so powerfully that he lit up like a light bulb. That level of spiritual anointing wouldn't happen again until the Sun Sword was whole, though. Still, it was enough.

Daniel suddenly felt connected to Gabriela and Seren. Then

Ben, like a candle blinking on in the dark, connected to the Spirit as well.

The Spirit turned his sapphire eyes toward Gabriela. Daniel couldn't hear words, but he felt reassurance and love passing between them. A sense of understanding welled up from within Gabriela: her need to trust in the Three even when she couldn't feel or hear them, and trust in their love and guidance even when they seemed far away; reassurance that her family in Aguas Calientes would be saved, and to wait only a little longer.

A shallow stream dries in the drought, Gabriela, he heard the Spirit say. *But a river, deep and wide, will endure for an age.*

Gabriela nodded her head and closed her eyes. It was the first time he'd seen her truly at peace since she joined them.

The Spirit turned to him. Daniel took a sharp breath. Now that he looked directly into the Spirit's eyes, he noticed something strange. He wasn't looking at the Spirit but through him. His eyes were windows, and on the other side, the Son. Daniel couldn't tell if he saw the Son visually, or in his mind. Either way, he was there, somehow, and through *him*, as though from a great distance, the Father. He appeared as a great fire—consuming, pure, holy beyond measure, infinitely good, unending, and more alive than Daniel could comprehend.

The Spirit's gaze drifted down to Daniel's leg.

Will you heal me now?

Why was your leg broken? the Spirit's voice, quiet and calm, asked within his mind.

It was the same voice that had always spoken in his prayers. He remembered being surprised to learn that when praying to the Father, it was the Son who spoke—who interpreted the Father's voice. Now, as the Spirit asked his question, Daniel sensed it was again the Son who spoke through the Spirit on behalf of the Father.

Because Seren didn't think before she attacked Raylin and the demons at Newgrange. It caused chaos, and the ruins collapsed in the battle.

Why did we allow this to happen?

I don't know.

The pain in Daniel's leg returned in a rush. After being without it for a few minutes, its sudden presence made it seem as though the break had just happened.

But it really hurts again! Why? Please heal me!

Who else is in pain?

Daniel was immediately aware of Seren, still astride the Spirit and looking down at him. From within her, he felt a deep sense of loss, regret, shame, and anger. It was faint. Locked away somewhere—temporarily sealed away by the Spirit's power.

Seren.

How can she be freed from this?

Daniel thought for a moment before Ben's thoughts broke in.

She needs Raylin's forgiveness. And mine, Ben said.

Daniel nodded. *I need to forgive her, too, I guess.*

The Spirit craned its long neck around and breathed on Seren. She stirred as though from a dream. *Being forgiven and accepting forgiveness are two separate things. Seren and Raylin both struggle with shame and guilt, which make receiving mercy and grace extremely difficult. She needs to experience both in her relationships with you so that she can navigate her relationship with Raylin.*

And you, the Spirit continued, *if you are to lead others, you must learn to bear with them in their pain and weakness.*

Something welled up from within Daniel's chest, and he found himself talking before he knew what he was saying. "I'm sorry for being angry with you, Seren. Please forgive me. And I forgive you for my leg. I know it was an accident."

Daniel looked down and saw a dark spot appear on his shirt. A shadowy form eased out of his chest and fell to the ground. It was smaller than Daniel but otherwise shared all the same features. It scowled up at him, then gawked, terrified, at the Spirit.

"All that stuff I said in the Mist," Ben began from behind. "I … I'm sorry. I was a real jerk." Daniel sensed him reach up to touch Seren's hand. "And I forgive you. I know you've been worried for Raylin, and Daniel's leg was an accident."

A coughing, sputtering noise brought Daniel around. Another shadowy form, dark and hissing, had just fallen out of Ben's chest, too. It joined up with Daniel's; the two creatures scurried over the ground until they found refuge, clinging to one another, behind a bowling-ball sized stone half-buried in the field.

Shadows, Gabriela thought. *Just like in Khireshwar.*

Daniel recalled the one that had emerged from Seren just outside the village—forced out of the deep, hidden chambers in her soul. What had Granny called them?

The Hollows, Ben's voice broke in, apparently discerning Daniel's thoughts.

The sun's morning rays streamed through the clouds as Seren drew her bow and shot an arrow at the stone. The binding shell of light encased it, as well as the two cowering Shadows.

Daniel hobbled to their side and swung the Sun Sword, shattering their forms like dirty glass. The shards floated up into the air and disappeared like vapor.

And now, the Spirit's voice brought Daniel around, *bind his wound.*

Before Daniel could take in his meaning, Seren drew back the Celestial Bow and fired an arrow straight at him.

It passed the Spirit's head and froze midair. He breathed out, infusing it with a complex nexus of gold. In the next second, the arrow whizzed through the air again and crashed into Daniel's leg.

Daniel jumped back in fright and nearly fell over, but the strength in his leg returned even as the pain left. An eight-pointed star flamed to life on his shin, then sank beneath the skin. Relief spread throughout his leg, and then his entire body. He took a deep, pain-free breath.

He let his crutches fall to the ground and rushed back to the Spirit, running his hands through the gray and blue iridescent fur, feeling, in each strand, the eternal bond between the Three. He could've stood there forever, woven into their union like a small thread in a universe-dwarfing tapestry.

Thank you, Daniel said.

The Spirit nodded its head, then pulled away to approach Tyr and the White Lady.

Seren slipped off his back and joined Daniel and Ben as they followed in the Spirit's train.

The White Lady goggled in abject terror at their approach and was so horrified that she stopped moaning and froze.

Tyr's haughty sneer quickly fell into a look of childlike fear. The blood drained out of his face, and his arms and legs shook despite the binding casing of the Celestial Bow.

"Get away from me," Tyr whined. "Don't come any—"

The Spirit shook his mighty antlers and fixed Tyr with a steady gaze.

Tyr whimpered into silence.

Daniel, the Spirit said. *Use the Sun Sword and witness the Enemy's plan.*

Daniel wasn't sure what the Spirit meant but obeyed immediately. Before Tyr could protest, he swung the Sun Sword, supercharged with the Spirit's power, through Tyr's chest.

The Enemy's spirit, black as ink, exploded out of Tyr like a raging serpent. It arched over as if to strike at Daniel, but simply crashed back into Tyr's body.

Daniel puzzled over this. He lifted the Sun Sword over his head, let the power of the Three flow into it, and stabbed the ground, sending a powerful Fire Strike radiating outward.

The White Lady shrieked as the shockwave reached her. She, and all the malevolent spirits within her, were instantly purified. A pile of rags, tattered and ancient, were strewn across the lawn. Within seconds, they had crumbled to dust while a mass of whimpering, whining spirits tore off into the sky.

As before, the Enemy's spirit burst out of Tyr's chest like a snake, then immediately returned. A Sunstorm yielded the same result. Even when Seren was in her Shakti form, it had taken several minutes to be refilled by the Enemy. But with Tyr, it was as though the Enemy's presence never completely left him.

"He is in me. My spirit is his spirit," Tyr spat through clenched teeth. "We are one! Without the image of the Three, my master's spirit cannot be banished, and I cannot be subjected to judgment. I am free of you and your power!" He gleamed triumphantly with his declaration.

I am not the Judge, the Spirit replied, calm and unaffected by Tyr's rage and arrogance. *But I do banish you. Go back to your master; though, he may not be as proud of you as you are of yourself. But know this: there is always mercy and forgiveness with the Three. Repent. Run to the Son and you will find salvation from your bondage.*

Tyr twisted up his face into a look of utter hatred. "Never!" he screamed. "I don't need your forgiveness!"

Nevertheless, it is there and free. Gabriela?

She stirred and walked around Ben to be parallel with the Spirit's head.

Take the Hammer of War. Do not fear to touch it.

Tyr squinted his watering eyes as Gabriela, the tongue of fire blazing over her head, knelt down to take the Hammer of War from his clenched fist.

"Keep away! The hammer is a Dark weapon like the Voidblade. Touch it at your peril!" Tyr's voice rose higher in pitch as he moved from haughty threats to whining, impotent badgering. "The Master hallowed this weapon for me! It's mine! No! Stop!"

Gabriela gripped the Hammer of War, which hissed at her touch like a live coal in a bucket of water.

The corners of the Spirit's mouth twitched with mirth. *Throw it into the sky with all your might.*

Tyr looked as though he might pop with fury. "GIVE. IT. BACK! My Master will kill you! He'll destroy you! I'll destroy you!"

No one paid attention, which seemed to infuriate Tyr even more.

Gabriela eyed the hammer with a puzzled look. *As hard as I can?*

The Spirit nodded.

This should be good, Ben said.

Gabriela reared back, took a deep breath, and put her entire body into hurling the hammer straight up.

The hulking, skull encrusted weapon left her hands with a sonic boom, and within a second was nothing but a speck of black, streaking through the clouds.

The Spirit turned his attention back to Daniel and the others, and said in a quiet voice that didn't reach Tyr, *How long do you think it will take the Enemy to find it if I hide it behind the moon?*

They all laughed. This sudden display of mirth surprised Daniel at first, but then it seemed natural. If the Three were the source of all good things, that included happiness and joy. Even jokes.

I am the funniest Being in existence, the Spirit said matter-of-factly.

Ben and Daniel caught each other's eye and laughed again.

And one day, when you all are with us in Heaven, we will spend an eternity exploring joy. But for now, he took a step closer to Tyr and shook his antlers, *we have more serious matters to attend.*

The binding of Seren's arrow slipped off Tyr like a cloak and flew a few yards away to where Raylin lay, still restrained by the red chain. It covered her in an instant, and the circlet of fire appeared on her head. The red chain binding her clanked to the ground, buzzing and whining with irritation. Tyr had only just begun to sit up when the chain snaked across the lawn and coiled around him like a python.

He screamed at its touch but struggled in vain against its power. A portal whirled opened beneath him.

Remember, Tyr, my forgiveness and mercy are always free. Remember this when you are before the Enemy. Call out for my help, and I will be with you.

"Never!" Tyr bawled as the portal sucked him downward and he disappeared.

The lawn was suddenly quiet. Daniel looked around. Off in the distance, downhill from the castle, was a tiny village bathed in sunlight. The wind picked up, blowing away the mists of the night.

Gabriela's thoughts broke the silence. *That is what the Enemy wants to do to all the Vessels?* she asked. *Make it impossible for them to be purified?*

The Spirit walked on silent hooves toward Raylin. *Yes. But as you have been told, that is impossible for any within the Celestial Family. He believes he has the power, though, so he would nevertheless try.*

But even now, the Spirit continued, *Tyr can repent.*

Daniel remembered Rhiannon's matter-of-fact explanation of the painful future the Enemy had planned for them and heard it play through all their minds in unison.

Seren stepped closer to the Spirit's head. *Won't the Enemy just free Tyr once he gets back to the Abyss?*

The Spirit's facial expression didn't change, but something about him told Daniel he was smiling. *Yes, but I sent him on the long way back. He won't bother you again on this quest.*

That's a relief, Gabriela said. *One less General to worry about.*

They reached Raylin, who lay shimmering with the Celestial binding. Her wild eyes flitted back and forth between everyone's softly glowing forms, then focused steadily on the Spirit.

Daniel raised the Sun Sword and looked to the Spirit. He nodded for Daniel to continue.

As soon as the sword touched her, a mass of dark spirits billowed out and covered the entire area in a nightmarish miasma. Daniel hoped no one in the village was paying attention. Maybe it was still too early for anyone to be up.

Raylin's face, usually so strained and inhuman, looked normal again. Her green eyes glinted with recognition.

"Guys," she whispered, her voice raspy and weak. "Please help me."

Tears welled up in Daniel's eyes.

Malevolent whispers swirled around them. Shapes, a few familiar, but most grotesque and awful in their strangeness, slithered and eddied around the bright light radiating from within them. Daniel thought he saw the elongated, centipede body of the Nightstalker creeping through the churning cloud and the grasping claws of the Devourer reaching toward them. He knew without being told that a mass of demonic spirits this big meant Raylin had absorbed a horde of monsters—and not just the run-of-the-mill kind, like snake and bat demons, although he saw a few of those, too. These were powerful beings on par with the Pitwolf and Ravana.

Should I summon the Triune Shield? Ben asked, calm only because of the Spirit's presence.

Daniel knew if they had been alone, they would have been freaking out.

No, the Spirit replied. *You will not be harmed as long as I am physically with you. And the Triune Shield will not keep her from being filled again. The Voidblade is a conduit for her possession. As long as it is bound to her arm, she cannot be free. Even if I were to transport her somewhere else, these spirits would be drawn to the Voidblade and absorbed again.*

Seren stepped forward and knelt down beside Raylin, placing a gentle hand on her forehead. *Can't you purify her?* She turned to the Spirit. *You're one of the Three; you have the power.*

As long as Raylin chooses to retain the Voidblade, she is choosing possession. In a way, it, too, is a demon—grasping, self-consumed, and filled with malevolence.

Seren turned a cold, angry gaze over the black sword grafted onto Raylin's arm. If looks could kill, the Voidblade would have been obliterated.

I could overcome her will, but once I left, she would return to the Voidblade again, or something worse, and simply be refilled with its evil. She is like Tyr in that way: choosing the Enemy's power and the loss of her soul.

The Spirit bent its towering head down to Raylin. He breathed on her. For a moment, her body relaxed, and she was at peace. In the next, though, a steely look settled into her eyes. With a great effort, she jerked her head away and stared into the woods.

The Spirit raised his head and backed away. *You see? Raylin must choose to abandon her quest for revenge, take up the Abyssal Staff of her own will, and be purified. Until then ...*

Right on cue, the miasma plummeted toward the Voidblade—sucked into the dark world of the sword. Raylin's face resumed its look of terrible emptiness and pain. She strained, trying to break the bonds of the Celestial Bow.

Gabriela frowned at the sword. *She broke the power of the Celestial Bow earlier. How can we transport her to the Abyss if she breaks out again?*

She broke its power because its power was incomplete, the Spirit said. *Seren is a cleansed Vessel now, and the power of the Celestial Bow is greater.* He nodded to Seren. *Nevertheless, shoot once more.*

Seren obeyed and drew back on the invisible bowstring. Another arrow glittered into being.

Bind! the Spirit said. The word was filled with power. Daniel felt it move through the air past him and connect with the arrow. It flared brighter and hummed with power.

Seren released the string, and the arrow struck Raylin's side. Three rings of gold appeared around her body, each with the eight-pointed star at its center. They tightened around her chest, waist, and legs.

Raylin's face darkened with rage for a moment, but it soon passed, and her eyes closed in sleep.

She will rest now, and in her dreams, she will be free from the darkness of the Voidblade.

Is she in pain? Ben asked.

She will see her true self in her dreams, and that is always painful. But the misery of possession will not reach her.

The Spirit plodded forward and turned. Everyone immediately sensed it was time for him to depart.

I will awake her when the time is right. Go now to Stonehenge and enter the Abyss. Find Raylin's Weapon of Power. Once there, she will be offered freedom. Pray that she takes it.

The Spirit's body suddenly morphed into a living flame, which divided and flew toward each of them, enlarging the smaller flames already hovering over their heads. A great wind swirled around the lawn, bending the trees and howling through the castle.

I am always with you, my children. I am always protecting and loving you. In me, you live, and move, and have your being. I in you and you in me, and you will be one with the Father, as we, the Three, are one.

The foundation for the entire universe was manifested in his words as if they contained the instructions to the very law which bound all space and time together. In an instant, an image of the cosmos flashed through everyone's mind, still connected by the Spirit, and they saw the Three holding creation together simply by their presence. Without them, everything would simply cease.

It was mind-blowing, and Daniel felt he was close to burning out with the power surging through him.

And then the Spirit was gone.

Where, he didn't know, exactly, but a portion of the Spirit remained in him, even if he didn't feel it. That much he knew. The gentle illumination within each of them dimmed and then ceased altogether, except for a soft glow that somehow still emanated from their faces. And each had streaks of white through their hair.

"Whoa, guys," Ben said. "I don't know how you're going to go out in public. Your hair looks crazy wild and your faces—"

"You too, Ben," Seren shot back. The edginess and anger were gone from her voice, but she was still the same old Seren.

"What? Oh man, I'm going to get made fun of at school. Great!"

Daniel patted Ben on the back but looked past him to Seren. "You've got some explaining to do, by the way. Like, where did the Spirit find you? How did you end up riding the Spirit out of the Mist? What did he say to you when you were alone? We want to know."

Seren nodded. "Once we're on the move. Sure."

"And Ben," Daniel flashed him a sarcastic smile, "if you'd like, I could start calling you names now, if that would prepare you for school."

"Oh yeah, that'd be a great help. Thanks, Buddy. What a pal."

Gabriela touched Daniel's arm, and all thoughts of messing with Ben were put on the backburner.

She had Raylin hoisted on to her shoulder and smiled at Daniel. "Leg feel better?"

The soft and easy-going nature he'd fallen in love with in Peru was back. "Much. You? Do you feel better, I mean? Not your leg."

Gabriela giggled quietly. "Yes, I do. Very relieved."

Seren and Ben joined them.

"Stonehenge?" Seren asked.

"Stonehenge," Gabriela said. "And then … the Abyss."

Ben plopped his hands on top of his head and blew out a long, slow breath. "Oh, man. This is going to be bad, isn't it?"

"Probably," Daniel said as Gabriela opened the Mist. "Mom and Dad are going to flip out."

"Definitely."

11

The Stonehenge Telethon

Now that Daniel wasn't in such pain, he was able to appreciate the beauty and mystery of the Mist. Their progress was much faster, too. With the Sun Sword guiding them, Daniel led the way, following its pull between the great trees looming out of the star-lit darkness.

"Well?" Ben said after a while, sidling up next to Seren. "You going to tell us what happened after you left us, or not?"

Seren shrugged. "When I left, I ran. Not sure exactly where or for how long. I just kept running. I don't know what I thought was going to happen, but I didn't really care. I wanted to find a way out and go save Raylin by myself. I guess I thought you all were going to give up on her (and me). Like we were too much trouble." Her ears colored red from blushing, but she continued. "Before long, I heard something chasing me—thudding of paws, breathing, the occasional rustle of a branch."

"Was it a demon?" Ben asked, his eyes wide with excitement.

"You look like you're watching a Saturday morning cartoon. No, it was the Spirit."

"Oh. Yeah. That makes more sense."

"Remember, an ordinary demon can't open the Mist," Gabriela said. "The Enemy could force it open. His Generals and Leaders, too."

Daniel followed the Sun Sword to the base of an ancient tree, where the sword stood up on end and pointed to the ground. "We're here. Everyone ready?"

"Guys," Ben snapped. "We're at the best part of the story. Go ahead, Seren. You can finish now."

"Oh gee, thanks," Seren replied in a deadpan voice. "Anyways, the Spirit found me. He still looked like a huge hound. We talked. Figured out some things. Purified me. And there you go. Next thing I knew, he'd changed forms, and I was riding him through the Mist and out at the castle."

Ben sighed. "Talk about bare bones. I want the juicy details! What did he teach you? What sins did you have to confess? What deep spiritual insights can you share with us?"

Expressionless, Seren listened to Ben's whining. After he was done, she put a hand on her hip. "Don't be a jerk. Accept forgiveness. Give forgiveness. Trust the Three. Don't trust myself. Pray. Rely on others. There, are you happy?"

"Ugh. No." Ben sighed and went to stand next to Gabriela. "That was disappointing."

Daniel laughed. "Well, that's Seren. Now, what's the plan? Is the Mist going to open at the entrance to the Abyss?"

Gabriela shook her head. "It never extends to where the Weapons of Power are hidden. Definitely not into the Abyss itself."

"Where is the entrance?" Seren asked.

"In the side of the hindmost trilithon."

Ben looked confused. "There's a telethon at Stonehenge? What, are they trying to raise money or something?"

"Tril-i-thon," Gabriela corrected. "What grade are you in again?"

"K-4," Daniel answered.

Ben punched him in the arm.

Gabriela drew a picture in the air with her finger to explain: two invisible, vertical lines parallel to one another, and one horizontal line above them. "It's two standing stones with one stone across the top. Like a doorway. Only, with this one, there's

only one stone still standing. The other two fell a long time ago."
Seren listened, her face solemn and intent. "And how do we open it?"

"Raylin's hand," Gabriela answered.

"And then what?" Daniel asked. "Transported straight to the Abyss?"

Gabriela repositioned Raylin on her other shoulder. "That, I'm not sure. We'll just have to play it by ear."

"I'm sure it'll go off without a hitch," Ben interjected. "But let's not forget that the Enemy said there were going to be some baddies waiting for us. What's the plan to get past them? I mean, if we were still with the Spirit, I'd say just bust up in there firing our weapons and shielding some stuff. But," he flicked his hands back and forth above his head, "last time I checked, I was no longer a candle."

Daniel nodded. "We should expect the entrance to be surrounded. Once we get our bearings, I'll lead the charge with a Sunstorm. Seren—"

"I'll advance right behind you, binding anyone that doesn't get taken out by the blast," she finished.

"I was going to say, 'Fire Celestial Arrows like a maniac,' but your idea sounds more specific. So, yeah. Do that."

Ben leaned against a tree and pulled out his daggers. "I'll stay back on Daniel's left and be ready with the shield. Gabriela, since you're carrying Raylin, you should be in the middle of the three of us."

Gabriela nodded. "I agree. I'll only fight if I have to. Keep in mind: our priority is not to defeat these enemies, just to get to the Abyss."

Daniel scratched his chin. "Can they follow us in?" He had flashbacks of Shakti's razor-sharp claws digging into his neck.

Gabriela shrugged. "We should assume they can if they're right on our heels. But if they're bound or knocked out, we should be okay. I think the entrance will close behind us once we're through."

All four looked at one another in silence. Apparently, there wasn't anything else to discuss.

"Okay," Daniel said, stretching his back and shoulders before taking the Sun Sword out of guidance mode. "We ready?"

"Ready," Seren and Gabriela said simultaneously.

"Not really," Ben mumbled.

Daniel nodded to Gabriela, and she parted the Mist.

Stonehenge stood under a clear sky and fast-rising sun. Or, at least, the fake Stonehenge projected by the Orb of Concealment did. Daniel scanned the area. There were no tourists around, which wasn't surprising. Normal people tended to avoid areas where an Orb had been cast, even though they couldn't see them. Occasionally, cars passed on the highway near the monument, but they wouldn't notice anything different either.

"Oh, boy," Ben groaned. "Here we go."

They approached the border. Daniel timidly reached out his hand to touch the surface of the Orb.

It pulsed and then suddenly expanded around them.

The scene inside was eerie. Stonehenge's imposing circle towered above them. An outer ring of stones surrounded an inner horseshoe of trilithons and fallen slabs. About half still retained their capstone—a horizontal, rectangular stone bridging the gap between the monoliths—while the others stood unadorned, their crowns half-sunk in the ground beside them or shattered into weatherworn fragments against their fallen comrades.

Like a total solar eclipse, the sun shone black through the Concealment, casting an auspicious light over the ruins. A crowd of men and women dressed like druids milled in a circle among the standing stones. Hoods hid their features, but their jerky movements, rasping conversations, and raking claws gave away their identity.

Creeps, Daniel thought. *Perfect.*

A fluttering movement from the top of an encircling boundary stone drew his attention. A murder of crows, eerily silent, flew in a swirling, weaving pattern among each other. In their midst, the figure of a woman formed from their bodies. Except for her face, she was covered in their glinting, ebony feathers. Her eyes, orange pinpricks of light, stared unblinking from behind a mask of red down as her crows continued to whirl around her. She surveyed the Creeps with a black-toothed smile, each fang the shape of a crow's beak.

Opposite of her, sitting on one of the fallen stones in the midst of the Creeps, was a man dressed in leather armor and a red cape. He played with a short sword, tossing it from one hand to the other or periodically flipping it in the air as if he was bored. He looked like some Roman soldier, except for the stag horns sprouting from the sides of his head and flitting deer eyes with rectangular pupils.

Daniel looked from Gabriela, to Ben, to Seren, and held his finger to his lips. Somehow, no one had marked their appearance.

Gabriela nodded and pointed to a standing stone across the clearing from them. It was among the inner horseshoe and stood alone without a capstone.

Her meaning was clear. That was their destination—the entrance to the Abyss. And, of course, it was smack dab in the middle of the Creeps.

A woman rose up out of the crowd and approached the stone. She was taller than the surrounding Creeps by at least two heads and carried a spear with a razor-sharp bronze tip. She, too, wore armor, though hers was made of animal bones and rawhide. Her skin was a pale gray, and her hair cascaded down her back like a blood-red waterfall. Solid green, pupil-less eyes gleamed under the blackened sun—merciless and void of life. She was beautiful but radiated the same evil as every other demon Daniel had faced.

"Weren't there supposed to be some Generals here, too?" Ben whispered.

Seren nodded, looking around. "I don't see them, though. Maybe they're busy in Babylon."

"Not that I'm complaining," Ben replied.

"Ready?" Gabriela whispered.

Ben shrugged.

Seren and Daniel nodded.

Daniel raised the Sun Sword to fire a Sunstorm when two

things happened simultaneously. The flaring Sun Sword brought all three demons and the entire force of Creeps spinning, and an unfortunately familiar crackling noise split the air right before Daniel felt an overwhelming nausea and sickening pain rack his body.

"Have you missed the Bolt of Pestilence?" a woman said in a thick, Indian accent.

Daniel had immediately crumbled to the ground, but he guessed at what Ben and the girls had seen when they spun around. The missing Generals, likely stepping out of some stupid portal that had opened up silently behind them.

A moment later, Daniel felt the wave of pain and nausea pulled into the Sun Sword, and a green bolt of lightning sizzled down the blade and into the ground, where it zigzagged across the grassy ground until it collided with the rest of the Bolt of Pestilence.

"I am Vinaash," the woman said as the pale emerald lightning arced up and over her shoulders. A six-foot-tall halo of gold swirled behind her, rising out of a puke-green cloud, suspending her a few feet off the ground.

"This," she gestured to the General they'd seen with Tyr outside of Granny's, "is Chiuta. I believe you've met him before."

Chiuta said nothing but cast a blank, gray-eyed stare at Daniel and the others. The Whirlwind of Famine eddied around each of his arms, back, neck, and head, like some midriff hoodie made of vitality-sucking wind. He, too, hovered just above the ground.

"And Wanu," Vinaash continued, waving lazily to the woman to her right. She had dark brown hair like Gabriela, olive skin, dark eyes, and a mouth full of teeth filed down to sharp points. She spun the Scythe of Death, with its knobbed handle and jagged, black blade, around her like it was a baton. Daniel hoped she didn't have flying powers, too.

Vinaash smiled. "The Master bid us—"

Daniel fired three Sunstorms in succession, one for each General. He knew they wouldn't be exorcised, but it might at least buy some time.

"Let's go!" he said in a commanding but quiet voice to Ben, Seren, and Gabriela.

The companions fell into formation, quickly darting between the standing stones as they plunged into the crowd of Creeps.

Seren summoned the Celestial Bow and fired an arrow straight toward the crow-woman. The cloud of birds simply parted to let the arrow fly through before swarming up into the air above Stonehenge.

Daniel fired another Sunstorm through the Creeps. This, at least, connected. A vast swath was cleared in front of them, and each exorcised Creep quickly vanished in successive flares which lit up the Concealment like camera flashes.

Ben held both golden daggers, using their hilts and his fists to batter away remaining Creeps trying to flank them as they made a beeline for the entrance to the Abyss.

Gabriela, with Raylin hoisted onto her shoulder and bouncing around as though she weighed no more than a doll, kept to the middle between Ben and Seren, but occasionally spun around to deliver a powerful kick or punch to any assailant attacking from behind.

They were in the middle of the ruins now, with the entrance about twenty feet away, when everything went wrong.

The Scythe of Death suddenly pierced up from below the ground and sliced open the lawn directly in front of Daniel. Everyone bumped into him as he skidded to a halt.

Where the blade sliced, the very fabric of reality flayed open. Wanu jumped out of the opening, which snapped shut after she passed through. She spun the scythe, slicing open the air all around her. One ripped open near Daniel. With a quick motion he barely had time to follow, she swung the scythe through an opening next to her, and the blade zinged out of the portal nearest Daniel.

It would've caught him in the side had not a Creep rushed him at that second.

The Creep exploded into a cloud, which immediately condensed into a vaporous gray ball that hovered over the Scythe of

Death wherever Wanu spun it. The blade instantly grew longer.

"Not who I was aiming for," Wanu tittered, a maniacal look on her face. "But it gets the job done."

"I know this is obvious, but don't let the scythe touch you!" Seren shouted even as she fired two arrows at Wanu, who sliced open a portal big enough to catch both. They were redirected through another opening and harmlessly crashed into a standing stone. "The Scythe of Death lets its wielder temporarily steal power from your soul. One knick, and you'll be just like that Creep—packaged and ready for delivery to the Enemy."

"It's like the Voidblade 2.0!" Ben shouted as he beat back another assailant.

Seren bound three more Creeps. "Exactly."

"I wasn't planning on getting chopped up by the thing, but thanks for the info!" Daniel replied. He charged a Fire Strike and stabbed the ground.

The shockwave extended outward for fifteen feet. Wanu's portals whined as the purifying power of the Sun Sword washed over them, smoothing them shut.

Wanu calmly retreated into one before it closed and appeared on top of a standing stone a second later.

Ben immediately erected the Triune Shield just as the Whirlwind of Famine and the Bolt of Pestilence stormed against the barrier simultaneously.

A cloud of crows attacked from the opposite side. Their beaks pecked against the shield as the horde parted slightly, letting the crow-woman through. She cackled and began muttering to herself. The words were in a strange language Daniel had never heard, and each took shape in a string of etchings that shone silver on the surface of the shield. She took a deep breath and blew outwards. A loud *BOOM!* resounded over the plain, and the entire shield wobbled and temporarily lost shape.

"This is not feeling good!" Ben gasped. "That was almost as powerful as when the Enemy attacked me."

"Keep up the spells, Morrigan," Chiuta shouted. "Don't stop until I give you the command."

The crow-woman snapped her head toward the General and begrudgingly nodded. "As you wish," she said in a thick Irish accent that couldn't hide her hatred.

Daniel and Seren immediately sprang into action.

Three Sunstorms blasted through the shield with a scattershot of Celestial Arrows around them.

Morrigan whispered another spell, and her words formed into a shield for her and most of her crows. About a third of the birds got caught in the blasts and were bound, purified, or both. She let out a combination scream and caw as she flew around to attack from a different position.

Daniel charged the Sun Sword and supported Ben with a Fire Strike before going back on the offensive.

"Anymore of those you can spare are greatly appreciated!" Ben said.

"Oh, sure, no problem!" Daniel gasped before returning his attention to their enemies.

With a series of quick shots, Seren bound several Creeps, but a group of ten had run around the shield and gotten behind their attacks. She spun around and fired a volley at the band when the stag-man and the woman with the spear vaulted out from behind them, weapons held high. After slashing and stabbing at the Triune Shield in one spot, they dashed in opposite directions, attacking the barrier every few steps. They moved like seasoned warriors accustomed to fighting alongside each other.

The attacks came from every side.

For a moment, Daniel froze, overwhelmed by the chaos.

Father. Give me guidance.

The brief prayer was enough to ground him. He opened his eyes. "Seren. Fire in a circle at Vinaash as fast as you can.

In a blur of movement, a circle of Celestial Arrows flew toward the General, forcing her to hover in the air without moving as the arrows sped around her. She attempted to summon the spinning halo in front of her to form a shield, but the arrows struck it before it could move.

Daniel's Sunstorm followed the barrage a split-second later.

Vinaash's shriek of surprised anger was cut short as the blast hit home.

Seren sent one more volley of arrows at Vinaash's falling form, encasing her before she hit the ground.

She tilted her head toward Daniel. "I doubt that'll hold Vinaash longer than a few minutes. What next?"

"Chiuta," Daniel whispered, "same attack."

But Chiuta seemed ready. With his usual blank stare, he simply moved the Whirlwind of Famine in front of him as the volley of Celestial Arrows flew by, obscuring Daniel and Seren's view.

As before, Daniel fired a Sunstorm, but Chiuta was already flying forward out of the arrows' entrapping trajectory and shot skyward before the Sunstorm could hit.

That same moment, Wanu popped out of a dimensional tear next to the shield. She was quickly joined by the warrior woman.

"Agrona. Strike the shield in one spot," she ordered.

The demon immediately complied with a torrent of slicing and jabbing attacks.

"Belatucadrus," she barked toward the stag-man. "You, too!"

He jumped to Agrona's side and delivered a blinding flurry of strikes with his short sword, perfectly timed between her own attacks.

Wanu quickly joined in as Daniel and Seren turned toward them, momentarily leaving the horde of Creeps, Morrigan, and Chiuta unchecked.

"I don't think I can do this much longer," Ben shouted. "What's the plan?"

Daniel and Seren both fired a stream of attacks toward their assailants, but that same moment Wanu sliced open another portal to let the arrows and blasts pass through. They were redirected through another tear left open behind the battle and flew off into the air. With a strained grin, she swung the Scythe of Death with all her might, slicing through the Triune Shield; she, Agrona, and Belatucadrus jumped through before Ben, groaning from the blow and exertion, closed up the rend.

"I can't keep this up forever!" Ben panted. "And they're inside me in case you haven't noticed!"

Seren sent a round of Celestial Arrows toward the intruders, but Wanu nonchalantly redirected them while muttering orders to the demons attending her.

Daniel heard a soft thud behind him, and Gabriela was next to his ear.

"Both of you. Fire straight toward her again. Quickly."

Daniel didn't know what she had planned, but he complied. Seren too.

Wanu opened the dimensional tear slightly wider to redirect the blasts just like before, but the Sunstorm's blinding approach hid Gabriela as she charged the enemies from behind it.

Wanu didn't have time to react when Gabriela, leaping over the portal, punched her in the jaw. She flew through the Triune Shield and collided with Morrigan on the other side. Both fell to the ground, dazed, in the cloud of crows.

Seren fired two Celestial Arrows after them, while Daniel slung two Sunstorms to seal the deal.

Gabriela didn't stop to watch the effect of the attack. Instead, she had immediately changed directions and bore down on Agrona. The warrior-demon tried to jump back, but Gabriela was faster. With one quick motion, she caught the spear in her hands and yanked Agrona toward her, meeting the demon with another powerful jab.

The blow sent her careening toward Chiuta. He seemed ready, however, catching her in the Whirlwind of Famine and ricocheted her into a standing stone several feet away. She hit its side with a loud *Smack!* and slid down the surface of the stone to the ground.

Daniel sent a Sunstorm to meet her. Her spear clattered to the ground as her demonic spirit joined Morrigan's in the air before both tore off toward the entrance to the Abyss and disappeared into the side of the trilithon.

With a belting war cry, Belatucadrus charged Gabriela from behind, but a Celestial Arrow followed by a Sunstorm caught him before he could take two steps. He was exorcised, leaving behind the short sword and cape before his spirit went screaming toward the trilithon.

Gabriela then jumped out of the Triune Shield entirely, catching Chiuta by the ankle as he flew overhead. Her trajectory carried them both to the ground outside the shield, where she slammed him into the earth with rock-cracking power. He was momentarily stunned but broke away from Gabriela's grasp with a powerful kick. The Whirlwind of Famine immediately separated them, pulling Gabriela into its vortex and slinging her through the air to crash into a standing stone next to the Triune Shield. She gasped and fell to the ground, wan and weary, looking as though she hadn't eaten in a week.

Daniel took two steps toward her and nearly broke into a run.

"Stay focused!" Seren commanded. "Chiuta."

Daniel understood and concentrated all his firepower on the General approaching Gabriela with the Whirlwind raging before him. Chiuta, teeth bared in rage, hurled the Whirlwind toward the fiery blast, slowing its flight as he shot into the air above it.

Crackling thunder was the only warning they had that Vinaash was free of her binding. The Bolt of Pestilence rained down on the battlefield. Gabriela weakly flung herself away from the standing stone and fell through the Triune Shield just as a bolt shattered the ground at her feet.

The Creeps who were left had scattered in fear. They apparently knew Vinaash was in no mood to discriminate between friend and foe. Chiuta circled the Triune Shield like a vulture while Vinaash kept up her attack. The binding around Wanu suddenly shattered, and she jumped to her feet, spinning the Scythe of Death like a maniac.

Gabriela lay emaciated at Daniel's feet. He knelt down and cradled her in his arms. "Gabriela? Can you hear me?"

She nodded weakly and then passed out.

Daniel felt her pulse. It was weak and irregular. He looked wildly around. Three Generals were still on the loose. They were no nearer to the entrance to the Abyss. Gabriela was out of commission and seemed to be dying. And Ben could likely hold the Triune Shield only a few more minutes.

His mind raced through the scenario, but all his thoughts and prayers could only focus on Gabriela.

"I need some backup!" Ben shouted. "Daniel. Use a Fire Strike."

"Daniel!" Seren joined in.

Their shouts seemed distant and quiet. If Gabriela died, he didn't care what happened to them.

12

Mad Dashes and Dilemmas

Slap!

Seren raised her hand again, apparently ready to rain down as many blows as it would take to bring Daniel to his senses.

"Daniel!" she shouted. "Snap out of it and use a Fire Strike. It'll purify the effects of the Famine."

Daniel shook his head, and his eyes flew open in understanding. If it worked with the Bolt of Pestilence, why not against the Whirlwind of Famine? And it would strengthen Ben at the same time.

He jumped to his feet and channeled every ounce of energy into the Sun Sword before stabbing it into the ground. The shockwave washed over Gabriela, forcing out what looked like a small whirlwind, before crashing against the borders of the Triune Shield.

Ben's glow brightened, and he immediately shrank to let the tiny tornado out of the shield. It droned and whined its way back to the larger Whirlwind of Famine tearing around Stonehenge at the bidding of its master.

Color returned to Gabriela's face. She sat up, rubbing her stomach. "Okay. So, that felt awful. I've never been so hungry in all my life." She jumped to her feet like she hadn't just been on the verge of death.

Daniel almost laughed with relief, but his feelings of jubilation were short-lived.

"Guys. Something's not right," Ben cautioned. "Where's Wanu?"

Daniel and Seren scanned Stonehenge, but she was missing.

"I think I feel …" Ben's voice faltered.

Gabriela walked toward the center of the shield where Ben's outstretched form was just above her. "What is it, Ben?"

"Raylin!" Ben shouted. "Wanu is—"

The Scythe of Death sliced upward from the ground next to Raylin like a shark fin, and Wanu popped out of the dimensional tear. The scythe spun once more and stabbed into the bottom-most star adorning the binding circlets around Raylin's body, but couldn't cut through. Wanu gritted her teeth and spun the Scythe of Death again, in one motion, slicing the other two stars and the circlet of fire around Raylin's head.

Nothing happened.

Daniel felt like he'd been holding his breath—frozen in surprise by the sudden attack. He sprang into action, and Seren and Gabriela followed close behind.

Wanu seemed more perturbed by the lack of effect her attack had on Raylin's binding than their approach. She casually sliced open a dimensional portal behind her and backed through. It zipped itself up just as Celestial Arrows and another Sunstorm came flying by.

Daniel and the others skidded to a halt next to Raylin. He dropped to his knees to examine her body. The binding was still in place, and she didn't seem hurt.

Wanu appeared outside the shield, with Vinaash and Chiuta hovering just above her. Vinaash studied them through the barrier. "Did it work?"

Wanu licked her pointed teeth and swung the Scythe of Death up to inspect its blade.

"Couldn't cut through," she hissed, testing the edge against her thumb. "Yet."

Chiuta shrugged and casually sent the Whirlwind of Famine raging against the Triune Shield again.

Vinaash flashed a smug grin at Wanu. "Useless." She floated higher on her cloud and hurled the Bolt of Pestilence at the shield.

"If I didn't know any better, Vinaash," Wanu hissed, "I'd think you were talking about me, not the scythe." She fell to spinning the scythe like a maniac. "I'd be careful if I were you. One small move and I might accidentally slice you." She popped in and out of portals that appeared around the shield and began assaulting Ben from all sides.

Vinaash flashed a wicked smile as if the thought of fighting Wanu to the death pleased her. But that was obviously an activity for another day, because she doubled her attacks on the shield.

"Plan, please," Ben snapped. "And quick!"

Daniel jumped to his feet and summoned two Fire Strikes. "Any ideas?"

Gabriela didn't look too eager to jump through the shield again. She snapped her eyes shut and began to pray.

Daniel followed suit.

Seren was too distracted by the recent attack on Raylin and kept searching her body for cuts.

Run.

"Gabriela," Daniel said. "I must be hearing the Three incorrectly. They want us to run?"

Gabriela, her brows furrowed in confusion, replied, "That's what I heard, too."

Both turned to look at the storm of Famine, Pestilence, and Death raging around the Triune Shield. One step outside the shield, and they'd be toast.

"We've got a problem!" Seren shouted, dashing to their side.

"Another one?" Ben screeched.

"It's Raylin. She's free!" Seren gasped.

Daniel and Gabriela spun around just as the last binding star faded, and the circlet of fire fizzled out around her head. Her wings shot out beneath her, launching her into the air.

There was nowhere to hide. They had to make a mad dash for the trilithon or stay locked in with the Voidblade.

"Run it is!" Daniel shouted as loudly as he dared. "Ben, release the Triune Shield and get ready to run!"

In a split second, Ben was by his side, and all four took off toward the entrance to the Abyss.

Seren and Daniel fired as many arrows and Sunstorms as they could. None of them landed, but it distracted the Generals long enough for them to get halfway to the trilithon before the Bolt of Pestilence stopped them in their tracks.

Vinaash floated down in front of them. "What's the rush, little—"

Raylin careened into Vinaash with the Voidblade extended outright. The General screamed in pain but wasn't sucked into the sword.

"You should know by now," Vinaash gasped in anger. "That I don't have a soul. And there's no end to the Master's spirit within me."

She gritted her teeth and grabbed the Voidblade with her bare hand, slowly pushing it away.

Raylin showed no signs of shock by Vinaash's ability to touch the blade. Expressionless, she punched Vinaash backward and jumped out of the way as the Whirlwind of Famine came tearing by. In the next second, she was hacking away at Chiuta, who was blocking the Voidblade with his bare arms. The attack clearly weakened him, but the effect lasted only a moment. With a flourish of his hands, Famine stormed between them, hurling Raylin into the air.

Its power didn't seem to harm her. Rather than hunkering down in starvation mode, she tore through the air straight back at the Generals.

Wanu popped out of a dimensional tear next to Raylin and swung the Scythe of Death straight for her heart. In one blur of motion, she batted the scythe aside and rained down a flurry of blows onto Wanu, driving her back through her own portal. Raylin followed her through, continuing her barrage all the way to the other opening closer to the ground.

"Now's our chance," Gabriela whispered. "Run!"

They sprinted across the remaining ten feet, scurrying over fallen stones and swerving around one giant slab lying on its side. As they neared the trilithon, a handprint, etched into the side of the stone, appeared at eye level with Daniel.

"Don't we need Raylin's hand for that?" Daniel asked frantically. He spun around just as Raylin and Vinaash came flying by, locked in mortal combat. Chiuta attacked from above them, driving Raylin down to the ground. She flipped, planted her feet on a stone, and launched herself through the whirlwind back toward Chiuta.

Wanu appeared above her, chopping downward.

Raylin grabbed the scythe's handle with one hand and blocked the arcing blade with her sword. The force of the momentum drove her back down to the ground.

Without warning, Gabriela darted forward and uppercut Wanu so hard she careened into Vinaash and Chiuta, who had both regrouped above to prepare another barrage of Pestilence and Famine. All three spun into the air in a tangle of arms and legs.

In the next split second, Gabriela grabbed both Raylin's arms and yanked her free hand toward the imprint on the trilithon. Raylin wrenched her arm free, but the opening had already activated.

The ground beneath Stonehenge immediately disappeared. A circular stairwell, the circumference of the entire ruin, spiraled down into the earth below them. Daniel found they were already standing on the topmost stair, behind which, and beside, the Abyss plunged into the depths, where a tiny pinprick of red light glowered up from the darkness.

Ben, who was standing on the very back edge of the step, flung out his hand and grabbed Daniel's shoulders to steady himself. "Where's the ground?"

"If you're going to fall," Daniel gasped, becoming unsteady and pulling Ben with him as he crumbled to the steps, "do it by yourself!"

Seren and Gabriela were unaffected by the sudden change and calmly steadied themselves by stepping away from the back edge onto the stairs below.

Several screams of rage and grunts of effort drew Daniel's attention skyward. The Generals were suspended in the air above the center of the Abyss. Wanu had hooked the Scythe of Death into an open dimensional tear, desperately trying to pull herself up, but she was weighed down by Vinaash, who clung to Wanu's legs, and Chiuta, who clawed frantically at Vinaash's feet.

All were outstretched as if a powerful force sucked them downward.

Raylin hovered in the air just above the topmost step, flapping her wings in a frenzy to stay aloft.

"The power of the Abyss draws evil into it," Gabriela explained. She reached down and yanked Daniel and Ben to their feet. Pulling them further down the steps, she said, "I think we need to move."

"Why?" Ben asked, looking backward. "Everyone seems pretty occupied at the moment."

No sooner had the question left Ben's lips, than Raylin lost the battle and crashed into the topmost steps with a dull thud. The force knocked the wind out of her, and she lay gasping for air.

"Don't let go!" Vinaash suddenly screeched. "Wanu! If you let go, I'll destroy you! Pull us up!"

"Oh, shut up!" Wanu shouted back, her hands slipping down her scythe. "How can I with you worthless fools dragging me down? Let go!"

The muscles in Chiuta's arms bulged with the strain of hanging on. His grip slipped until he clung only to Vinaash's two big toes. "Idiots! Wanu. Let go … and … open a portal … below us … as we … fall," he gasped.

But it was too late.

Wanu's grip failed. She slid the rest of the way down her scythe handle, and all three plunged toward the red light below, screaming and bellowing curses to each other. The scythe hung from the portal a moment longer, but the sucking power of the Abyss gradually pulled it from its perch to plunge after its mistress.

Ben peered over the edge of the steps. "Kind of seemed like a bunch of snot-nosed kids bullying each other on the playground, not crazy-strong Generals in the Enemy's army."

Daniel recalled Tyr's behavior once the Spirit had bound him. "Take away their power, and they're just a bunch of self-centered brats."

"Guys," Seren said, irritation edging the word. "Now's not the time to psychoanalyze the Generals." She nodded her head toward Raylin, who had laboriously pulled herself to her feet and was glaring at all four with murderous intent.

Raylin took an arduous step forward and raised the Voidblade. Ben and Daniel backed down another step. Raylin's next move was quicker as if she were adjusting to the gravitational pull of the Abyss.

Gabriela spun around and started down the staircase. "The Spirit said he'd unbind Raylin at the right time. Well, the Generals are taken care of for now, the Abyss is open, she's unbound and following us. Get a move on!"

Daniel and Ben snapped to attention and followed her down.

Seren hesitated. "Raylin, can you hear me?" she asked in a quiet voice. "Do you ... do you remember me?"

Raylin slashed toward her with the Voidblade, narrowly missing her stomach.

Daniel rushed back up the stairs and grabbed Seren by the arm. "Come on. Let's get her to the Abyssal Staff, and she'll be fine."

Seren nodded and silently hurried down the steps after Daniel.

With grunts of effort, Raylin picked up the pace to follow.

The farther they descended, the more the stairwell widened— like a bottle or a vase, Daniel thought. Within half an hour, the opposite wall was about a football field away. By an hour, it was hard to make out the details of the other side. And still, the steps spiraled downward toward the angry red light.

"Is this ever going to end?" Ben puffed. He cast a look over his shoulder.

Raylin lagged behind now, following so slowly that, for once during this quest, she didn't seem to pose any threat. She plodded after them, her ragged, inky wings and the Voidblade both dragging on the ground while her eyes remained fixed, unblinking, on Seren.

Ben risked a pause and carefully peered over the edge of the stairs down to the center of the Abyss. "How far is it?"

Gabriela didn't turn around. "I don't know, but it's a long way yet. And I don't think it can really be measured in miles, exactly. We're not in the physical world anymore. It's more like a different dimension connected to the space inside the earth."

Daniel hurried down to be next to her. "Kind of like how the Mists are linked to the space all around us."

"Exactly."

"Come on," Seren said as she passed Ben. "You don't know when she might get a burst of strength."

Ben watched Raylin trudging after them. Her lips were drawn tight over clenched teeth, and her face flushed a deep crimson from the strain of each step. She was ten feet from him now, and, with great effort, started swinging the Voidblade in his direction—like a tiger clawing the air for a piece of meat it can't reach.

Ben shuddered and ran after Seren.

While the stairwell kept widening, Daniel noticed another change, too. With each revolution down, the gravity of the Abyss felt stronger. Even though it didn't seem to affect them as much as Raylin and the Generals, it was still noticeable. At first, he thought it was just his imagination, but his breathing grew more labored by the two-hour mark, and each time he took another step down, it felt as though his feet were metal drawn down by a powerful magnet. The change was more obvious in Raylin. She was now almost doubled over, and the Voidblade, once dragging the ground behind her, now angled toward the edge of the Abyss, pulling her right arm in front of her as it was sucked toward the red light below.

Only Gabriela, with her superhuman strength, plodded down the steps as though unaffected.

Ben wiped sweat off his face. "Is this ever going to end?"

"Eventually," Gabriela replied. "But we can't rest as long as Raylin is—"

With little more than an angry grunt, Raylin slid off the stairs and into the center of the Abyss, where she was quickly drawn straight down and out of sight.

Daniel imagined he heard a metallic din as she hit the bottom somewhere far below.

Everyone froze, looking at each other in confusion. They turned toward Gabriela.

Seren looked panicked and trudged to the side of the Abyss.

"Um ... is that okay?" Daniel asked after a moment, pointing after Raylin.

Gabriela thought for a moment. "I don't know, honestly," she said, shaking her head. "I'm sure she'll be fine physically."

Seren hurried past her. "That's just a guess. We all know what's at the bottom of this place, so let's get a move on."

Daniel shivered despite his exertion and the growing heat of the Abyss. He *did* know. The Serpent. Seven giant heads and a seriously bad attitude. If the Sun Sword didn't have the power to completely purify the Generals, what effect could it have on *him?*

None, that's what. Uh, Father? How is this going to work out exactly? And is Raylin okay? I mean, that looks kind of far. Was she supposed to get sucked down there?

He paused for a moment. The Spirit had said he would unbind Raylin when the time was right. Surely he wouldn't have let that happen only for her to be harmed somehow by her fall into the Abyss.

"Daniel!" Seren shouted, she, Ben, and Gabriela nearly on the opposite side of the Abyss. "Get a move on!"

He continued listening for any reply from the Three as he slogged his way down to catch up, but nothing came, only the ever-increasing power of the Abyss, drawing them down with its crushing power.

Another hour passed by, and the temperature of the room began to rise considerably. Instead of the chilly air funneling down from Stonehenge, it was a hot, dry air with no hint of a breeze. The next hour crawled by, and finally, the group found themselves slowly circling the bottom from a few stories up. The crushing power here was so strong that each step Daniel took felt as if a twenty-pound dumbbell was strapped to his feet. Even his eyes couldn't help but be drawn continuously to the bottom.

A slab of furiously red metal stretched from wall to wall. Infused just below its surface, a string of fiery letters streamed across its face from one end to the other. They were in the same language as the barrier outside Granny's, which struck Daniel as odd. He always figured the Abyss was a place of evil because the Enemy was there, but maybe that was wrong.

A dark line spanned the middle. It was a thick, raised lip of some black metal with another stream of glowing letters continuously flowing within its margins.

In the dead center of this, four figures lay stretched out on their backs, squirming angrily. Three griped continually at one another while one struggled silently, but all were bound by the power of the Abyss. Daniel couldn't make out their faces from his distance, but their weapons were visible enough to distinguish each from the other.

Gabriela and Seren were the first to reach the bottom step. They hesitated, then carefully stepped off onto the huge metal slab. Both threw out their arms and tottered like they had almost lost their balance. Daniel and Ben, walking a few steps behind, paused at the bottom step.

"Is everything okay?" Ben asked the girls.

Seren turned around. "Yeah, it's just that … well, step off. You'll see."

Daniel and Ben exchanged worried glances and joined the girls.

The second their feet touched the metal floor, the spiraling staircase disappeared. Instead of the confines of the Abyss wall, wide as it was, the base stretched as far as they could see in every direction. At the horizon, it curved slightly. Daniel had never been to the ocean before, but he imagined the unhindered view would look similar.

The visual change was so sudden, Daniel lost all bearing. Ben, too. They reflexively threw out their arms to steady themselves.

Ben's eyes were wide as golf balls, but he couldn't help but laugh. "This place is weird." He glanced around. "No dragon, though, so that's good. Anybody see the Abyssal Staff? Seems like a good time to grab it and go, what with the Three Stooges being tied up and all." He jabbed toward the Generals with his thumb.

Gabriela put her hands on her hips and pivoted around to scan the entire scene. "Call me crazy, but maybe this isn't the bottom."

"You're kidding," Ben exclaimed, throwing up his hands. "What, is there another staircase somewhere? Fifty miles long this time?"

Daniel waved for Ben to be quiet. "I think she's right. Look." He fought against the gravity as he stepped up on the black lip and trudged the ten or so feet to its center. There, hard to see from a distance, but obvious upon close inspection, was a seam running the length of the lip. It wasn't one but two giant slabs forming the ground.

He felt a sense of dread as he turned toward the others. "I think this is a door, and I bet I know what a door this size is meant to keep shut in."

Ben looked disgusted. "Of course."

Seren joined Daniel in studying the lip, then raised her eyes to Raylin and the arguing Generals. "Kind of looks like they're in the dead center. What's that?" She stumped toward them.

"What's what?" Ben griped. "Wait. Never mind. I don't want to know."

Daniel and Gabriela hurried after Seren and found her walking in a circle around the glaring Generals. Wanu and Vinaash were going back and forth, blaming one another. Chiuta, sullen and pouty, watched them with a look of revulsion. Only Raylin seemed unbothered by the binding gravity of the Abyss and the miserable company of her fellow prisoners. She simply followed Seren with her eyes—silent and expressionless, like some reptile watching its prey.

"You think you have beaten us," Wanu screeched as Daniel passed her by. Her mouth twisted into a hateful smile. "You have done nothing! How dare you worms," she spat the word, "look down on us and gloat. We are—"

"No one is gloating, you shark-toothed freak," Daniel shot back. "Go see a dentist and leave us alone. We're trying to figure something out."

Wanu was so taken aback, she actually fell silent.

"Finally," Vinaash whispered to Chiuta. "I thought she'd never shut up."

"You're both annoying hags," Chiuta replied, turning his head away from Vinaash with great effort. "Can't be around each other for a minute without fighting like brats. Grow up."

Vinaash narrowed her eyes at the back of his head, then joined Wanu in glaring at the Vessels.

Pestilence, Death, and Famine hovered harmlessly near the Generals' feet. Daniel and Gabriela followed Seren, giving the weapons a wide berth just to be safe. They walked around until they were a couple meters down and to the left of the captives.

"Look," Seren said, quickly kneeling to the ground and pointing to an indentation in the ground. The metal was so black it was hard to see unless you were right on top of it. "It's rounded like the bottom of a sphere. And this one," she walked back to the opposite side of the Generals, "is arced." She thought for a minute. "I bet there's another one—"

"It's right here," Gabriela said, pointing to the floor several feet above the General's heads.

Daniel and the others joined her. The indentation was a small slit.

"That's a keyhole for the Sun Sword," Daniel explained. "There were several in Peru."

Ben nodded. "Which means the spherical one is for the Triune Shield, and the arced one …" He looked at Seren.

"Is for the Celestial Bow," Seren finished. "I guess when we put all the Weapons of Power in them, the bottom of the Abyss will open."

"Are you all ready?" Gabriela said, taking a deep breath and adjusting her wrist guards.

"No," Ben flatly stated even as he moved toward his keyhole. "But when has that changed anything? Let's just get this over with."

"Are we going to fall when this thing opens?" Daniel asked. He didn't expect anyone to have the answer.

Ben snorted. "Probably. And right into one of the Enemy's giant, stupid dragon mouths."

Seren's eyes lingered on Raylin. "What happens to them? They're right in the center."

Everyone looked back and forth at one another, no one certain of the answer.

Gabriela closed her eyes in prayer. Daniel and the others did the same.

Summon your weapons. Do not fear.

The words came before Daniel could even form a coherent thought. There was a sense of certainty and urgency as well.

He opened his eyes and summoned the Sun Sword.

Ben's eyes flew open, and he transformed into the Triune Shield.

Only Seren hesitated, her attention drifting back to Raylin. Daniel wasn't sure what she had heard, but he knew her hesitation wasn't for herself.

"Seren, don't fear," he said. "This is all for Raylin, remember? This is the only way. Whatever happens, it's for the best."

She nodded her head and took a deep breath. Her brow shone brightly as the power of Celestial Bow manifested. The light flew down to her open hand and expanded into the brilliant, recurve limbs. She pressed the weapon into her keyhole.

Daniel stabbed the Sun Sword downward. The moment it

clicked into place, iridescent, red-gold lines shot from one keyhole to the next, forming a triangle. Outside this, behind and around the Vessels, an expansive eight-pointed star blazed up from the ground.

A deep groan vibrated through the Abyss, and the doors parted so quickly, Daniel and the others were wrenched away from the keyholes and left staring into the bottom of the Abyss. It had to be at least a mile below them and was lit with the same unnerving red of the door. The effect of the gravity on Raylin and the Generals was now so strong, they were immediately pulled all the way down in an instant.

For some reason, even though Daniel could feel the increased force, he and the others floated down more slowly. Below them, glaring up with more anger, hatred, and malevolence than Daniel could even process, was the Serpent.

"See? Right into one of its stupid mouths!" Ben shouted, changing back into his normal form. "I hate being right."

13

The Serpent's Abyss

Daniel took in the scene below in an instant.

The Serpent looked exactly as it had in India. Its size was difficult to process; the Abyss offered no frame of reference. Daniel had thought the stairwell vast, but this portion of the pit—the true Abyss—might have been as immense as the entire earth. And the Serpent took up most of it. Massive coils undulated and slithered around themselves, each with giant, razor-sharp ridges running the course of its back. Seven snapping heads, colossal as mountains, bared thousands of massive, jagged fangs. Rows of knife-sharp horns grew from the sides of each face, forming serrated ridges lining its cheeks, eyebrows, and temples. Two titanic horns, curved and ribbed like those of a ram, sprouted from the side of all seven heads. Five sets of eyes were forced shut by the binding eight-pointed star—the result of its fights with Vessels in each previous age. In the center of those foreheads, a human figure—arms outstretched, featureless, and black as tar—lay as if bonded to the Serpent's scales. The unblinking, fiery-red eyes of the two unbound heads alternated between Raylin and the Generals, and the falling Vessels. The human figure outstretched between their foreheads flickered like smoldering coals.

Each time a head turned toward Daniel, a hot wave of hatred, malevolence, and a horrifying mixture of consuming fear and chaotic confusion buffeted his whole being. He shuddered and looked away. Every negative emotion and terrible memory he had ever experienced burst in on his mind. His breathing quickened, and he broke out in a sweat. He tried to recall the images of the Son as he'd seen him in India: peaceful, radiant, and brimming with holy power. But no such soothing image could be recalled, as though nothing good was allowed here.

He shut his eyes tightly. *Father, Spirit, Son. Where are you? I can't ... I can't see you. Help me.*

He looked around at the immense walls of the Abyss. He now realized they were peppered with thousands of alcoves, each filled with towering figures, with their names carved in multiple languages at the top of the niche. His immediate perception that these were statues was quickly abandoned when he realized they were moving. His eyes were drawn to four: Supai's schizophrenic form, alternating between angelic and demonic; the giant, four-armed Shiva; Arawn, bedecked with clattering bones and ghastly skull mask; and the strange lion-man he'd seen at the White Lady's castle. The others were equally dreadful. In one, he saw a giant man with beady, slate-colored eyes. Icicles protruded from a dull crown of iron, which held back long, pale-blond hair. A snow-encrusted mustache nearly covered his furious mouth. Drab gray chain mail chinked as he shifted to scowl down at the Vessels. He wouldn't have seemed as horrible as the Enemy's other forms, except that his mere attention sapped Daniel's body of all warmth, hope, and memory of light. The spindly letters above his alcove spelled the name *Cernobog*.

Daniel turned away but found no matter where he looked, one of the Enemy's hideously dreadful forms exerted its awful power to make him miserable. A figure named Elrik occupied this alcove: a gigantic man with a bear head, growling and slavering, and crowned with human bones. In that recess stood Ahriman, a toothy, fork-tongued beast with giant horns protruding from his forehead, feathers draping his shoulders like a cape, and ragged claws that raked the air in front of him. Across the Abyss, there was Malsumis, a great, black wolf with baleful, yellow eyes, teeth so long his mouth wouldn't close, and fur alight with a ghostly fire. Then, Al Puch, Mot, Balor, Mantus, Huitzilopochtli …

Daniel went from one figure to the next but found no reprieve, only more monsters, demonic faces, and terrible power. These were the forms the Enemy used when walking the earth, organized in the walls like clothes in a closet, ready to be worn as the occasion demanded. The weight of their combined attention was crushing.

And still, below them and growing closer by the second, was the Serpent: the source of all evil in the world. Swells of vile hatred, so foul Daniel could almost taste them, surged upward from the coiled Enemy.

Beside him, Ben, Gabriela, and Seren stared in horror around the room, mouths agape and the whites of their eyes glimmering red with the glow of the Abyss.

Finally, Daniel felt something stir within him—some whisper of hope and guidance. He shook his head and realized he and the others crouched as though on their hands and knees in midair. He straightened out his legs while reaching out for Ben and Gabriela. Both stirred at his touch, and then they, too, instinctively stretched out their hands to Seren. Now forming a circle, Daniel closed his eyes and prayed out loud.

"Father, we are powerless here. We feel crushed by the Enemy's evil."

"Crushed," Ben repeated fervently.

"We are too weak. We need you to fill us with your Spirit, or else … or else we might …"

Seren took over, "Die here. And then we won't save Raylin."

"But even if we do die," Gabriela finished in a small voice, "we accept your sovereignty over our lives. We accept what you allow. We're your servants."

Daniel nodded his head. "We accept it."

"Even death," Ben echoed sadly.

Seren made a whimpering noise and seemed to be in internal agony. Daniel opened his eyes and saw her trembling.

"I accept what you allow," she finally whispered.

Suddenly, in Daniel's mind, he saw the Spirit as he had last appeared: a powerful, living flame. He burned among the four, still in a circle with hands joined.

Peace filled Daniel's heart, and in his mind's eye, spread to the others.

Everyone breathed quietly, but more easily.

"Amen." They all spoke in unison.

Laughter—deep, rasping, and devoid of all happiness—rebounded through the Abyss. It seemed to come from the Serpent initially but was taken up by hundreds of the horrible figures peppering the walls. The moment of tranquility vanished like a candle flame before a scorching gale, but the strength the Spirit had brought remained.

"Prayer to the Father? In my presence?" the Enemy said, his voice appallingly deep and filled with evil. "Fools. Come closer so we can talk."

"Don't answer him," Gabriela said, locking eyes with the others.

Everyone nodded. They weren't here to fight the Enemy, or even talk to him.

Daniel's gaze drifted down to the Serpent, still at least a thousand feet below. Written on the ground, a circle of heavenly letters spun around his coils. At first, the letters appeared as they had so many times: wispy and indecipherable. The more he looked, though, they began to change until he could read the entire message:

"Judgment ~ Cursed above the beasts of earth ~ The full number of thy days ~ Consume dust upon thy belly ~ Enmity between thou and the Woman ~ Enmity between thy progeny and hers ~ Thou wilt strike his heel ~ He shall crush thy head ~ Judgment."

"Judgment?" Ben muttered. He pointed at the ground around the Serpent and twirled his finger. "What's that about?"

Seren floated closer to them. "It's the curse the Father laid on the Enemy after he deceived mankind. It keeps his physical form here."

"Two questions," Daniel said. "How did you float yourself over here? And, the Enemy doesn't seem too bound to me! In case nobody's noticed, he's been getting out lately."

"That was one question and one statement," Ben said. "You should pay more attention in grammar class."

Daniel rolled his eyes but was glad for the joke. It brought a little mirth to the situation and grounded him.

"We can fly here," Gabriela explained, moving closer to Daniel. "Granny told me about it a while ago. It'll help us when we have to fight the Serpent. Just pick a direction in your mind, and your body will follow."

Daniel floated closer to Gabriela. "Hey, it works. I'd probably be excited if we weren't slowly descending toward a seven-headed dragon. So what about the Enemy's body being *kind of* bound but not really?"

Seren gestured toward the walls with the Celestial Bow. Each of the Enemy's giant forms glared down at them. "His spirit can leave. He just picks one of his fake bodies and puts it on."

"What about when the Serpent popped over for a visit in India?" Daniel asked.

"Yeah," Ben agreed. "He didn't seem too bound then."

Seren shrugged and looked to Gabriela.

"That was still his spirit," Gabriela replied. "His true body always remained here, and it's here we have to fight him—during the last quest, anyway. Once the last Spirit of the Age is bound into his body, then he'll be completely imprisoned here. No part of him will be able to leave until the Three allow it."

Seren narrowed her eyes as she studied the Serpent's form. "When I served him," she began with a shudder, "we would transport here to speak with him in person."

Two of the Enemy's coils slithered around each other and then separated. A five-pointed star, red and glowing, burned on the ground at the very center of his undulating body.

"There," Seren continued, pointing at the smoldering shape.

"He would transport us to the star, and as long as we stayed inside it, we'd be free of the crushing power of the Abyss. The Generals will try to get there."

Even as she explained, one of the Enemy's unbound heads turned toward the Generals on the Abyss floor. He blew out a deep, rattling, hissing breath. Another five-pointed star appeared on the ground under each one. Although it didn't seem to break the power of the Abyss entirely, the gravity they felt must've lessened because they were able to turn over on their stomachs and crawl toward the center of the Enemy's body.

Daniel pointed with the Sun Sword. "Should we do something about that?"

"No. Leave them be," Gabriela replied. "We're here for Raylin."

Raylin's wings and arms remained outstretched, pinned to the ground, and unable to move under the crushing power of the Abyss but beyond the Serpent's reach.

"And *that*," Gabriela finished.

They were now only a few hundred feet above the Serpent, which was nauseatingly gargantuan at this distance. The Abyssal Staff—black as obsidian but emanating a pure light from its circular head—floated in front of him. It was tiny in comparison, like a speck of sand before a whale, and Daniel could barely make out any details of its appearance. Every few minutes, the Serpent shuddered, and a faint aura of darkness was drawn into the staff's head from his body.

The five-pointed star at the center of the Serpent's coils burst into flames, and Amira and Abida appeared. They quickly bowed before their master and began talking. Almost at the same time, the Generals pulled themselves, panting and sweating profusely with the strain, into the confines of the star. The gravitational power of the Abyss apparently didn't extend there because they immediately jumped to their feet and joined in the conversation, throwing up their hands apologetically. One of the Serpent's bound and blind heads tilted toward them as if listening to their conversation. The three Generals talked over one another while splitting their attention between the twins and the Serpent, regarding each with a mixture of fear and expectation—like children begging their abusive parents for food. The sound of their voices didn't reach Daniel and the others, but he could tell from their gestures and periodic glances toward the Vessels that they were giving their masters an earful of excuses and complaints. Then, as if tattle-telling had been their only task, the Generals and the twins disappeared from the star.

The Vessels were now eye level with the Serpent. His two unbound heads locked their gaze onto their descent, while the others bobbed, blind and unfocused, on their undulating necks. Each was tilted to the side, probably listening for the slightest sound so they could join in the fight Daniel knew was about to come. A wave of malevolent power buffeted them, pushing them backward.

"What now?" Seren whispered. "Do we go for Raylin or the ..."

All five of the Serpent's blind heads immediately zeroed in on Seren's location. She paled and fell silent.

The Serpent lowered one toward Raylin. Three red stars blazed on her chest, and she slowly lifted into the air. With a nod from the giant head, her body floated toward him.

"Guys!" Daniel said, regardless of the noise. "We need to grab her. Now!"

All hell broke loose.

Before they could move, the Serpent took a deep breath, and both unbound heads belched a storm of raging green flames toward them.

A split-second before the fire engulfed them, Ben had summoned the Triune Shield and encompassed them in a perfect sphere.

The world flashed green for a full ten seconds before the Serpent took another massive breath.

"Ben! You okay?" Gabriela shouted.

"For now. What do we do about Raylin?"

Seren flew to the borders of the shield. "Can you fly while keeping the shield up?"

Daniel joined her to get a better view. Raylin was nearly within the Serpent's reach. "Ben, if you can, go! And hurry!"

"Give me a second. I think I can manage it." Ben's outstretched, featureless form on the top of the shield slid down its borders so it was facing Raylin. The Triune Shield floated forward uncertainly, then gradually picked up momentum.

The Enemy opened his terrible mouth.

"Got it!" Ben cried triumphantly, darting underneath the next hurricane of green flames and tearing through the air toward Raylin.

The Serpent's head nearest her snapped hungrily, its titanic fangs crashing together with ear-splitting clangor.

Daniel summoned as many Sunstorms as he could and fired each one at the top of the Serpent's head. He doubted it would have any purifying effect, but maybe it would be enough to distract him from Raylin, who was now only ten feet from being consumed.

The bright flames neared their mark, but the Serpent simply swayed its head, weaving between the blasts without even looking at them.

The other unbound head was suddenly next to the shield, its enormous, skyscraper tall pupil staring directly at them. Daniel's assault may have temporarily interrupted the Serpent's attack on Raylin, but their descent had carried them within reach of its heads.

"Below us!" Ben shouted.

Daniel glanced down and saw the other unbound head rearing toward them, leaving Raylin to one of its blind counterparts.

"Seren! Take the eye!" Daniel shouted while he flung two Sunstorms at the head coming from below. One landed on the Serpent's neck with an orange and yellow explosion.

The Enemy bellowed in anger but didn't slow his attack.

Daniel straightened up into a Firestrike to prepare Ben for the inevitable.

With blinding speed, Seren began a barrage of Celestial Arrows.

The Serpent's eye blinked shut just as the arrows landed, and it reared back. The head froze for a moment as the binding light spread across its face.

The striking head was now directly below them and opened up his mouth. The entire floor of the Abyss was blacked out by the gaping jaws threatening to engulf them.

Seren joined Daniel in concentrating all their firepower on this next threat.

"Higher, Ben!" they screamed in unison.

"I'm going out," Gabriela stated.

Before Daniel had time to process her intent, she'd flown outside the shield and was making a beeline for the attacking head.

The jaws snapped shut but froze as the binding of the Celestial Arrows took effect.

The Triune Shield suddenly lurched to the side, and the world went half-dark—one direction offered the dreadful view of the Abyss, while the other was caged between the mammoth teeth of the first head which had broken the Celestial binding. In the moment of surprise terror, time slowed. Every detail of the Serpent's mouth registered in an instant—the forest of teeth so large that each could be a redwood, two prominent fangs that dwarfed the rest by a hundred feet, the gap toward the front of the mouth where one tooth was broken, the city-sized tongue, the hissing gale of rancid breath that somehow made it through the Triune Shield.

Daniel spun around, flinging Sunstorms into the roof of the Serpent's mouth.

The attacks landed, and the Enemy groaned, but its hold on the Triune Shield didn't slacken. A green light shone from within its cavernous throat.

"This isn't a good thing!" Ben shouted. "Daniel, aim for the teeth or something. Maybe they'll shatter, and I can break free."

Daniel did as Ben suggested, but the teeth held fast.

The world flashed green as flames engulfed the Triune Shield. The smell of sulfur filled the air and burned Daniel's eyes.

"I can do this … I can do this …" Ben repeated to himself, and then, "Nope, nope, nope! Oh, Father, I can't do this. Please help me!"

"Let them go!" Gabriela's voice rose above the roaring flames. "Haaaaaaa!"

A bone-shattering thud reverberated through the Abyss.

A shudder went through the Serpent, and his mouth unclamped just enough for the flames to shoot the shield out of its mouth like a cannonball. At the same time, the Serpent reared up and back.

Now free of the blinding fire, Daniel saw that the head which had attacked from below had crashed into the neck of the head intent on broiling them. And Gabriela, flying below, was poised as though she had just put all her strength into a Herculean punch.

"Gabriela!" Seren cried while unleashing seven arrows in close succession at the Serpent. "Raylin!"

With a curt nod, Gabriela dropped like a stone toward Raylin, who was now feet from the Serpent's mouth.

Daniel surrounded her descent with Sunstorms, praying they would be strong enough to dissuade another striking head from attacking her.

The Serpent pulled back its blind head to avoid the blasts. They exploded on the ground around Gabriela, who now crouched beside Raylin.

Careful to avoid the Voidblade, she gripped Raylin below her shoulders and tried to pull her back out of the Serpent's reach. Whether because of the Enemy's power or the downward force of the Abyss, Raylin wouldn't budge. Even from his height, Daniel could see Gabriela straining.

The Serpent's blind head nearest Raylin rose slightly and angled downward as though it could still see. Daniel didn't doubt it retained some spiritual ability to sense its surroundings. "The little girl from Aguas Calientes," it said, its cavernous mouth opening only slightly to let out the sound of its sickening voice. "How strong you are. And yet, not strong enough. Powerless to save your friend, and powerless to save your parents."

Gabriela fell to her knees and covered her ears and shut her eyes. "Get out of my head. Get out of my head!" she screamed.

"Despair." The Serpent's mouth glowed green.

"Gabriela! Fly out of there!" Daniel shouted in warning.

Seren's eyes, wild and filled with terror, were fixed on Raylin. She attempted to fly out of the shield to her aid, but at that moment, the two unbound heads redoubled their attack, both bathing the Triune Shield in emerald flames.

Raylin and Gabriela were beyond their help now. Daniel flung prayers of desperation to the Father while channeling all his strength into a Fire Strike. After a few moments of being completely shut off from view, the flames covering the bottom of the shield parted slightly, just enough to see Raylin straining to raise the Voidblade even as the green inferno stormed around them.

In terror, Gabriela fell back while shielding her eyes.

14

The End of Hope

The flames never reached her. Swirling into the sword like water down a drain, the fire quickly vanished into the Voidblade.

"Guys, they're okay!" Daniel yelled above the roar of the fire. "They're okay. The Voidblade protected them."

Seren looked like a ten-ton weight had been lifted off her shoulders, and even Ben sighed in relief despite his strain.

Flames covered the Triune Shield again, and Daniel's view was utterly blocked. The attack seemed to last an eternity, but the knowledge that Gabriela and Raylin had survived strengthened him. He summoned three Fire Strikes in a row. Despite his support, though, the shape of the Triune Shield began to wobble and shrink.

"We need to get out of here!" Ben wheezed with effort. "I'm flying out of reach."

The head attacking the shield from below paused to take a breath and darted up to block their escape. It prepared to fire again even as the other attacker ceased its onslaught to speak.

"Do you think you will escape me here? Many other Vessels believed they would, only to—"

Daniel fired as many Sunstorms as he could summon directly into its mouth. "I don't really care!" he gasped, certain he would've collapsed to his knees in exhaustion if he hadn't been flying.

"Same!" Seren shouted while simultaneously firing an unending barrage of arrows at the head blocking their path.

Ben shot up through the air out of the reach of the other heads.

"No, Ben!" Daniel cried. "We have to rescue Gabriela and Raylin! Fly down!"

"Just give me a second!" Ben panted.

The Triune Shield shot away from the Serpent and dropped like a cannonball straight toward the floor. They were beyond the Enemy's snapping jaws, but Daniel didn't doubt another fiery assault could reach them. His only thoughts at the moment were getting to Gabriela and Raylin.

The blind head attacking the girls shook with fury. "You dare use the Dark Blade I created against me?" It lowered itself to the ground and slithered as far forward as it could go, snapping and striking the air to get to Raylin.

Gabriela still strained against the forward pull of the Serpent's star. Snatches of her desperate prayers for strength and help echoed up to Daniel. He joined in her frantic pleas.

Seren sent a cascade of Celestial Arrows at the blind head. Several reached their mark; the binding shell of light began to spread like blotches of purity on blighted skin.

The shield finally reached the floor of the Abyss, and Daniel knew it would be seconds before all the Serpent's heads convened in one spot.

The vast, fanged mouth straining for Raylin opened again, ready to spew out another torrent of fire. Daniel was so exhausted he wasn't sure he had the strength to fire another Sunstorm. Ben, too, was obviously about to give out. He panted and grunted with the exertion of keeping the Triune Shield summoned.

Seren kept up her frenetic volley of Celestial Arrows, but even she was slowing down.

The Serpent's head froze in place, temporarily under her power, but the green flames came pouring out like a river bursting its dam.

Ben flew forward to encase Raylin and Gabriela.

A split second before he reached them, Raylin raised the Voidblade again. A huge fireball, emerald and boiling with raging power, appeared at the tip of the jagged sword. She swung it forward.

The fireball flew like a comet, gathering up the stream of flames from the Enemy and exploding into his blind, bound head.

All seven heads bellowed as the conflagration spread down the neck and over the body of the Serpent.

Ben finally reached the girls and quickly surrounded them with his borders.

Seren immediately fired four arrows into Raylin's chest, halting her forward momentum.

Daniel, his feet now touching the floor, ran forward and summoned a Firestrike. He stabbed the Sun Sword down into her body. Its power was weak and only spread out four feet from its epicenter.

It was enough. The five-pointed star beneath her body sizzled angrily, then, with a pop, it faded and disappeared. The crushing gravity of the Abyss took over again, and Raylin's entire body was drawn to the ground with a hard *thunk!* Without the added force of the Enemy's power, however, Gabriela was able to drag Raylin backward. Seren ran to help her, and within moments, they had pulled her out of the Serpent's shadow.

The Enemy chuckled, his voice now seven-fold as all the heads spoke in unison. "Look, little Raylin. Your friends still desire you back, even after all the *dreadful* things you did. My, my … how touching."

Ignoring his comments, Daniel dashed around to push on Raylin's feet. The Voidblade, drawn downward as if by a magnet, dragged along the rocky floor of the Abyss, rasping and complaining as it scraped the stone. If the Serpent decided to fire from all seven heads, they'd still be in range, and the sword wouldn't be any help. Ben inched backward to keep everyone within the confines of the Triune Shield.

The blind head bound by Seren's many arrows finally broke free and shook from side to side, seemingly in a fog. "I could bathe you in fire again, of course," the seven voices said. "But I would much rather watch you struggle and wear yourselves out. After all, I still plan on removing the Father's image from you." He paused and hissed out a laugh. "But the Peruvian girl has no use for me, other than entertainment. Perhaps I will give her to Abida as a slave."

Daniel felt an anxiety attack rattle through his body. Gabriela had already been taken by the Enemy once. He couldn't bear it again. But even now … even now … she was as good as captured. He was watching, helpless, as Abida dragged her away through his portal. Hissing, growling Creeps bound Daniel, Ben, and Seren hand and foot and prepared to perform some terrible experiment on them.

Daniel released Raylin's legs and turned to face the Enemy.

The Serpent's two sets of unbound eyes glowered through the remaining smoke of his last attack. "What a shame. You are already defeated. Raylin is completely ruined by my power and beyond redemption. Gabriela is carried to slavery."

Seren, in a daze, dropped Raylin's shoulder and fell to her knees.

"The Three are locked in battle at Babylon and cannot come to your aid. My power there is too great; they will be utterly defeated, and the earth will be mine forever."

The glow of the Triune Shield flickered, and a sigh of despair drifted down from Ben's outstretched form.

The Serpent was right. They were all defeated.

"Snap out of it!" Gabriela shouted. She balled up her fist and punched the ground. *Boom!*

"He's just getting inside your heads. Now stay focused and help me with Raylin!"

The sound of her voice more than the crushing punch brought Daniel back to his senses. The Serpent's spell vanished like a bad dream, and he looked to Gabriela like a beacon of light on a foggy night. She wasn't captured. All hope wasn't lost.

"Oh man," Ben gasped quietly. "What a jerk! He's not happy just breathing his rancid breath all over you. He's got to make you miserable, too."

"I can't believe I served him all those years," Seren griped, redoubling her efforts to help with Raylin. "Miserable little worm."

Daniel smirked. Hearing the others make fun of the Enemy somehow made the situation seem less dire.

"No wonder he opted for seven heads," he whispered. "Only way he could have friends."

The others smiled as they continued laboring with Raylin.

Gabriela smiled. "Had a rough childhood," she added. "Poor little thing."

A deep rumble went through the Enemy. "I hear you." His voice shook with barely controlled rage. "Your irreverence is new to me."

Daniel and the others locked eyes, then began pushing and pulling Raylin's body with all their might.

They were a few feet from the spinning circle of the Enemy's curse. Daniel was sure the fire could still reach them here, but every inch counted in lessening the force of the fiery torrent.

"Your disrespect," the Serpent continued, all seven heads trembling in disbelief and anger, "will be punished!"

Daniel pushed with all his might; Raylin's feet crossed the streaming words, and he fell over the line just as the world behind him exploded into green brilliance.

Ben shouted with the strain of keeping the Triune Shield summoned, but in the end, his strength gave out. The sphere of the shield collapsed into Ben's scintillating form, which fell to the ground beside Raylin.

Daniel spun around and lifted the Sun Sword. Maybe, somehow, it could absorb some of the Enemy's fire like the Voidblade had.

A wall of pure white light shot upwards from the spinning words. The emerald flames crashed against it harmlessly. The Serpent paused in his assault and stared, glaring at the wall. All seven heads spewed another river of flames, only to have them thrown back by the barrier once more.

He reared his colossal heads, flailing them around the Abyss and roaring so loudly the floor shook. The unbound eyes rolled back in furious protest, and the Serpent's ridged tail beat the ground like a drum.

"You cheat!" he shrieked to the air. "The curse marks are not to bind my power! That was the rule you put in place." The heads stared intently into the darkness above as though he expected an answer. When none came, he fell back to raging. "You believe yourself to be so pure and truthful, and yet you lie? You deceive and then judge me for deceiving! You are just like me!"

The Serpent paused and shuddered as the Abyssal Staff drew in another portion of his power. This seemed to anger him even more. "I hate you!" he raged over and over. "I HATE YOU!"

Daniel and the others covered their ears while the Serpent continued his seven-fold rants. At least for the time being, the Enemy was focused on something other than them.

Daniel moved closer to the group so they could huddle together.

"What now?" Ben asked in a harsh whisper. "We've got Raylin, but what do we do about the staff?"

All four turned to look at the Weapon of Power floating directly in front of the Enemy and occasionally being engulfed by a stray stream of acrid flame.

"One of us is going to have to go grab it, then hightail it back here before getting roasted," Daniel said. He looked askance at Ben. "You up for covering me?"

Ben, still trying to catch his breath, put his hands on his head and nodded. "In a minute, but it'll have to be quick."

"It needs to be me," Seren said. She had moved to Raylin's head and was cradling it in her lap. With a gentle stroke, she drew the hair away from Raylin's stony face, which stared, unblinking and full of hate, back into Seren's eyes. "I need to be the one to take the Abyssal Staff into myself."

The Serpent's angry shouting finally ceased. "Very well. If you will not allow my fire to reach them, will you bind my power entirely, I wonder?"

Daniel looked up at the Serpent. Three of the heads were angled downward and muttering something inaudible. Oh well, whatever he was planning, at least he'd stopped raving like a lunatic, and they could hear themselves think.

"Now hang on," Daniel protested, going back to the conversation. "Why don't you stay here with Raylin? I can—"

"I don't need your heroics, Daniel. She's my sister, and I'm going to do it. Besides, I feel the Spirit," she patted her chest, "telling me to. This is my quest ... well ... our quest," she finished, letting her gaze fall back to Raylin's. "It needs to be this way, I think."

Gabriela nodded and gestured for Daniel to back off, then knelt down next to Seren. "Here's the plan. First, we pray. Next, Ben covers you with the shield. Fly straight in as fast as you can, but don't fire any arrows until the Enemy notices you."

"Pfft. That shouldn't take long," Ben muttered. "The jerk's got seven sets of ears and two sets of working eyes."

Seren gave a curt nod like she had received orders from her commanding officer. "Grab the staff and come straight back here."

"Straight back," Gabriela echoed. "No arguing with the Enemy. No listening to his words. No confrontation if it can be helped. While you're doing that, Daniel will fling Sunstorms at the Enemy while I fly higher along this protective barrier acting like I'm about to attack him. Hopefully, both distractions will be enough for you to get in and get out."

"We all have to be touching the staff for it to work on Raylin, right?" Daniel asked quietly. He glanced back at the Serpent, who had stopped muttering to himself and now had all his eyes closed.

Gabriela noticed the change as well and suspiciously watched the Enemy out of the corner of her eye. "All three of you, anyway. I don't have the power to activate it."

Remnant tongues of the Serpent's fire smoldered on the ground within the barrier, casting dancing shadows on the walls of the Abyss. Out of the corner of his eye, Daniel noticed darker shapes sliding against the walls nearest them.

The floor of the Abyss shook, and Arawn towered above them while his spectral dogs crouched with fiery hackles raised, snarling and reading to pounce. The earth rumbled again, and Shiva stood by his side, smiling down at the group with feigned serenity. Daniel, in horror, looked up to meet their eyes just as Supai eased out of his niche and jumped down, slamming into the ground so violently Ben and Gabriela were knocked onto their backs. Seren sprawled onto her side.

Ahriman, the beast-man and Malsumis, the demon wolf, slipped from their alcoves across the Abyss, vanished, and rematerialized beside the other incarnations in the blink of an eye.

More and more dreadful figures leaped from their resting places, bringing a miasma of spiritual horror with them.

Daniel jumped to his feet. Splitting up wasn't an option anymore. "We stay together. Ben!"

Ben summoned the Triune Shield and rose into the air. Daniel and the others floated upward as well, while Raylin's form lay sprawled at the bottom of the shield, kept immobile by the crushing gravity of the Abyss.

"To the staff," Daniel whispered urgently.

Ben took off toward the cursed circle, but Arawn's dogs pounced before he made it ten feet, driving them to the ground beneath spectral paws.

With a shout of exertion, Ben slipped the Triune Shield out from beneath them and flew backward. Supai was ready and delivered a crushing blow with his fist.

"My old friends!" he shrieked with wicked glee. "How I missed you."

The Triune Shield was knocked to the ground, where it bounced like a ball back into the air within the space of the curse marks.

The Serpent was ready with a double dose of hellish flames. Daniel and the others were flung around within the Triune Shield as it was bandied about by the Enemy. The pounding force of the fire drove them back out of the encircling curse marks and into all four of Shiva's hands. He gripped the Triune Shield and squeezed.

"Daniel!" Ben cried out with pain. "I can't—oh, get your hands off me, you four-armed freak!"

Daniel, finally able to get his bearings, summoned a Fire Strike as fast as he could. Then another and another.

"Give up your striving," Shiva urged, his voice lilting and calm. "Surrender to my peace!" He flung the Triune Shield toward Malsumis, who spewed forth a torrent of black spirits from his mouth.

The wailing ebony onslaught slammed against the Triune Shield like a battering ram, driving them back toward Arawn. His bone-encrusted fingers raked the shield. "Come out, children! Be obedient to your Master and come out. I promise the punishment will be horrible and unending." Each word filled the surrounding air with dark spirits. His eyes, burning with cold flames within his skull mask, bore into them.

Gabriela flew to the top of the shield and punched Arawn's hands, flinging them off of Ben and allowing the Triune Shield to drift free.

Seren followed with a volley of Celestial Arrows, momentarily binding both Arawn's hands and hounds in place.

After another Firestrike to strengthen Ben, Daniel fired a Sunstorm directly into Arawn's face.

The blast exploded, encompassing most of his head. When the flames cleared, Supai, now in his angelic form, towered over them. "So naïve. Does the Father care so little that he gives you broken weapons and sends you against a host of gods? Come and submit, little ones. Submit."

The word was taken up by all the Enemy's incarnations. "Submit," hundreds of voices said.

The words reverberated through the Triune Shield with crushing, hypnotizing power.

Gabriela floated backward, eyes blank and glossy. "I think ... I ..." Her voice trailed off into quiet gibberish.

Seren dropped the Celestial Bow to her side and fell to her knees.

Ben flickered. "Daniel," he muttered. "I want to go home." The Triune Shield wavered and collapsed back into the form of Ben's body.

Raylin would have been drawn immediately down to the Abyss floor had not Ahriman jumped in and grabbed all five in his enormous, clawed hands. His touch was ice cold, and Daniel felt all hope drain away the moment he made contact.

Hope. Joy. Peace. Love. Friendship. Even the concept of struggling against the torture he now experienced—they were now only words he remembered. No experience of any such thing could be recalled. No good thing at all. All was darkness, despair, and eternal death. He was alone.

Someone wept near him. He turned his head and found that Ben, Gabriela, Seren, and even Raylin had tears streaming down their faces. Cold drops slid down his own cheeks; his tears had been drained of all warmth—all comfort they might have given.

"Submit," all the incarnations said again. Ahriman, grotesque and beastly, spat the words through curled and humongous fangs. His breath singed Daniel's skin like toxic gas.

Daniel struggled against the overwhelming power, but the Enemy's voice, magnified now beyond anything he had experienced in Peru or India, echoed back and forth within his mind.

Supai, Shiva, Malsumis, Arawn, and a dozen other nightmarish giants crowded around Ahriman, grinning down at the Vessels and Gabriela as they plodded toward the Serpent.

Daniel's eyes fell on Seren. Through her tears, she reached out for Raylin, stretching her arm helplessly toward her sister despite the distance of nearly ten feet that separated them. *Why?* Daniel thought. *Why struggle against such power? Why struggle when nothing exists to struggle for.* Daniel searched his memories for any reality beyond doom, death, and utter ruin, but he could find none.

But then ... a memory. The Spirit, as he had appeared at the White Lady's castle. Tall, gray, and in the form of a majestic stag. His eyes, sapphire and lit from within by a pure power, stared back at Daniel. Immediately, Daniel was reminded of another person. The Son, standing in the Chamber of the Moon, wielding all the power of the Father; life flowed out of him and into the entire cosmos. Daniel recalled something of the sound of his voice and re-membered that he spoke for the Father: almighty, ancient, unend-ing, possessing raw and purifying power cloaked in goodness, joy, and fatherly love. Hope existed within *them*. Love. Joy. Peace—they all dwelt within *them*. Daniel still couldn't feel these things, but the knowledge that they existed somewhere, in Someone, was enough. He called out to the memory as if it were the Three themselves.

"Help," he whispered.

"Please," Ben murmured several feet away.

Daniel wondered what he saw in his mind. Some fleeting vision of a far-off salvation? Some uncertain and unlikely illusion of hope, if such a thing actually existed outside their imaginations.

Gabriela's eyes were wide open, but she prayed in an unending stream of Spanish. He wasn't sure what she was saying, but her ur-gent and desperate tone needed no interpretation.

Seren wept, muttering words under her breath between the sobs. Daniel thought he caught Raylin's name several times. And then, a little louder: "Take me instead."

Daniel had already watched Ben sacrifice himself, he wasn't about to watch Seren do the same thing for any of them. Still on his back, he lifted the Sun Sword above his face and channeled en-ergy into the blade. With as much remaining strength as he could muster, he plunged the fiery blade into Ahriman's black hand.

The shockwave barely spread under Daniel's body. The Enemy didn't blink, flinch, or give any indication he had noticed the attack at all. He simply plodded forward, with the other incarnations, leer-ing and frowning down at them, to present Daniel and the others to the Serpent.

The giant coiling body dwarfed the Enemy's other forms. All seven heads angled downward, hissing at the offering and laughing through fanged teeth. "Take them to Babylon and remove the im-age of the Three."

Daniel remembered what that meant: pain and death.

Ahriman's beastly eyes lit up as he plodded around one of the

Serpent's massive heads toward the five-pointed star in the center of his coils.

At that moment, the Abyssal Staff, now directly above them, pulsed and drew in another portion of the Enemy's spirit. Ahriman's hand, and the bodies of the other incarnations, flickered like a loose light bulb. For a second, Daniel felt the hope-draining power of the Enemy waiver. And at that moment, direction and certainty from the Three.

"Seren. Go!" Daniel, Ben, and Gabriela shouted in unison.

Seren jumped to her feet and flew toward the Abyssal Staff, shooting arrows in every direction she could.

Ben encompassed Daniel and Gabriela and skimmed along Ahriman's hand so Gabriela could scoop up Raylin. Within two seconds, they streaked through the air after Seren.

The effect of the staff ceased, and the Enemy closed in from every direction.

"Capture them!" the Serpent shrieked, seeing Seren close in on the Abyssal Staff. Each word was spat with a torrent of fire.

Every incarnation in the Abyss leaped from their alcoves to join those already chasing the Vessels. Daniel tried to ignore the thousands of maniacal, demonic giants charging from above and right, and the Serpent with seven flame-spewing heads attacking on the left.

"Father! Help!" Daniel flung a weak Sunstorm somewhere off toward the Serpent. There was no telling where the greatest danger was coming from; any direction would do. He tried another off to the right, maybe toward Malsumis, who lunged with slavering maw toward Seren, or maybe Elrik, who suddenly had a jagged, pine tree-sized spear of dirty, gray ice brandished over his head. The purifying power slid off the Sun Sword with barely a spark.

The Serpent now belched all his fire toward Seren.

Gabriela lifted Raylin over her head and hurled her like a football toward Seren. "Raylin, I know you're in there somewhere," she shouted after her. "Save your sister!"

Time slowed down as Raylin, Seren, and the Enemy's encircling onslaught simultaneously reached the staff.

Seren and Raylin disappeared between a raging emerald inferno and a hulking, crushing mass of frenzied monsters.

In the space of breath, everything froze in Daniel's mind.

Suddenly, the Voidblade appeared amid the fire, sucking in the churning, swirling flames of the Serpent. The gravity of the Abyss overpowered Gabriela's throw and yanked Raylin down to the floor, pulling the stream of fire with it. She landed with a dull thud ten stories below.

Daniel caught sight of Seren's body, outlined darkly against the light of the blaze, clutching the Abyssal Staff with both hands, eyes clenched shut.

The head of the staff hummed with energy, and now siphoned off a steady flow of power from all the Enemy's incarnations on the one side, and the Serpent on the other.

The Serpent ceased its fiery barrage and reared back with bared fangs. Daniel also noticed that one of the unbound heads shuddered, and a strange light glowed through its eyes—pure and white in place of its usual sickening red.

The Enemy's many forms were frozen in their attack, their gigantic hands, paws, and raking talons, mere feet from Seren's body.

Elrik's spear shattered. He gasped, spat out a curse in some unknown language, and jumped backward away from the group.

Malsumis yelped and snarled, frantically backing away from the tangle of giants while his hackles bristled out in every direction.

Supai transformed back into a demon, shaking and shrieking with rage.

The other incarnations followed suit, halting in their attack if only for a moment.

Daniel, Ben, and Gabriela finally reached Seren, encompassing her in the relative safety of the shield, before diving at breakneck speed toward Raylin.

Seren opened her eyes and looked around. "Praise the Three," she muttered. "Where's Raylin?"

Daniel pointed below them. "I don't know how much time we'll have to purify her before the Enemy attacks again. Let's make it count." He looked up to see the Serpent, recovered from the attack now that the Abyssal Staff was moved farther away, slithering his titanic heads down toward them.

The incarnations had also regained their composure and were summoning wicked-looking weapons.

"They're all going to attack again," Ben said, his voice desperate and exhausted. "But we all three have to be touching the staff to exorcise Raylin, right? I have to release the shield."

Seren looked at Daniel, her eyes fraught with fear and uncertainty.

They reached the floor of the Abyss, and Raylin was encompassed in the faltering glow of the Triune Shield.

"Yes. And there's no time to debate another option. Do it now!" Daniel shouted.

Gabriela looked up at the approaching enemies. "I could try to fight them to buy you some time."

Gabriela must stand between you and the Enemy. She must intercede in prayer.

"What?" Daniel shouted out loud, confused. Seren looked at him sideways.

The Serpent took another huge breath, and his mouths lit up with fire.

The Triune Shield collapsed into Ben's form. He ran toward Seren and grabbed the staff. "She said she would—"

Daniel gripped the staff between Ben and Seren's hands. "Not that. Quiet for a moment!"

What do you mean intercede?

She must not fight. The battle is spiritual, not physical. She must stand in the gap, between the Vessels and danger, and pray.

But that's suicide!

She must intercede.

Malsumis prepared to belch another spume of dark spirits, and

Ahriman joined most of the other incarnations by pulling a wicked looking weapon out of another dimension.

"The Father wants you to stand between us and the attack, Gabriela!" Daniel replied as the flames descended toward them. Apparently, the Serpent was putting his plans for keeping them alive on the backburner now that they had the staff. "He wants you to pray for us! To … to intercede, but not to fight! Now!"

Pale and shaking, Gabriela nevertheless leaped into the air, ten feet above them, and spread out her arms. "Father!" her voice rang out clear and loud, "protect us!"

The flames descended like a blinding blanket of destruction, throwing back Gabriela's shadow. The incarnations flung their weapons or spewed forth some evil power.

"Protect us!" Gabriela shouted, and then quieter, "Protect."

Daniel, Ben, and Seren watched, their eyes wide with terror, none of them able to focus on Raylin amid the attack.

After everything he had been through, Daniel trusted the Three. But he still feared to see the girl he loved risk her life—feared as he would if he stood on the edge of a cliff and the Three bade him jump. Or feared had the Three told him to stretch out his hand to grab a venomous snake, or leap into a fire.

The encroaching destruction was yards away. Daniel gasped. Would the Three really allow Gabriela to sacrifice her life? They had allowed Ben—required it even. Was he about to watch her be consumed by the Serpent's flames and then shattered and broken by his weapons? The air in front of Gabriela shimmered with heat and burst into flame.

15

The Abyssal Staff

"It's the Spirit," Ben panted in relief.

Daniel glanced down at him, still clutching the Abyssal Staff while kneeling below Seren, and back to Gabriela. The flames in front of her were a mixture of bright blue and yellow. They grew larger and changed into the form of a giant stag—familiar, but taller than he'd appeared before. He shook his mighty antlers, and a line of glowing people shimmered into being on each side of Gabriela, stretching off into the distance. Unlike her, they floated face down, backs to the onslaught. The two closest to her grasped her hands, and on down the line, each clutched the hand of the person next to them.

The Serpent's fire crashed against the Spirit and the line of people like a wave against a dike. The weapons and other blasts of power did the same, shattering and dissipating as soon as they touched the Spirit's boundary. The Serpent roared and belched another torrent of green, acrid fire; his incarnations, likewise enraged, clamored to attack, shoving one another aside to try new weapons or blasts of power against the Spirit and the line of interceders. Their efforts were in vain, and the Serpent's fire did nothing but envelop his own allies in flames.

Stunned and in shock, Daniel, Seren, and Ben gaped up at the scene.

Daniel found himself staring at two people. The Enemy's attacks were so over-stimulating and jarring to his senses, it took him a moment to realize he was looking at his parents. Recognition finally set in. "Mom? Dad?" he muttered. His voice probably didn't reach them.

Ben flashed Daniel a confused look. He followed his gaze upward and gasped.

Daniel could hardly process seeing them in the Abyss. Their eyes were wide with disbelief. They both gave furtive glances behind and above them to see the Serpent and all his incarnations wailing with hatred and dancing around in rage amid the burning chaos. They simultaneously snapped their heads back around, mouths moving in an unending stream of barely audible supplications for protection.

Beside them, Daniel recognized others. There was Janice, who for once seemed wide awake and aware, her magnified eyes focused and calming. She smiled down at Daniel. Beside her, head bowed and eyes closed in prayer, was Ms. Julie. She didn't seem aware of her surroundings. Daniel scanned the line of almost a hundred people. Nearly all the rest were like her, engaged in quiet prayer to the Three but oblivious to the Enemy's frenzied wrath. Some were familiar: people from church or school, an old man from the neighborhood, a couple of his teachers, and even a classmate or two. Daniel scanned to the right of his parents and focused on one woman: thin blond hair, brown eyes, skinny, early to mid-thirties. She gazed back at Daniel with tears streaming down her face. Like the others, her mouth moved in urgent prayer, but she could also see the spiritual battle taking place. Something about her struck Daniel as familiar, but he wasn't sure where he'd seen her before.

A pained moan escaped from Raylin's lips, and the Spirit's voice drifted into the Vessels' minds.

Use the Sun Sword to purify Raylin. If repentance is her choice, she must renounce the Enemy's power now. I will lend you strength.

Daniel turned his attention back to the task at hand. Tongues of fire burst into flame above their heads, and he felt the Spirit's illuminating power flow into everyone's bodies. All doubt and weariness fled away. A quick glance at Gabriela told him she was likewise infused with power. Around them, the Enemy in all his forms continued their assault, but the line of interceders, empowered by the Spirit, stood strong.

Daniel summoned a Fire Strike and plunged the blade into Raylin's heart. She convulsed for a few moments before the Enemy's spirit was forced from her body. As at the White Lady's castle, a great cloud of hissing, whispering darkness billowed out of her mouth. The seething darkness forming her wings evaporated up to join the mass, and the Voidblade unbound itself from her arm. She suddenly took a deep, calming breath, and the wild, lost look left her eyes. She was silent, but Daniel knew she was aware of her surroundings.

"Raylin," Seren's voice rang out clear and strong. "Raylin. Leave this power and renounce your path of revenge. Let go of your anger toward the Father and … and please forgive me."

At Seren's last words, Raylin clenched her jaw, and she suddenly sat up. "Forgive you? Why should I forgive you? You don't deserve forgiveness!"

The mass of darkness above her grew more tempestuous.

"I know," Seren replied. "I don't. But please, be free of your bondage. Be purified. Come to the Three and be washed of your past."

"Washed of my past. You mean, like you? All pious and filled with power even though you're nothing but a traitorous villain who'd sell her own sister into slavery as soon as look at her. Why should I want anything that lets you off the hook? He …" Raylin paused and cast a hateful glance up at the Spirit. "*He* let you off."

"The Three forgave me and rescued me, Raylin. I didn't deserve it, but neither did Daniel nor Ben. No one does. We're all lost in darkness until the Three rescue us. Please come and be free."

A dark tendril snaked down from the seething mass above Raylin. It licked her shoulder like a snake's tongue, and her left eye went black for a moment. She shook her head angrily and slapped it away.

Daniel was suddenly aware of a more focused malevolence directed their way. He looked away to see one of the Serpent's unbound heads staring at Raylin. Keeping his left hand on the Abyssal Staff, he summoned a Sunstorm and flung it at the wisp, disintegrating its entire form up to the main body of seething, possessing spirits.

Raylin threw her shoulders back. "I don't need your help, Daniel," she snapped. She lifted the Voidblade. "I can handle this on my own." Despite her attempt at confidence, her voice wavered with uncertainty.

"No, Raylin," Daniel replied, trying to keep his voice calm and soothing. "You can't. I couldn't either, neither could Seren." He looked down at Ben. "Seren's right. We *all* needed help."

Ben, still kneeling, wrung his hands. "Raylin. Don't you hate the Voidblade and the Enemy? He's got you all mixed up and stuck. Don't you see that? You're completely controlled by all those terrible spirits, and the Voidblade keeps you bound. Turn away from all that and come back to the Three. Come back to us."

Raylin brushed a stray strand of snow-white hair out of her eyes. She focused on Ben and, for once, seemed to waver. Another tendril of darkness snaked down and touched the base of her neck. Both eyes went black, and she froze.

"Raylin!" Seren pleaded. "Resist it. Don't let it back in!"

Daniel raised the Sun Sword, but Raylin suddenly shouted and started swinging the Voidblade around.

"Get off me!" she screamed. The sword connected with the tendril which now clung to it like a heat-seeking missile. The metal forming the hilt turned amorphous and crept up her arm. Her eyes went back to normal, but when she saw the darkness seeping into the jagged black blade, and felt the sword grafting back to her arm, she panicked. "No! NO! Get off!" She swung the sword around as if trying to fling the spirits onto the ground, but it was futile. A dozen more slithered out of the mass to search for the blade.

Daniel fired another Sunstorm. The blast forced the darkness to regroup and knocked Raylin to the ground.

She rolled backward into a crouch. Like a wild animal, cornered between two hunters, her eyes flitted back and forth between the darkness and the Serpent, and the Vessels. All the while, the Voidblade's hilt continued sliding up her wrist like a cancerous growth. Raylin pulled at it with her free hand, trying in vain to resist its claim on her.

"You belong to me." The Serpent angled his head to be directly behind the mass of spirits. "Let me in, Raylin. I take away the pain and give only power."

The Enemy's incarnations suddenly ceased their attack and focused on Raylin as well. "Let us in. We give only power," they intoned, putting all their power into the spell.

Raylin shook her head and covered her ears. "No. Stay out of my head."

The Serpent persisted. "It would be so easy. Submit, and let—"

"Be silent." The Spirit's voice, now audible, was quiet but filled with all the authority and power of the Father. He slowly walked from the line of interceders toward the Vessels.

The Serpent shook with mad rage but immediately obeyed.

The Spirit stopped in front of Raylin and breathed on her forehead. For a moment, the terror and madness left her eyes, and she calmed. Daniel half expected the Voidblade to immediately reverse its hold on her arm, but it continued its slow progress upward. The Spirit turned around and gazed up at the Serpent, who quickly averted his eyes. "She heard your offer. She hears ours. Now she must choose. Do not interfere again." He joined Daniel and the others and stood behind them.

Daniel felt the Spirit's power coursing through his own body more strongly and once again heard Ben, Seren, and Gabriela's thoughts flowing into his mind. Ben was focused solely on Raylin, waiting for her choice while uttering a steady stream of prayers for her deliverance. Seren's thoughts were no less intense but vacillated between Raylin's salvation and her own continual confession of her sins, begging the Three to keep them from being an obstacle for her sister. Gabriela seemed to be in a trance of sorts, fiercely continuing her prayers of intercession for protection.

If Daniel listened hard, he could also hear his parents' silent prayers, Ms. Julie's, and even Janice's. And then …

Please protect him, Father. Don't let him die now that I've finally found him. My son. My beloved son.

A voice Daniel had never heard—never heard, but somehow knew. He turned away from Raylin to study the line of people. His focus lingered over the blond woman he'd noticed before. She continued weeping, her hands folded in prayer while returning Daniel's gaze.

Does he know me? Does he recognize me? Father, is he angry? Please let my son live so we can meet. I want him to know how much I loved him. How much I love him even now.

Understanding finally clicked into place. This was his biological mother, brought here by the Spirit's power, to intercede for their protection. His protection. A thrill zipped through his body like a bolt of electricity. She did, and always had, loved him. And, if she was here, that meant she belonged to the Three.

Daniel caught the Spirit's sapphire eye. *You will have time with her soon. Intercede for your friend.*

Nodding, Daniel turned back to the battle. If he hadn't been filled with the Spirit, there'd be no way he could focus now. As it was, the purity coursing through his body filled him with a singleness of mind and purpose. The Spirit would arrange for him and his mother to meet. First—Raylin. He tightened his grip on the staff and poured out a stream of prayers for her salvation.

She stood, shaking, with the Voidblade held up in front of her.

"Let it go, Raylin," Seren pleaded. "Turn away from the darkness. Ask the Three for forgiveness, and they'll give it to you. Then you can be free! You can come live with me. I'll make up for everything I did. I promise!"

Raylin dropped the Voidblade to her side. "Free?" She said the word like it was the first time she'd ever heard it or believed it to be a real option. "With you?"

"If you want. If not, that's okay, too. Anywhere you want. Just please, give up on your vengeance. The Three will take care of the Serpent. I promise."

This caught Raylin's attention. She twitched the jagged, black sword and cocked her head to one side. "You mean they'll keep fighting against him and letting people suffer."

"No," Ben jumped in. "The Three will bind the Serpent's power permanently. We're a part of that, and you are, too."

Raylin stared back. "Permanently?" she repeated.

Seeing her hesitate, Seren nodded her head and persisted. "Permanently. And it's your job to seal away the Spirit of the Age. Only, you have to turn away from your past—the hatred and darkness—your sins."

"*My* sins," Raylin muttered, now avoiding Seren's gaze. She frowned. "It wasn't my sins that started me down this path." She clenched her teeth and stuck out her chin.

Seren nodded eagerly. "I know. It was mine, Raylin. I sinned against you. It was my fault. But I've been freed from my past now. You see? And now, I'm trying to make things right with you in the only way I know how. Follow the Three, Raylin."

"It's the only way," Ben joined in.

"It is *the* Way," Daniel added. He suddenly felt his skin prickle and a familiar, overwhelming power push at his back. He turned and saw exactly what he expected. As if Daniel's statement had been an introduction, the Son—*The Way* to forgiveness and eternal union with the Three—approached from behind. Each beam of light from the Abyss caught in the surrounding air was purified and refracted into a robe of atomic radiance. The golden sash Daniel had seen in the Chamber of the Moon still flowed around his chest like an undulating river of liquid life. A great halo of fire, wood, electricity, water, and a hundred other elements rotated behind him.

Flowers and grass sprouted from the ground at his feet, and his eyes glittered with every color imaginable. Daniel felt he was staring into a vast ocean simultaneously reflecting the sun and all the stars in the universe.

The Son reached out his hand toward the Spirit, who stood between him and the Vessels.

The Spirit became a giant tongue of white fire. He flew to the Son's hand, spiraled up his arm, and blossomed out from behind him into an immense blue circle of vibrating, pulsating, life-kindling light. Within it was a perfect triangle, each line exactly the same length. In turn, the halo of elements fit flawlessly within the triangle, while the Son's form fit within it. Without being told, Daniel intuitively understood the symbolism. In his mind, he, Seren, Gabriela, and Ben simultaneously pronounced its meaning as though reciting the Son's credentials.

Three in One. Triune God. Inhabiting Eternity. Incarnate Word within Flesh of Man. Creator within Created.

Daniel and the others all knelt. Raylin, too, though she shook so violently, Daniel thought she might collapse.

The mass of spirits went berserk, seething and churning within their cloud.

The Serpent and all his incarnations sent up a deafening scream and threw themselves to the ground. The Serpent spit fire while writhing on the Abyss floor, his now flaming coils weaving in and out of one another until Daniel thought he had tied himself into one titanic, incendiary knot.

His incarnations groveled in a pile, scratching and clawing at one another.

"What do you want with me?" the Serpent and his incarnations demanded in one unified, whining voice. "Have you come to torment me before my time? Will the Father also descend from his Mountain to cast me into the Lake of Fire?" All the Enemy's forms took one enormous breath. "It is not my TIME! What do you want with me?" they screamed again.

The Son raised his hand, and the Enemy fell silent, except for the constant scraping and scratching noise of his myriad scales, claws, and horns rasping against the ground.

"He who has seen me has seen the Father," the Son said as if this dismissed the Serpent's question. He turned to Raylin. "I am Alpha and Omega. First and Last. Beginning ..." he paused, and at that moment, the veil between them and reality drew apart. The Father's Mountain appeared behind the Son. "... and End," the Father said in his cosmically deep voice.

The Abyss shook violently.

The Serpent hissed and groveled. "Not my time," he whined. "Why have you come here? Why? Why? Not my time."

The Three completely ignored the question.

Raylin lifted her eyes and stared up at the Mountain. "I don't understand." Her voice was flat and confused. "He fears you. He bows." She limply gestured toward the Enemy, shaking her head. "Why don't you destroy him now? If your power is this great, why did you let me suffer? Why didn't you rescue me?" Tears streamed down Raylin's face, and her voice fell to a shaky whimper. "I was scared."

Daniel didn't have to guess at Raylin's meaning. He knew she now spoke out of her childhood trauma—the terror of being sold as a slave and exposed to atrocities he could only imagine. Even with never knowing his biological parents, Daniel had never experienced even half of what she went through. He let his eyes drift to his biological mother, then to his mom and dad, all still praying fervently for his protection. If he had ever thought his life hard, one glance at Raylin's blew that notion right out of the water. He'd been sheltered and protected. She'd been exposed to the worst of reality.

"Some are called to suffer, Raylin," the Son said, still standing at the base of the Mountain. "Among the Three, mine was a path of sorrow."

Images flashed through all their minds. A life of ridicule and poverty. Foreknowledge of an inescapable, painful death. The Enemy in various guises, haunting every step like a nagging ghost, kindling every demeaning comment. Unjust accusation. Torture. A Roman cross soaked in blood. Descent into the darkness of death and hell. And, worst of all: separation from the Father.

But then …

Light. Life. Inheritance. Redemption of countless people—a vast sea of children pulled out of darkness and into a world of light, an innumerable host of men and women flooding the plains of Heaven. All because of the suffering, death, and resurrection of the Son. In one burst of understanding, Daniel saw the terrible things experienced by the Son as unworthy of comparison with his great work of redemption.

"*Your* suffering was not purposeless, either. Nor will it be in vain. Through it, you will find compassion for others who suffer, and you have won immense strength. Repent of your anger, Raylin. Sin no more. Come to me and find rest."

Daniel knew he was a son of the Father, but he felt he now understood redemption on a completely different level than he had before. His own repentance and conversion at Intipuncu seemed based on a childlike faith in comparison to what he understood now. Maybe that was all he was capable of then—a simple surrendering, an acknowledgment of the Father's sovereignty over his life, recognizing his sin. And yet, the Three's grace was sufficient to save him despite his lack of understanding then.

Gather your strength and focus on the Abyssal Staff.

The command was clear and forceful. Raylin's decision was upon them, and they needed to be ready.

Ben stirred. "Raylin, please leave the Enemy's power behind. Turn to the Three and confess your sins. Be free of your darkness."

"Please, Raylin." Seren's voice was small and pleading.

Raylin shook her head as if trying to wake from a dream. Her eyes rolled back and forth between the Serpent, his incarnations, and the Three. Finally, they landed on Seren, and something seemed to settle in her mind. She nodded her head. "Okay," she murmured.

"I … I'm sorry for …" the words caught in her throat, and she had to take a deep breath. "I'm sorry for hating you, Seren."

A Shadow oozed out of her back, took on her shape, and skittered over to join the dark spirits.

Raylin slowly stood. "I'm sorry for taking on this stupid sword," she said in a louder voice, shaking the Voidblade still fused to her wrist.

The ebony sword began to vibrate and whine.

This seemed to give Raylin hope. "I'm sorry for letting all those spirits live inside me," she said with a louder voice.

The Voidblade, the Shadow, and the dark spirits moaned and screamed as if her confession pained them. A black tendril slithered down toward Raylin, but she turned to face it before it made contact.

"No! I give you up! I don't want you anymore!" The tendril blanched and drew back. She spun around and stumbled toward Seren, Daniel, and Ben. "I give up my hatred for you all—my jealousy. I'm done with you too!" she shouted at the Serpent. Pointing at the Son, she cracked a desperate smile. "I'm going to let HIM take care of you. I give up on my revenge!"

Another Shadow popped out of her chest and fled toward the dark mass.

With a scream like an injured animal, the Voidblade unraveled from Raylin's wrist and flew, spinning, into the spirits.

She clutched at her hand as if it were a baby rescued from danger.

"Raaayyyllliiinnn!" the Voidblade and the dark spirits moaned together. "You belong to us! Let us back in!" they wailed.

"Never!" Raylin cried in defiance. She stumbled away from the seething mass of spirits, drawing up in front of the other Vessels and falling at their feet. "I know it was wrong to serve the Enemy in Peru, and I'm sorry for betraying you," she said to Daniel and Ben. She cast an anguished look to the Son. "I know I hated my father for …" the words caught in her throat, and she sobbed. "For leaving us alone. Abandoning us. For taking his life. I'm sorry for my anger and hatred." She locked her gaze onto the Mountain. "Forgive me for everything, Father. Please take it all away from me!"

One more Shadow slid out of her chest and darted toward its counterparts, now huddled together in the middle of darkness.

"NOOOOOO!" wailed the Voidblade and the spirits in unison. They shot through the air toward Raylin. The spirits snaked around her ankles, yanking her prostrate and coiling around her neck as if to cut off all confession she could still utter. The Voidblade stuck in the ground near her right arm. "Take us back!" they demanded. "Use us for revenge. Destroy. Punish! Empower yourself!"

Daniel, still anointed with the power of the Spirit, nevertheless felt a twinge of uncertainty. Ben and Seren also looked shocked, glancing back and forth between the Three and Raylin's form.

"Save me," Raylin choked, her hand stretched out toward the Three. "Please!"

Daniel felt his hands suddenly stick to the Abyssal Staff and its surface grow warm. His resonance with Ben and Seren told him they, too, experienced the staff's activation.

Iridescent green swirls glowed from beneath the surface of the staff, glinting into being before disappearing and reappearing at some other point within its depths. The staff, once a solid piece of black obsidian with a half-foot-wide circular head, changed shape. The rim of the head unlocked itself along previously invisible joints and expanded into circular fragments, bound together by some invisible force and orbiting in a perfect ring. Similarly, triangles of light appeared within the head. They, too, began to orbit, only in the opposite direction. A point of darkness appeared within the very center of the staff.

The spirits and Shadows screamed in terror as portions of their miasma were violently sucked through the eye of the staff. The Voidblade moaned and sunk itself deeper into the Abyss floor to keep from being drawn in. The tendrils around Raylin's neck disbanded and swirled into the eye. Those around her ankles were next.

She gasped for air as more and more of the darkness disappeared. Finally, with one last desperate scream, the cloud of malevolent spirits disappeared completely. Like ink sucked off an old piece of paper, the black color siphoned off the Voidblade. The sound the sword emitted was like grinding metal mixed with ghostly screams. Within seconds, it had lost its darkness entirely, until nothing but a sickly yellow remained.

The Serpent watched from outside the line of intercessors, shaking but silent. One of his open eyes flared white. He threw back his head and screamed. Eight points of matching white light appeared over the eye. He writhed and rubbed it against his coils. One of his blind heads even spit fire on the eye as if he thought he could incinerate the lights. Daniel immediately knew they would one day be connected in the form of a binding, eight-pointed star—once their quests were over, and they had bound the Spirit of the Age within him.

The Serpent continued his frenzy, but Daniel turned his attention back to Raylin and the Voidblade. The power of the Abyssal Staff ceased, and Raylin slowly stood. She breathed hard and shook, but then lunged for the staff with an outstretched hand. Once she made contact, Daniel felt his hand repelled.

He, Ben, and Seren stepped back as she gripped its surface. A tongue of fire blossomed over her head as the power of the Spirit rested upon her. She took a deep, calming breath and faced Seren. They hugged and, despite the peace that Daniel felt within them, both wept quietly in each other's arms.

"Raylin." Seren sobbed her name. She held her at arm's length, staring into her face in disbelief. "I'm sorry. Sorry for everything."

Raylin returned her gaze with a look of calm acceptance. Daniel had never seen her so at peace. Once the Spirit's anointing no longer rested on her, he knew she would still have some issues to work through. They all did. But now, at this moment, she was able to experience the calming assurance of the Three's power, unhindered by her personal feelings.

"Me too," she finally said, her voice quiet and deeper than Daniel remembered. "Forgive me?"

Seren almost laughed. "Do you have to even ask?"

Ben stepped closer, hesitated, then finally reached out to touch Raylin's shoulder. With a quick look of apology to Seren, he drew Raylin into a hug. "It's good to have you back," he said. "We missed you."

Raylin smiled. "It's good to be back. Hey, you've gotten taller since India." Her smile fell. "I never did thank you for protecting me there. I mean, you died and all. That should've been me."

Ben shook his head. "Nope. I was supposed to die for you." He cleared his throat awkwardly and quickly released her. "I mean. It was kind of my destiny to die and resurrect. Part of the whole Triune Shield thing. So … anyway. Glad you're back."

He shuffled back toward Daniel while Raylin and Seren embraced again. Something within Ben felt different. It was a familiar sensation, just odd that it emanated from within *him*. Daniel craned his neck to see Gabriela, who was still in the line of intercessors, protecting them all from the furious attacks of the Enemy's incarnations. He glanced back to Ben, whose eyes were locked on Raylin as if he could prevent her from disappearing just by keeping her in sight.

"Aha," Daniel murmured, nudging Ben with his elbow. "Now, I get it."

"Shut up," Ben said.

Seren said something that Daniel couldn't hear. With a nod, Raylin turned to face the Voidblade. It whimpered like a hurt puppy rejected and beaten by its master. Without warning, Raylin charged the sword. In response, the Voidblade shot into the air and brandished its point, whispering and hissing its siren song for Raylin to take it back. Now deaf to its pleas, she spun the staff expertly around her body to gain momentum and attacked.

The sword parried and blocked, but Raylin seemed to anticipate each move. If a sweeping strike with the staff's head was caught by the blade, she immediately switched directions and attacked with the butt, slamming the Voidblade down against the ground. When the sword stabbed toward her, she expertly blocked it with the center of the staff and used the momentum to push her body out of the way. Without missing a beat, she redoubled her attack from a different angle.

Daniel watched in awe. It had been so long since he had seen her in her right mind, he'd forgotten what an expert martial artist she was.

"Why doesn't she use the staff's power?" Ben asked.

The Son's voice drifted into their minds. *Because the Voidblade is no longer possessed with the Enemy's spirit. His power, however, still flows through the sword, and the Abyssal Staff will nullify it. Watch.*

Right on cue, Raylin jabbed the sword dead on its hilt. There was a loud cracking noise, and what looked like an iron ring, previously invisible, snapped and fell off from around the sword. It crumbled to dust as soon as it touched the Abyss floor.

The Voidblade wailed, then flew at Raylin. It made wide, unbalanced sweeps with its blade, sloppily arcing over her head.

She ducked, slid under the blade as it flew overhead, and swung the Abyssal Staff up, catching the sword on the very center of its edge with the staff's head. Another ring appeared, cracked off the Voidblade, and crumbled to dust.

Like a caged animal, the sword alternately made desperate attacks on Raylin before attempting frantic escapes, only to find its path blocked by the barrier put up by the intercessors.

Raylin was merciless. With a shout of victory, she unleashed a series of blinding jabs with both ends of the staff until she caught the sword on the very tip of its jagged blade. A third ring appeared and shattered.

The Voidblade expanded until it was a monstrous fang. It crashed into the Abyss floor, cracking the ground under its immense weight. If Daniel thought the Serpent hated them before, he now gave them a look of such venomous revulsion that he felt sure it was capable of burning them to ashes had not the Spirit empowered them from within.

"You belong to me, Raylin!" the Serpent hissed. "Mine! I will steal you back and punish you. You will suffer—"

The Son appeared next to Raylin, and the Serpent instantly fell silent. He put one hand on her shoulder, and with the other, touched the surface of the fang. "I have won her. She is mine. *This* is yours." He made a slight motion with his hand, and the fang jettisoned through the air toward the Serpent.

It crashed into his mouth with a sickening, bone-crunching noise, filling in the gap in the rows of teeth Daniel had seen earlier. The impact slammed the Serpent's head back into his tangle of coils and extra heads.

Not bothering to watch the Enemy's reaction, the Son turned Raylin away and led her back to the other Vessels.

At his touch, Raylin trembled and dropped her eyes. Daniel and the others bowed as the Son left her with them and walked toward the Mountain. The Father's deep voice—filled with infinite, vibrating power—rumbled down from the blinding light at the peak. Now filled with the Spirit, Daniel and the others could understand it without the Son's interpretation. "He shall lose none that I give him. All who look to the Son will have eternal life and will be raised up."

The Son spread his hands and turned. "There is more to be done, but for now, your task is over. The final phase of this age will be set in motion when I go to our Father. But be of good cheer, we will be with you until the end."

He stepped through the triangle of light behind him. His body became an image of blinding brilliance, which shot through the air toward the top of the Mountain. Once within the peak's radiance, the verdant slopes faded away, leaving the companions in the dull red glow of the Abyss.

The circle and triangle morphed back into a huge tongue of fire, which made their shadows dance wildly on the floor behind them.

The Enemy's incarnations had ceased their attack and now glowered, along with the Serpent, at the Vessels. Daniel knew this was only because attempting to get through the barrier of intercessors was futile. He scanned his parents' faces. They were still in fervent prayer, their mouths moving in unceasing supplication while their eyes focused in on all the Vessels. He followed the line of people until he found his biological mother again. She concentrated on him alone. Her tears had dried up, and a smile of relief had lifted the tension and fear he'd seen earlier. Gabriela, body glowing with the warm light of the Spirit, still faced the Enemy. He couldn't see her expression, but he sensed she was at peace and calm. But what would happen once that was gone? The Enemy would be in a flurry of murderous rage at being thwarted yet again. Daniel hoped the day wasn't going to end with a desperate battle to flee the Abyss.

"Come," the Spirit said aloud, still in his form of fire. Ben, Raylin, and Seren moved immediately toward him. The line of intercessors dimmed and then, one by one down the line, faded away. Janice waved before disappearing. Daniel's parents, concern still evident on their faces, were quick to follow. It was only his biological mother left, as if she clung to the very sight of her long-lost son. But soon, even she disappeared, until there was only Gabriela. She floated down slowly until, spinning around in the air, Daniel could see her face again.

"Glad that's over," she gasped, panting as if she'd just run a race at a break-neck pace. Her feet touched the ground. She reached out and put a hand on Daniel's shoulder to steady herself.

His skin prickled at her touch. He nervously helped her walk toward the others. "You okay?"

"Fine. Better than fine. I'm great, actually, because of him." Gabriela nodded toward the Spirit. "I just feel like I've been plugged into an electrical socket for the past fifteen minutes or so. But it's good."

Daniel nodded. He understood the feeling.

Seeing the barrier of people gone, the Serpent unleashed another volley of fireballs toward them, while his incarnations hurled a vast array of projectiles their way—spears, swords, hammers, belches of dark spirits mixed with black fire.

The Spirit didn't seem bothered by the attempt. Without so much as an acknowledgment of the Enemy's attack, he instantly transported them all high above the fray.

The Enemy, in all his myriad of forms, angrily scanned the Abyss until he found them. One of the Serpent's heads coiled toward the five-pointed star. Sparks flew from its crimson lines, and the twins appeared. By their side, three of the Generals knelt in obeisance. Tyr, still wrapped up in the red chain, writhed in anger and embarrassment on his back. The Serpent glared down at him for a moment before simultaneously roaring out his orders from every head and every incarnation's mouth. "Attack the Holy City. Turn it to dust! Declare war from each stronghold we have, in every country. If the Three's servants are present, I want them persecuted. I want them captured. Remove the image of the Three from every hostage!"

The Enemy's incarnations began disappearing with loud pops—a thousand gone in ten seconds. Daniel had a feeling they'd be reappearing all over the world to carry out their orders.

The Serpent's orders were so violently given that flames spurted from his mouth. Amira and Abida threw themselves to the ground to avoid incineration. The Generals covered their faces, except for Tyr, who couldn't move. Even from their distance, Daniel could see his hair singed into a poofy bouffant.

"Bring all the holy people to me in Babylon. Every. Last. One of them! Without the Three's image, they will be abandoned. They will worship me. Me! And then I will break the Great Prophecy. The end will not come. IT WILL NOT COME! I have that power. It is mine now." This last part to the Spirit. All seven heads hissed and nodded in agreement. "I can do it. I can break the Word of the Father. Then your power will be undone, and the entire universe will unbind itself from your influence."

The Spirit's voice, quiet, but audible in every corner of the Abyss, spoke out of the tongue of fire. "The universe would melt if we took our hand away for one moment."

"I will remake it! Refashion it without all your pathetic fleshly life. There will be only spirit, rock, and fire. The way you fashioned it in the beginning. The way you should have left it!"

The Generals looked back and forth among each other, clearly concerned about this last statement. Even the twins looked confused. None of them dared to question the Enemy in his present state of wrath.

"Our Word endures forever," the Spirit announced, his voice still quiet but so filled with power that the walls and floor vibrated and shook. Several of the Enemy's Incarnations were thrown to the ground. The Serpent's tall necks swayed as if in a gale.

The great, brazen doors of the Abyss crashed shut below Daniel and the others, and the scene was gone.

16

The Spirit Says Goodbye

Daniel hadn't realized they were already so high. If possible, the Enemy was probably even more furious at having the door slammed in his face, but Daniel didn't care. It was just a relief to be away from his oppressive presence. He relaxed his shoulders and released the Sun Sword.

As before, their surroundings abruptly changed the higher they rose in the air. The gigantic doors disappeared, and instead, the enormous spiraling staircase materialized around them.

"Oh, man," Ben sighed. "I sure am glad we don't have to climb back up."

"That makes two of us," Daniel absently replied. He focused primarily on Gabriela, who stood so close to him that their arms brushed.

Raylin rested her head on Seren's shoulder, and together, they watched the Spirit as he carried them higher still.

In a matter of seconds, they reached the top of the staircase. The rocky ceiling fast approached, but its solidity melted away like fog. They passed through it and into the crisp night air. The towering trilithons of Stonehenge loomed black against the starry night sky, and the wind swept like ocean waves over the wide plains around the ruins. Daniel scanned the scene and scratched his head. Their time in the Abyss hadn't seemed long enough for nighttime to have already come. He furrowed his brow and shrugged. Maybe time flowed differently there.

The power faded from within Daniel and the others as they came to rest on the solid, cold ground. The tongues of fire over their heads flew to the Spirit, who then floated higher above Stonehenge. His form morphed from purifying flames to gray goose. Without the snapping, crackling of his blaze, everything was suddenly quiet and still.

"Are you leaving us?" Raylin murmured sadly. Her voice fell flat among the stones. She clutched at her heart, and Daniel thought he saw starlight reflected in tears on her eyelashes. "But I need you. It hurts."

Daniel felt it too. Old feelings flooded back in—memories of past hurts, locked away someplace deep within, found their way out to creep around the mind. The realization that there was still life to live, hardships to face, and issues to work through was *felt*. It wasn't as though those things had been forgotten, they just seemed trivial and powerless in comparison to the Spirit's hope-filled, healing power.

Seren gripped Raylin's hand and patted her back reassuringly. "It'll be okay, Raylin. I'll be with you."

"We'll all be with you," Ben added eagerly. He hurried to Raylin's side and hesitantly reached out to put a hand on her back. "I promise."

Even in the dim, gray light of the Spirit, it was evident he blushed.

Raylin's brow furrowed as if these small acts of kindness were foreign to her. Which, Daniel realized, they were.

She didn't seem to know what to say or how to process through everything she felt. Like Seren immediately after her conversion from Shakti to a normal human, Raylin probably fought against an overwhelming wave of shame and doubt now that the Spirit had lifted his power from them. But Daniel knew the Spirit was still within all of them, even if the powerful anointing of his presence wasn't felt, and that the Three would help her sort that out.

Gabriela joined Ben and Seren, gripping Raylin's hand and giving it a comforting squeeze. Daniel shuffled closer to them, but something held him back from reaching out to Raylin. He stood behind them, gazing up at the Spirit.

"Will you tell us what happens next?" he asked after some time. "Will the Enemy attack this 'Holy City' right away? Are we supposed to go defend them or something?"

The Spirit floated, wings outstretched but unmoving, above the very center of Stonehenge, the soft light emanating from his gray feathers bathing everything in a gentle blue-gray. His still, quiet voice wafted into their minds like whispers on the breeze. *The next and final quest will be to seal away the Spirit of the Age. The Holy City is defended even now; you will visit there, but do not concern yourself with its fate. Its Prince keeps its boundaries and watches over its people. He is able, and his right hand is upheld by the Father.*

Daniel rubbed the back of his neck and ambled forward. "I see," he said slowly, even though he didn't quite understand how some prince could defend a city against the Enemy and his servants.

"Michael," Gabriela whispered to Daniel, seeing his confusion. "He's the Prince, and he's a Firstborn like Inti, only much, much, much more powerful."

"Ooohhh. Wow. Okay." If there was a Firstborn that much more powerful than Inti, then he guessed the Holy City could hold its own.

For now, the Spirit continued, *return to your home and wait. The next quest will come quickly, but you will have some time to rest.*

A sharp wind whistled through the ruins, and Raylin shivered. Ben pulled a jacket out of his backpack and offered it to her. She eyed it uncertainly, as though it were something strange, and hesitantly took it from his hands to drape it over her shoulders.

"Um, Spirit, Sir? I don't suppose we could get a solid date on that?" Ben asked, shifting uncomfortably from one foot to another. Despite himself, he kept glancing from the Spirit down to Raylin.

The quest will begin when the Father decrees. It is not given to you to know the times and dates.

Ben nodded his head and found his feet very interesting.

Do not let shame and doubt cloud your mind, Ben. On this quest, you discovered that you, too, are a leader. When Daniel was wounded, your courage, flexibility, and—he let his gaze fall to the jacket on Raylin's shoulders—*willingness to sacrifice your own comfort sustained the group. Turn a deaf ear to the Shadows within your heart and listen to my voice.*

Ben silently nodded.

Seren. The Spirit slowly turned his unblinking eyes onto her. She stood up, one hand lightly touching Raylin's arm as though fearful she might disappear again. *You still carry a heavy burden.*

Seren absently played with her ponytail, pulling it over one shoulder then the next.

But your sins are forgiven. Will you not turn from shame and condemnation and accept this?

"I know the *Three* forgive me. That's easy to accept, but it's harder to forgive myself. This whole quest was a bit of a mess. I was angry the whole time, got Daniel hurt, ran off by myself, and just stumbled my way through the last battle. I kind of feel like everything *I* tried went wrong or just made things worse." She threw up her hands. "I felt so powerless!"

The Spirit laughed and cast his eyes toward the sky as if sharing a private joke with someone invisible.

Oh, Daniel thought. *He probably was.*

You are powerless without my indwelling presence, Seren, the Spirit explained. *Being a Vessel does not mean you are capable of fighting the Enemy on your own. You will never be strong enough to do so. Did you not see his power?*

"I … I did. But didn't we mess things up? I mean, you had to show up to help, Gabriela had to put herself between us and the Enemy and call all those people to protect us. Without all that, we would've failed."

Daniel felt the Spirit's attention on him, even though he seemed to still focus on Seren. He thought he understood.

"Seren," he said, ambling toward her slowly, "when I was on the quest for the Sun Sword, it was a total debacle. First off, I had no idea what was happening, and I outright refused to even look for the shards of the sword until Gabriela had been captured."

"Glad to be of service," Gabriela laughed.

Daniel shrugged. "Not to mention, we were chased all around Peru by a bunch of monsters, and then totally tricked into giving up the Sun Sword at the end. I mean, it was almost over before it even started."

Raylin blanched at Daniel's words and hung her head low. She took a step back and sat on one of the fallen stones. For some reason, that seemed like the right response. It was good to see that she truly felt bad about betraying them.

Daniel looked up to see the Spirit eyeing him curiously. He cleared his throat. "But, if it hadn't been for Raylin deciding to help us." He paused, and then added, almost as a question, "For Raylin responding to the Spirit."

The Spirit nodded in confirmation.

"Then me, Ben, and Gabriela would've been killed. And *this* quest. I mean, I was basically—"

"An invalid," Ben interrupted.

"An invalid," Daniel repeated through clenched teeth. "I had to be carried around while everyone else made the decisions. I couldn't really lead much. Mostly, I just had to let others help me, let *them* lead, and let go of control when they made mistakes. Which now that I'm saying this out loud, I realize this was probably what I was supposed to learn all along. And I guess if my leg hadn't been broken, I would never have taken a back seat to the whole leadership thing and learned patience."

Correct, the Spirit said.

Ben stood up and eagerly joined in. "Yeah, and I don't know if you know this, but the quest for the Triune Shield was basically one big fight between me and Daniel. He was such an arrogant jerk the whole time—"

"I'm standing right here, Ben."

"The whole time," he repeated, then continued meaningfully, "and *I* was angry and resentful. All the while, you were chasing us down with your stupid Pestilence. We were nearly killed several times, until I finally WAS killed."

Seren rolled her eyes to the sky. "Hey, I've apologized for that."

"Yeah, yeah. Anyway, it was only by the Three's power that I came back to life, and we escaped. With you, I should add."

Gabriela chimed in. "Let's not forget when the Enemy showed up on the plains of Khireshwar. If it hadn't been for all those Firstborn and the Three appearing, we would all have been destroyed. Truthfully, none of us have a great track-record for accomplishing much by ourselves, Seren." Her voice fell quiet, and a fond smile played at the corners of her mouth. "We're all just children, after all."

The Spirit took a deep breath and blew it out. All of Stonehenge blazed, suddenly alive with an intricate network of glowing, embossed veins of light. Swirls, webs, and complicated patterns that defied the eye glimmered on every surface, and power coursed through each line like blood, coming from …

Daniel followed the design from the grass to the stones and into the air, until he realized they all faintly connected to the Spirit. He let his eyes fall to the ground at his feet and saw that they even connected with his own body. For some reason he couldn't explain, he summoned the Sun Sword. The lines connecting to it blinked into being as soon as it formed in the air. Daniel studied the blade, tracing the lines to the Spirit, himself, and … He furrowed his brow. One particularly thick line trailed from the blade directly to the back of Raylin's head. What was that about?

She briefly noticed Daniel's scrutiny, but the line was out of sight. Shifting away on her stone seat to avoid his stare and to better take in the scene all around them, she studied the night sky, her mouth open in awe. Her breathing grew deeper and more relaxed.

Daniel craned his neck upward toward the Spirit for some explanation, but now that his eyes were more accustomed to the faint glow of the lines, he was immediately distracted. They were everywhere—literally connecting to *everything* around them. The flock of birds that flew overhead, the stars in the night sky, the planets that he was somehow able to see with the naked eye, the stones, the clouds. The connection between the Sun Sword and Raylin was probably nothing worth mentioning. After all, everything was connected anyway, and besides that, she did take possession of it once. The link was probably just a reflection of that.

All things are held together by our power, the Spirit explained. *All things are worked out according to our will. Your mistakes. The Enemy's choices. Your strengths and your weaknesses. Your triumphs and your failures. I live within you to accomplish the Father's will.*

Seren lightly touched the strings connecting to her heart and traced one that wound its way into Raylin's. "So it's normal to feel like a quest was just one big mess? Like you've somehow failed?"

"Pretty much," Daniel said.

Ben agreed. "One disaster after another."

The Spirit flapped his wings, flying slightly higher and changing direction. *Take heart, Seren. Your dedication and love for your sister was the vehicle of her salvation. It planted seeds of the Father's love, and the Father harvested them.*

Seren nodded and gave Raylin's arm a squeeze.

"What about me?" Raylin suddenly asked, nearly jumping to her feet. "I thought I was free and forgiven for everything when we were in the Abyss, but now I feel like I've got about two tons of shame crushing me. What do I do with that?"

You are saved from the Enemy and saved from yourself. The Spirit pronounced this with authority in his voice. *You are forgiven, but you are not free from your flesh. As long as you are clothed in mortality, shame will seek entrance into your heart. You are newly on the Way, Raylin. The longer you travel it, the harder it will be for the sins of your past to weigh you down. Go and sin no more, and remember the Son already paid for your sins. You can never atone for them yourself.*

The Spirit flew higher into the air. *I will be with you until the end. Do not let your hearts be troubled.*

"Wait!" Raylin pleaded. She broke free from Seren's grip and ran forward, jumping up on a fallen stone and reaching out her hands. "Don't leave! What am I supposed to do now? Where do I go? Do I really just start over like nothing happened?"

Believe in the Son; he is the Champion who has overcome all. Through him, you will overcome. Rely on your friends; they are his hands and feet.

The crackle of fire along the Sun Sword drew Daniel's attention down to the blade. He realized if he was going to ask the Spirit about the missing shard, he was about to lose his chance. "Wait! If we're going to start the new quest soon, don't I need to know where the tip of the Sun Sword is?"

A gentle breeze rattled through the grass, and the Spirit, along with all the connecting lines of holy power, were gone with a faint shimmer.

Raylin's shoulders slumped forward, and she plopped down into a sitting position on the stone. She hung her head and lay the Abyssal Staff across her lap.

Seren finally released the Celestial Bow and sat next to her.

Daniel followed suit and released the Sun Sword. Figures. Finding the lost shard was probably a part of the next quest. And he knew better than to keep asking. It was clear the Three didn't intend to tell him anything about it until the time was right.

Daniel followed Ben and Gabriela to the stone, where they all sat in a line, watching the heavens for any sign of the Spirit.

Raylin tilted her head to the side, narrowed her eyes, and gripped the middle of the staff with both hands. She took a deep breath, then slid them apart. The staff disappeared into her palms, both of which glowed with a dull, hunter-green light. Raylin watched her hands as they faded. She brushed stray strands of white hair out of her face and set her jaw in a line of determination that Daniel remembered seeing so often in Peru. "What now?" she asked matter-of-factly.

Gabriela clapped both hands on her thighs and stood. "We travel through the Mist to Newgrange, then transport back to Oregon." She lifted her hands and pushed them apart and down. The Mist opened; she stood to the side and gestured for everyone to enter.

"I wasn't kidding in the Abyss," Seren said, taking Raylin by the hand and pulling her to her feet.

Raylin cast a confused look her way. "Sorry, there's a lot I don't remember. My head's still fuzzy when I think about what happened down there. What do you mean?"

"I want you to come live with me in Granny's house. It's just me there. And Daniel and Ben come over a lot too, of course."

Raylin frowned as she considered this silently for a moment. Daniel wasn't sure what she was thinking, but one look at Ben made it obvious what was on his mind. He chewed his fingernails and waited for Raylin's answer with bated breath.

Daniel sidled up next to Ben. He lightly elbowed his side. "Don't make it *so* obvious. You look like you're in secret stalker mode. Chill out."

Ben punched his arm. "Shut up," he hissed. "Like you've got room to talk. When you were pining after Gabriela, it was so obvious, a blind man could've figured it out."

"All right, all right. Geez, so touchy. Let's talk later."

Ben mumbled something under his breath and walked through the opening to the Mist. Once inside, he turned and waited for the others to join him.

"Raylin?" Seren urged.

Raylin started as though roused from a daydream. "Back to Granny's, huh? Just like I never left. Except now, I'm undercover for the Three, instead of the Enemy."

"Not exactly undercover," Gabriela corrected. "The Joneses now know, and I suspect Janice does too. They were in the Abyss with us. In spirit, anyway. And they've been watching through the sphere I gave them at the beginning of the quest."

Raylin shrugged as if this information didn't really matter to her. "No idea who Janice is. I barely remember Ben's parents. I just go home and wait, then. We don't gather information on what the Enemy's doing? We don't make a plan? We don't go hunting down Creeps? We just wait."

"Well, me and Daniel go to school," Ben said, sticking his head out of the Mist. "See movies. Hang out with friends. That sort of thing."

"School," Raylin said as though the concept was completely foreign to her. "How old am I?"

Daniel laughed at the question, but quickly realized she wasn't kidding. "I don't know. You were like, what, fourteen when we first met? That was about two years ago. So you're probably sixteen."

"She's fifteen," Seren interjected. "She turns sixteen on December 9th. You'd be in the tenth grade."

"December 9th. My birthday," Raylin said slowly. "Do I have to go to school?" she finally asked.

Seren shook her head. "If you want to. If not, I could home-school you. When I was a General, I had to learn tons about how the world worked. It was mandatory. I've basically already been through college, though I don't have much to show for it. Anyway, I could teach you."

A barely noticeable smile appeared on Raylin's face for the first time since the Spirit left. "I'd like that."

Seren smiled back. They locked arms and walked into the Mist together.

Gabriela followed them through, with Daniel trailing close behind, and shut the opening with a wave of her hands.

The constant swishing of the wind through the grass around Stonehenge was gently replaced by the comforting forest sounds of the Mist. Daniel listened intently, but the song of Rhiannon and the Sons of Don no longer drifted through the woods. They must've still been fighting in Babylon. Other than that, everything was the same: ancient trees; bright, starlit sky casting a peaceful, dreamlike glow upon the glistening canopy; and the sleepy cadence of dripping dew, thumping on the thick carpet of moss and leaves.

Daniel leaned closer to Gabriela. "Do I need to guide us with the Sun Sword?"

"Nah. I know the way back." She wound around Ben, Seren, and Raylin to take the lead.

Daniel raised his eyebrows. "Figures. Broken leg, carried, and now my girlfriend doesn't need my help with directions.

Gabriela stopped and put a hand on her hip. "I don't recall ever saying I was your girlfriend."

"Thought I'd give it a shot. Just slip it in and see if it stuck."

"Is the Spirit of the Age sealed away? The world saved? My people freed? All of us survived?"

Daniel shrugged. "We've got Raylin back?" he offered hopefully.

Gabriela smiled. "Daniel," she began, but he cut her off.

"I know, I know. Just forget I said anything. But," he grabbed her hand and held it tightly, "even if you won't date me unless *everything* is perfect—"

"That's not what I meant."

"Sure. But at least you can hold my hand until we get back to the Transportation Pedestal."

Gabriela sighed and considered this for a few moments. "Or, I could just pick you up and carry you back. Or toss you into the brush, for that matter."

"Toss him. Toss him. Toss him," Ben chanted.

Daniel snapped his head around. "You keep out of this. Unless you want similar help with *your* situation."

Ben's eyes narrowed, and he skittered up to Daniel's shoulder. "A little discretion would be appreciated, Mr. Daniel, sir," he hissed. "I'd like to avoid being shot down before I even get started, thanks."

"Then you'll mind your manners," Daniel replied, poking Ben in the chest. "Got it?"

Ben rolled his eyes. "This is extortion." He turned to Gabriela. "Don't toss him. There, Daniel. You happy?"

"You better hope so," Daniel whispered in a quietly threatening voice.

Ben paled and fell back next to Seren and Raylin, who were still walking silently, arms locked, behind the group. Raylin now rested her head on Seren's shoulder.

Daniel noticed that, despite her threat, Gabriela hadn't let go of his hand. He smiled but kept his mouth shut.

They walked for three hours with only a few brief breaks before Gabriela opened up the Mist to Newgrange. The sky was still dark, and the stars were obscured by a thick blanket of clouds. A heavy fog rolled over the countryside, and the ruin of Newgrange was nothing more than a looming shadow in the distance with a few pinpricks of light.

Gabriela strode up to the standing stone they'd been transported to at the beginning of the quest and summoned a globe of light. She gestured for Seren to join her.

Raylin followed close behind. She eyed the stone distrustfully. "Is using the Transportation Pedestals still as awful as it used to be?"

"You bet," Ben said, walking between Raylin and Gabriela to lean against the stone. His eyes lingered on Raylin as if hoping she would continue the conversation.

She stared back blankly. "Is there something else you wanted to say?"

"Huh? Me? Oh, no. I was just …" he coughed awkwardly, "waiting for Gabriela to find the handprint." He pulled out his daggers and illuminated the blades. He turned and began scanning the stone himself. "Was there something you wanted to say?" he said with a backward glance.

"No." Raylin returned his fidgeting and insecure glances with a deadpan stare.

Daniel edged up to Ben with a smile. "So, Raylin. All that time alone, in silence, fighting the Enemy with no one to talk to—must make it hard to be back among friends, huh?"

"I was never alone. The spirits in the Voidblade," she shivered slightly, "were never silent." Her green eyes glinted in the light of Gabriela's globe.

Daniel hiked his backpack higher onto his shoulders and sucked in air through his teeth. "Yikes. Sorry I brought it up. But, I mean, wasn't that kind of what you signed up for by taking the Voidblade in the first place?"

Raylin narrowed her eyes. "I guess."

"What's your point, Daniel?" Seren said, an edge to her voice.

Daniel held out his hands apologetically. "Nothing, nothing! No point. It just sounded like Raylin was surprised with what happened with the Voidblade, but I thought she knew what it was going to be like when she took the sword. I mean, Granny spelled it out for us before she left, right?" He turned to Ben for help.

Ben raised his eyebrows. "Not sure what you're trying to prove. You're on your own with this one," he whispered.

Daniel cleared his throat and tried to catch Gabriela's eyes, hoping for some help, but she was preoccupied looking for the handprint on the standing stone.

A faint shimmer of light illuminated the area.

"Found it," Gabriela finally said.

"Good," Seren replied. With one more cold look at Daniel, she pivoted on her heel and strode toward the stone. She poised her hand above the print. "Ready whenever you all are."

Raylin, looking confused more than offended at Daniel's comment, shuffled after her sister.

Daniel turned, thankful for the interruption. He leaned in close to Ben. "Man, you've got your work cut out for you."

Ben shook his head and took a deep breath. "Tell me something I don't know. What you said to Raylin was super insensitive, by the way. You didn't have to rub it in."

Daniel threw up his hands. "Oh, good grief! I didn't mean it to be. Here, I'll go apologize."

"You should. She already feels horrible about *everything*. No need to slap her with a You-Should've-Known-Better."

Ben hurried past him; his reasoning became clear when Daniel saw that Raylin was blindly holding out her hand for the next person in the chain to hold. Ben grabbed it a little too excitedly, earning him another confused stare from Raylin.

Gabriela took his hand, and Daniel brought up the rear.

"Raylin," Daniel said after everyone was situated. "I didn't mean to offend you with what I—WHOA!"

The windy fields were jarringly replaced by a spinning vortex of light and discombobulating motion. Daniel felt his body dissolve and hurtle through space.

"This isn't so bad," he heard Raylin say. "I remember it being so much worse."

Seren's voice emanated from a streak of color up ahead. "Compared to what you've been through, this is nothing, I'm sure."

"Hm," was all Raylin said in reply.

Behind her, Ben, nothing but a mottled blur, moaned. "If my body has dissolved, how can I possibly feel nauseous? Almost there. Keep it all in. Don't hurl—OOP." A splash of green.

"Just like old times," Raylin commented wryly.

"Welcome back," Ben burped.

"I just pray," Gabriela said, "that whatever just came out of Ben isn't all over me when we get back to the cave.

"Raylin!" Daniel shouted above the constant commentary. "I was trying to apologize for what I said earlier. Didn't mean to rub you the wrong way."

"Heard you the first time," Raylin replied.

"Oh. Well, sorry. I didn't realize it." Daniel pushed his concern aside. If Raylin didn't want to talk about it, then he didn't either. Besides, what he'd said earlier was true: she knew what she was doing when she took up the Voidblade. Granny had warned her. Besides, she'd been working for the Enemy long enough to know what the sword would do to someone. There was no point in trying to bring it up again. Memo to self: avoid all discussion of Raylin's choices.

The cave on Pedestal Hill came into view. Seren materialized in front of him, and, one by one, each person took shape and collapsed on the ground behind her. The fiery circle of heavenly letters around the pedestal burned down and disappeared, leaving them in the dim light of the afternoon sun, peeking through the ivy vines of the cave.

17

Granny Bursts a Bubble

Alan and Mariah Jones were frozen, mid-stride, facing opposite directions as if they'd been pacing the cave. Mariah had the Orb of Seeing in her hands. It disappeared with a pop, startling her. Off in a corner, Janice jolted awake at the noise. She lay on the rocky floor, wrapped in an over-sized, mottled cardigan, and her hair, as frizzy as ever, stuck out from her face like rays from the sun. She blinked her magnified eyes in confusion before leaping to her feet.

"Look! They're all back. See, I told you that terrible dragon didn't eat them," she said, waving a hand at Alan and Mariah while jumping to her feet. A pile of knitted socks and underwear went flying into the air. "I just knit like crazy when I'm nervous. But look, here you all are and no worse for wear. Oh hooray! You brought Raylin home with you." She rummaged through the pile of socks and pulled out a stocking cap. "Made you something, dear. Absolutely saturated it with prayer. Go ahead and try it on. It's a bit chilly. And here you are, nothing but threadbare clothes and bare feet. Well, put on these socks, too. These gloves will warm your hands, and this muffler—oh goodness me. I'll do it." Janice descended upon Raylin before she had a chance to respond. After a quick embrace that caught Raylin off guard, Janice had her bundled up from head to toe. "There! Much better. Now you girls come here and sit out in the sun. Oh goodness, look at that white hair. So beautiful. And all of you have white streaks in your hair now," she added, her owl-eyes sweeping over the companions. "Like a bunch of old biddies. Goodness!" She grabbed Seren and Raylin by the arms and drew them toward the cave opening. "You've had nothing but chilly nights and foggy days since you left," she said to Seren. Then, leaning over to Raylin, "And you, why, you've just been full of sorrow and darkness, haven't you? Bless your heart, you poor thing. I know just what to do about that." Janice parted the vines and drew the sisters through into the sunlight.

"Soooo …" Daniel said, pointing after Janice, "she knows too, now? I mean, I did see her in the Abyss praying for us and all. Is she totally in the loop?"

Mrs. Jones completely ignored the question, and instead, rushed across the cave to pull Ben and Daniel into a bear hug. Alan joined them momentarily, then broke off to rustle the boys' hair.

"That was some adventure!" he laughed. "There were several times I thought you boys were going to be goners. When Daniel broke his leg—we were praying like mad then. That giant rock lady was nuts. Could you understand a word of what she said? And Arawn! What a freaky guy."

"You have no idea!" Daniel laughed, feeling relieved by his father's easy-going manner and jovial banter.

"How much of the Abyss did you see, Dad?" Ben chimed in.

"Nearly all of it. The Serpent—how huge was that thing? It was hard to tell through the globe, but when the Spirit brought us there, I thought I was going to freak out! It was terrible but exciting at the same time."

Ben shook his head. "It was so big, Dad. Bigger than a mountain. It was crazy!"

Daniel ran his hands through his hair. "I couldn't believe it when you all showed up. I thought we were all about to get fried."

"So did I," Gabriela chimed in quietly. "We haven't slowed down since then, so I haven't had a chance to even think through it all, but—yeah, I thought I was going to die."

"Looking death in the eye changes everything, huh?" Ben asked.

Gabriela took a deep breath and slowly blew it out. "Puts things into perspective, that's for sure. I just kept wondering why I'd been so worried about anything before. It was like all the little things in my life that bothered me were so small and insignificant."

Mrs. Jones threw her hands in the air and screamed. "How can you all be so calm about this?"

Everyone froze in silence.

"Dragons? Death? Demons? Teleporting? Broken legs? Do you know how many times you all almost died? At least five, that's how many. Not to mention that during each fight, you could've been killed at least a dozen times over! A dozen! Now listen to you all. You might as well be talking about a soccer game or an exciting day at a theme park. You faced off with *the* Serpent." She cast a dark glare toward her husband. "The Serpent, Alan! The source of all evil in the universe. Can you all take this a little more seriously?"

"Dear," Mr. Jones began, but that's as far as he got.

"Don't even start! I know they were protected. I know God heard our prayers for them. I know they had to do all this to save Raylin. But that doesn't mean I have to like it or pretend they didn't just nearly DIE!"

"Mom," Daniel said, pulling her into a hug. Daniel reached behind to grab Ben and yanked him around to hug his Mom from the other side, sandwiching her between them. "We love you. We're sorry you had to worry so much, but we're home now. Now you can protect us again."

Mrs. Jones stiffened, brushed away some tears, and eventually returned the hugs. She cleared her throat after some time. "Thank you for acknowledging how hard this has been for me. I hope there're no more quests anytime soon."

Ben cast Daniel a terrified look.

Daniel pulled his mom closer so she couldn't see his response and mouthed the words, "Not now."

Ben breathed a sigh of relief, then yawned fiercely. "Can we go home now? I'm so tired I could fall asleep on the Serpent's head."

"Tired and starving," Daniel added. Both boys released their mom from the hug. "I need eggs and bacon. And toast. Cereal, too. A couple donuts."

"Ten donuts! That sounds amazing right now. I—hey, where's Gabriela?"

Daniel spun around, searching the cave, but she was gone. A cold feeling of dread crept from his feet up to his head. "Oh, don't tell me she's disappeared again!" He darted for the ivy-draped doorway.

His dad reached out and grabbed him by the arm before he had a chance to burst through into the sunlight, spinning him around. "Daniel. Hey, calm down. She just slipped outside when your mom went cra—when she got upset," he corrected himself after a sharp look from Mariah. "Listen," he continued, drawing Daniel closer, "it's obvious you like her and she likes you, but don't act too desperate. She's told you what she needs before she can be in a relationship. Saw that in the globe, too. Respect her feelings and don't pressure her. And don't act so desperate! Did I already say that?"

"Yeah, you did," Daniel replied, somehow feeling relieved. It was nice to finally have some advice about Gabriela from someone with experience. "But I needed to hear it again."

Mariah joined the conversation. "Your dad's right. Now, walk out there confidently and *calmly* ask her if she'd like to stay at our house for dinner."

"Mm, food," Ben mumbled, pushing his way through the vines.

Daniel relaxed his body. "Ok. I got it." His dad held the vines aside so he could walk through.

Seren, Raylin, and Gabriela were all sitting quietly while Janice prattled on about something. It took a while before Daniel figured out what she was talking about. "I'll sleep on the couch. I can sleep anywhere, you know. Probably fall out right here mid-sentence if I'm not careful." She paced around the landing, waving her hands excitedly, periodically stopping to look over the side of the ledge into the forest below. "You girls can share the room just fine, I bet. Probably don't want to be out of each other's sight. Your story is just heartbreaking. Heartbreaking, I say! You need a mother for sure, and the Father told me in a dream that I can be that for you—for a little while, anyway. You both are so nearly grown. If only I could've known you as children. What fun we would have had! I saw everything that happened to you both while I was sleeping. Learned about the Vessels and the Serpent and your quests. We all are just going to have the greatest time!" She startled Raylin and Seren by pulling them up from their seats into a hug.

Daniel searched Raylin and Seren's faces, expecting them to be cringing at Janice's over-the-top barrage, but he was surprised to find both smiling warmly and leaning their heads on her shoulders. The coldness in Raylin seemed to melt away, and for once, she looked her age.

Seren looked relieved and even had a few tears rolling down her cheeks onto Janice's cardigan. "I think we'd like that," she said quietly. "Raylin?"

"I would. It's been a long time since we've had a mother, though. I might not be good at the daughter thing."

"Don't worry about that, you poor thing. You'll be just lovely. You both will." Janice continued nattering on in a quiet but never-ending stream of conversation.

Alan nudged Daniel toward Gabriela. "Go on, son."

Daniel stumbled forward. After an icy glare at his dad, he turned. "Gabriela, I don't know what you're supposed to do now, but you're welcome to join us for dinner."

Gabriela looked up into Daniel's face and smiled. "To tell you the truth, I don't know what the Three want me to do either. I've been praying about it, but not getting an answer. Yet, anyway. But," she glanced at the sky, "I know that doesn't mean the Three have forsaken me."

"It most certainly does not," a familiar voice said out of the air.

Everyone scanned the area, looking for the owner until Granny's fire-lady form appeared in all its blazing glory above the mouth of the cave. Mariah and Alan paled and fell back.

"Oh my! Would you look at that," Janice exclaimed, not the least bit afraid. "Nothing so terrifying as that Serpent, I'll say. Do you know her, girls?"

Seren nodded. "We all know her. She's a Firstborn that lived in the neighborhood for a long time. I live in her house, as a matter of fact."

Daniel folded his arms. "But she's been missing for a while and has some explaining to do."

"You better watch it," Ben said quietly. "She's bound to fly down swinging with her broom if you take that tone of voice."

"Or light you on fire," Gabriela joined in.

Daniel blanched, unfolded his arms, and tried to look disinterested and respectful.

The flames calmed as Granny floated to the ground, and died down completely when she turned into her old lady form—broom, blue nightgown, and all.

"I have nothing to explain to you, young man," Granny said to Daniel, one eyebrow raised while patting her broom handle.

"Yes, ma'am," Daniel squeaked.

"Granny?" Alan said, tilting his head to one side and then the other.

Mariah studied Granny closely before commenting, "So all those years walking the streets of the neighborhood and sweeping the sidewalks, and you're really a Firstborn."

"As you see," Granny replied. "It was my job to keep the Enemy out of the area to protect your son, and prepare things for Daniel, Seren, and now," Granny turned around and strode up to Raylin, "this young woman."

Granny took Raylin by the hand and pulled her into a hug. "Welcome home, young Vessel, and into the Celestial Family. Your Heavenly Father rejoices over your salvation."

The corners of Raylin's mouth curved upward into a barely perceptible smile. "He does?"

"He does. We all do. Now," Granny turned and pointed for everyone to gather beside Raylin.

Daniel, Ben, and Gabriela quickly obeyed. Granny's air of authority was so strong, in fact, that even Alan and Mariah didn't hesitate or ask any questions before skittering across the ledge to stand at attention.

"It will be only a little while before the next quest," Granny began.

A shocked intake of breath escaped from Mrs. Jones's mouth but was met by a sharp look from Granny.

"Janice has already explained that she will be living with you girls," she gestured to Seren and Raylin. "Through her prayers, the Three will continue to protect you from attacks while you wait for the quest to begin."

"Don't worry, boys," Janice said, patting Daniel and Ben's backs reassuringly, "you can wear the Prayer Socks, Prayer Beanies, and Prayer Underwear I knitted you. It'll protect you just fine."

Daniel cast a sidelong glance at Janice.

"Sounds itchy," Ben whispered.

Granny simply nodded her head. "Yes. Janice has prayed over a number of things, hallowing them with the Three's power. They will add to your protection in battle."

Daniel imagined himself fighting a horde of Creeps in nothing but Janice's Holy Underwear. It was so ridiculous, but Granny seemed to take it seriously, so he wasn't going to say anything to gainsay her.

"Boys, you will, of course, stay with your parents. But be on your guard; the Enemy will seek to infiltrate your school in the coming months. More than that, they will be dogging your steps whenever you set foot outside your house. Be careful, even in the neighborhood."

Daniel searched the ridge above and the woods below them. Try as he might, he couldn't help but feel a prickly sensation, as if watched by something within the shadows of the forest. "Before the quest, Abida attacked us right outside your house. He got through your barrier."

Granny looked irritated at this. "I am aware. The Enemy poured a great amount of power into him and his sister. Rest assured, I will shore up the barrier's power, and Janice's prayers will enlarge its boundaries as well." She pointed her broom handle at Mr. and Mrs. Jones. "I suggest you two get to work praying a stronger circle around your house as well. Morning and evening."

Mariah nodded her head repeatedly, her eyes big as saucers.

Alan rubbed his stubbly chin and nodded. "So that's all we need to do to protect them more? Keep praying for safety?" he finally asked, seeming to take the instructions more calmly.

Mariah pushed him aside so she could face Granny. "Will that really be enough? Should we buy more guns? I'm a pretty good shot. If that Abida man comes again, I'll send him packing with some lead in his pants! Alan!" She swung around. "I want my dad's rifle out of storage before bed tonight. I won't be able to sleep without knowing we've got some way to defend ourselves."

Granny reached out and touched her. "Mariah, do not fear. Even in the darkest times, the Three are with us. A gun would not work against Abida. Prayer is the most powerful weapon, even if we do not always see its effects right away. Besides, do you forget your sons and these young women are Vessels for the Weapons of Power?"

Mrs. Jones nodded, her mouth opening and closing, though she couldn't seem to find the words for a reply.

"You go through hard times, too?" Raylin asked, fixing Granny with a confused look.

Granny smiled. "Indeed. Firstborn take part in the fight against the Enemy. You know this. Even now, the one you call Inti is locked in battle with the Prince of Peru. Day and night, he prevents that ancient power from completely enslaving its people. But the fight is bitter, and Inti has undergone numerous trials while he waits for help."

Before Raylin could respond, Gabriela was at Granny's side.

"Inti has finally risen up? He's fighting now? How ... how long has he been fighting the Prince?" She stepped closer and put a shaking hand on Granny's arm. "Is he winning? Is my family safe? Have you seen my parents? I need to go back and help. I'll help with the fight. I'll fight any Creeps I find and," she held up her fist and gritted her teeth, "and I'll pummel any demons that are trying to hurt them. Please, you have to send me back!"

Granny touched Gabriela's brow. "Peace, Gabriela. Peace." A soft light emanated from Granny's fingertips. Gabriela visibly relaxed. "Do not be anxious. You *will* go to your people soon, once you have rested and eaten."

Daniel had been fishing through his backpack for his last water, but quickly dropped the entire thing to the ground. "She's leaving when now?"

"Tomorrow morning," Granny said.

"But ... but, but, but ... she only just got finished with the last quest!"

"Play it cool, remember?" Mr. Jones whispered in Daniel's ear. "Calm down."

Daniel waved his dad away and drew himself up to his full height. He wasn't quite sure what that would accomplish with someone like Granny, but he was past reason.

"Here we go," Ben muttered to Seren.

Seren rolled her eyes. "Oh, boy."

"She needs to take a break for longer than just one night! And if she's going back to Aguas Calientes, then I should go with her to help. You can't send her there by herself, Granny! That place is crawling with monsters and Creeps." He tossed his arms wide. "We can all—"

"You will all go." Granny's statement caught Daniel off guard, and he stuttered himself into silence. "Just not yet. The Three are sending Gabriela there to gain intelligence for you four," she gestured toward the other three Vessels with her broom handle. As

Daniel was nearest, she tapped him with it on the forehead, a mischievous gleam in her eye.

Daniel took the warning and backed down.

"She *will* walk through the Mist to her village and begin her personal quest tomorrow."

Gabriela's face lit up. "The Three opened the way to Aguas Calientes?"

"They have. Now is the right time to go. Before, it was too dangerous for you, and martyrdom was not your path. Once there, you will find the remaining free people fearful and terrorized. Hide them in your tunnels, fight off the Enemy with your strength, and pray for the Three to establish their presence there. They will work through your petitions, and the Enemy's power will be weakened."

"And us? When do we finally all go down to help?" Daniel asked, sullen.

"You will begin your last quest by freeing Aguas Calientes. It, and Machu Picchu, will become a stronghold for holiness, and many of the Father's children will flock there for safety."

Gabriela was utterly distracted now. Daniel could tell there was no way he'd be able to get her to focus on anything other than saving her town. His shoulders slumped forward. It wasn't that he blamed her: they were talking about the lives of her family and friends, after all. It was just that, he had been hoping she could've stayed in the neighborhood until the next quest began. To have that possibility now completely out of reach was a major letdown.

"If you really care for her," his mother whispered into his ear, "you'll care about what she feels is important." She squeezed Daniel's shoulder.

He met her eyes and smiled. She was right, of course. He needed to chill and support her in her efforts to save her people. Gabriela was asking Granny a slew of questions, but he hazarded an interruption by walking between them and giving her a hug. "I'll be praying for you. Every day. Every night."

"Same!" Ben joined in.

Seren smiled up at Gabriela. "Us too."

Raylin stood and put both hands on Gabriela's shoulders. "I know I played a part in Aguas Calientes's problems. I'm sorry for that. I promise I'll support you in prayer. As best as I can, anyway. I'm not exactly sure how it works. But when we come to help, I'll be sure to bring my A-game."

Daniel listened to Raylin's comment and frowned. He hadn't really thought about how she had contributed to the enslavement of Gabriela's people. Now that she mentioned it, she *was* partially to blame. And because of that, Gabriela had to leave. A hot wave of anger boiled up from inside him, but Daniel took a deep breath and pushed it back down. What was going on? It seemed like Raylin was a trigger for him. First, there was her comment about the Voidblade and his immediate sarcasm about her getting what she deserved. Now this? When she'd been AWOL, her past choices hadn't seemed to bother him as much. Now that she stood in front of him, however, he couldn't help but feel resentful—especially because of Gabriela's people. He shook his head. Now wasn't the time to process through all of that. Gabriela needed his focus, not her.

Gabriela took Raylin's hands and squeezed them affectionately. "Thank you all. Now, if you don't mind, can we head back? I'm starving."

Everyone wearily agreed.

Granny ambled to the other side of the ledge and rose into the air, resuming her fire-lady form. "Gabriela, I will meet you in the Mist at sunrise. We can discuss your strategy then." With that, she disappeared.

Silence.

Ben was the first to climb up the slope from the ledge. "Food. Food. Food. Food."

"That's my cue," Mrs. Jones chuckled. "Come on."

Everyone else quietly followed.

18

Goodbye ... Hello

Gabriela let go of Daniel's hand and parted the Mist at Granny's house. To his surprise (and utter joy), she had intertwined her fingers into his as they walked up the road to meet Ben and the girls at the ivy-covered house. The sun barely peaked through the trees over Pedestal Hill, which stood like an imposing sentinel crowned with the early morning light. As promised, when the portal opened, Granny blazed on the other side. Gabriela took a deep breath, her eyes fixed on the path through the Mist as if seeing all the way to Aguas Calientes. After a few moments of silence, she nodded to herself.

"I'm counting on your prayers," she said, her voice suddenly uncertain. She nervously fidgeted with her hair.

Everyone murmured words of reassurance, except for Janice, who had inexplicably already begun moving into the house and, at that moment, popped out onto the front porch. "Of course, we will!" she exclaimed. "Constantly. Oh, don't forget your poncho. Been working on one for several weeks. Didn't know why until now. Well, let me see where I put it," she reached into the doorway for her knitting bag and pulled out a black knitted poncho. "I couldn't for the life of me figure out why I was knitting it in all black. Makes sense now, though, since you'll be on a top-secret mission. Prayed over the silly thing every second I worked on it."

"Take it," Granny ordered. "It will shield you from the eyes of your enemies.

Janice flew down the steps and slipped it over Gabriela's head, then wrapped her up in a vigorous hug.

"Thank—thank you!" Gabriela stuttered, her surprise at Janice's sudden onslaught evident.

"Well, I'll let you kids say your goodbyes alone. Loads of organizing to do inside. Farewell!" Like a tornado of frayed yarn and frizz, she whirled through the screen door, and all was quiet.

Raylin hugged Gabriela next. "I promise to make this right. As soon as we get the signal from the Father, we'll be by your side kicking butt."

"And shooting stuff," Seren added with a grin. "Thanks for all your help, Gabriela. Without you, we couldn't have saved Raylin. *I* wouldn't have been saved without you, for that matter."

Raylin's eyes fell to the ground, and she backed away as if the mere mention of the quest caused shame.

Gabriela waved Seren's comment away. "Say nothing of it. We're all part of the Celestial Family, so that makes us all sisters. Besides, Ben and Daniel helped a little, too."

"Oh wow, you honor us," Ben said, deadpan. "I can tell how much you truly acknowledge our efforts."

Daniel covered his cheeks in mock humiliation. "Stop gushing. You're embarrassing us."

Seren rolled her eyes. "Pfft. Yeah. I guess they were there too, but we all know who ran the show."

Ben pushed past Seren. "All right, all right. 'Bash the Boys' is such a hilarious game. Move it, it's my turn."

"Stay safe and knock 'em dead." He gave her a quick hug then went to stand beside Raylin, who watched the friendly exchanges as if studying a different culture.

Daniel felt a strong grip on his hands and found himself pulled into a warm embrace. Before he had time to realize what was happening, Gabriela kissed him on the lips then walked into the Mist.

"See you all soon!" she called back before the Mist silently shut behind her.

"What? Wait … I have to …" Daniel shouted, unable to finish his sentence while running forward and waving his hands up and down in a vain effort to reopen the portal. "That's … What just happened? Open this stupid thing back up! Gabriela? Granny? Open the Mists right now! That wasn't fair!"

Ben, Raylin, and Seren broke out into laughter.

"Looks like some crazy duck dance," Ben said. "Daniel, flap your hands harder. It'll probably work eventually."

"Shut it!" Daniel snapped, nevertheless taking Ben's advice.

Seren linked arms with Raylin, who was grinning silently, and walked toward the house. "Just be grateful she knows you're alive," she called over her shoulder.

"I'm exhausted," Raylin murmured.

"Me too."

On cue, Janice flung open the door. "Well, you come right in and climb back into bed, young ladies. Just sleep as long as you need because later today …" The rest was lost in the creaking of the screen door.

Ben watched after Raylin until she disappeared inside.

Daniel buried his head in his hands and groaned. "That was evil. Like dangling a hamburger in front of a starving man and then yanking it away. Girls are so mean."

"Cry me a river," Ben replied. He spun Daniel around and shoved him toward home. "At least she's made it clear she likes you. Raylin barely knows I'm alive."

"She barely knows anyone's alive except Seren. And maybe Janice. Can we please focus on my problems?"

"No. Your problems are stupid, and they don't matter, and they're stupid. The girl you like just kissed you. Be grateful. Cherish the moment. Move on."

"Does this mean Gabriela and I are dating?" Daniel continued as though Ben hadn't responded. "Because she said we couldn't until things are better in Aguas Calientes. But then she goes off and kisses me! Did I kiss her back? Seriously, did I even kiss her back?"

His voice rose to a crescendo. "I don't know! Oh great. What if she thinks I didn't like it? What if she thinks I'm not into her now? What if I'm a terrible kisser? Will she change her mind about liking me? Ben, did it look like I was a terrible kisser?"

Ben smacked his forehead. "This is going to be a long day. I'm sleeping on the couch tonight because I just know you're going to be blabbing about this in your dreams. Don't you have more important things to think about? Like your biological mother or something? Were you going to call her now that we're back? Dear Father, please let this distract him from Gabriela."

His mother!

Daniel fell silent and looked at Ben with narrowed eyes. "I heard that. And yes, I do need to call her. Or write to her. Although I'm still not sure what Mom and Dad think about it, so I guess I better talk with them." Daniel shrugged off Ben's hands. "Your prayers are answered."

***

Daniel gripped the arms of his chair and stared at the carpet. His dad was on the opposite side of the living room perched on the arm of the couch, nervously glancing out the window. Beside him, his mom stood up and paced around, then plopped back into her seat again. Ben sat on the stairs and leaned against the wall while staring blankly out the front door. Daniel knew they all felt nervous. For weeks this day had been approaching, inching maddeningly nearer at a snail's pace. Finally, it was here, but everyone was on pins and needles. Today, at lunch, his biological mother was to arrive for a visit. She wasn't going to stay the night or anything; his parents wouldn't agree to that, but at least they were okay with her driving over from Idaho. The plan was for them all to spend the day with one another, maybe dinner out somewhere, and then she would spend the night in a hotel and head back the next day.

Mrs. Jones had still been hesitant about the whole thing—that is, until Daniel explained he'd seen his biological mother praying for them all in the Abyss. Daniel suspected it was this that changed her mind. Even with that, and all Ms. Julie's reassurances that an adoption couldn't just be undone, they were nervous: the Joneses, that this would somehow disrupt Daniel's happiness with them as a family, and Daniel, that—he wasn't sure why. That his mother wouldn't like him? That he wouldn't like her? Maybe she'd be disappointed in him somehow? Or he'd find out something about his family that was embarrassing and shameful? He rubbed his temples and blew out another exasperated breath. If only there was a switch to shut off all his thoughts.

"She's here," Ben said. He didn't move from his lookout, but instead, kept peering through the glass front door.

Daniel jumped to his feet and ran to the window. His mother got out of a black car parked on the street, slowly pulled a purse over her shoulder, and walked toward the house. Even from this distance, he could see her hands were shaking and she was trying to calm her breathing. She looked just like she had in the Abyss: blond, brown eyes, petite. Her mouth moved as if in conversation. Probably praying, Daniel figured.

He stepped away from the window and absently wove his way around the furniture in the living room.

A quiet knock.

Daniel shut his eyes and counted to ten in his head. He didn't want to seem too eager and go rushing out the door into her arms, even though that's exactly what his brain was shouting for him to do.

He felt his father's hands on his shoulder and opened his eyes.

"Don't worry. She's going to love you," he said, his voice and touch reassuring to Daniel's nerves.

Mrs. Jones opened the door. "Good morning. I'm Mariah, how are you today?"

Daniel's biological mother stared at Mrs. Jones for a moment, almost in shock, before recovering. "I'm good, thanks. It's nice to finally meet you in person. I'm here to meet with Daniel. But of course, you already know that." An awkward laugh faded into silence. "I'm sorry, I'm just so nervous. I've been dreaming of this day for years."

Mariah reached out and took Leah by the hand. "Of course! We are, too, if we're being honest. Nervous, that is. Come in and let me introduce you to Daniel."

All the blood rushed to Daniel's head. His heart pounded so loudly he could barely hear what was said after that, but he found himself guided forward by his dad's steady hand. The next moment, he was staring into his biological mother's eyes.

"Hello."

His mother stared at him with a mixture of surprise and emotion. Tears ran down her cheeks, but she quickly brushed them off and fidgeted with her hands. "I figured I would cry a bit, but not so quickly. Hi, Daniel. It's nice to finally meet you." She reached out but then hesitated. "Is it okay if I … if I hug you?"

Daniel nodded and was immediately embraced. He worried it would feel uncomfortable and foreign, but those concerns disappeared. Instead, peace flooded his mind and brought a sense of calm as if his mother's touch were some missing puzzle piece in his life.

She seemed to force herself to release him and step back. "Oh, I could hug you for hours, but I'm sure a teenage boy wouldn't want that."

Ben sauntered up. "Please, he'd probably let you cradle him like a baby and rock him if you wanted. Ben Jones. Nice to meet you." He gave a casual wave.

"Young man," Alan warned, but Mariah beat him to the punch.

"Ben!" Her eyes flashed dangerously. "That was so rude. Apologize this instant, or you'll be up to your neck in chores for a year."

Despite how embarrassingly correct he was, Daniel felt that Ben's comment broke the ice. "Well, now you've finally met Ben. He's my annoying little brother. We normally keep him locked up in the attic except on special occasions."

His mother laughed and waved Mariah's concern away. "I'm glad to be one of those occasions. It's nice to meet you, Ben." She took his hand and gave it a hearty shake.

"Sorry," he mumbled with one eye on Mrs. Jones.

Leah winked. "Don't mention it."

Mrs. Jones gestured for them all to sit in the living room. "Would you care for anything to drink?"

"A glass of water would be perfect," Leah said, finding a spot on the couch.

"Ben." Mrs. Jones nodded toward the kitchen. "Do you mind?"

Ben ran to the kitchen and quickly returned with a drink as if worried he would miss something important.

Daniel sat on the opposite end of the couch. His dad and mom found their usual places in armchairs by the fireplace. After handing off the glass of water, Ben plopped down in the loveseat catty-corner to Daniel.

"I know you have lots of questions," Leah began. "And I did bring the life insurance check, by the way. The policy was pretty substantial, it turns out. Your half, Daniel," she reached into her purse and pulled out the thin slip of paper, "is for $500,000. I better go ahead and give that to your dad."

Ben snapped forward on the loveseat. "$500,000! What the ...? Daniel! You're rich!"

Mariah's hand flew to Alan's arm. "Oh, honey!"

"Wait. That's all mine?" Daniel stared at his biological mother, then at his parents. "Like, for a car and video games and whatever I want?"

Mr. Jones stood up to take the check. "Hold on, Daniel. Don't start spending all your money before it's even in the bank. Besides, as your parents, we have to hold it in trust for you until you're legally an adult." He tried to sound calm, but the stunned look on his face told Daniel he was just as shocked. "You'll have money to spend, don't worry. But, this will pay for your college, a car when you're sixteen, retirement ... and you'll probably have enough left over to put back toward a house one day." His voice rose with excitement. "We'll talk about investing it after it's been deposited in the bank."

Daniel stared at his dad. This was unbelievable. A couple years ago, he could only have dreamed of something like this happening.

He had his adoptive parents who provided for and loved him; his biological mother had searched for him and was finally here; his biological father was in heaven but had loved him enough to provide for him after his death.

Father, thank you for this, he prayed, closing his eyes momentarily. *Thank you for showing me that I was loved. That I AM loved.*

A sensation of peace welled up from inside Daniel and spread throughout his body.

He opened his eyes and found his biological mother watching him. "I know you have a lot of questions about your birth, your dad, why it all happened, but," she paused and nervously took a drink, "if you don't mind, I'd like to ask a question first. This is going to sound so weird, I just ... I have to know." She took a deep breath. "A couple days before you all called me, I had a—a vision, I guess. Oh gosh, that sounds so crazy!"

Daniel urged her on.

"I saw you and Ben, and three girls, and a line of people—Alan, Mariah, you were there, too—and this terrible dragon and all these monsters. It was so terrifying, like something out of a horror movie. But it seemed so real. I mean, I saw what you looked like, and now here you all are, looking exactly the same. I almost didn't know what to think! And then I saw you praying just now. I know this must seem crazy."

For a brief moment, Daniel wondered how much he should explain to his mother, but before he could even ask the Father, reassurance flooded his mind.

Tell her everything. She needs to know. There is work she must do.

Daniel looked at his mother and smiled. "It doesn't sound strange at all. In fact, let me—"

"Oh man," Ben chuckled as he leaned forward. "Listen, if crazy is what you're worried about, you've knocked on the right door."

As if on cue, someone banged violently on their front door. Everyone jumped at the noise, but as soon as Daniel turned around, any fright he felt vanished into a feeling of annoyance.

Gator, Barf, and Barth crowded the doorway, peering through the glass into their house.

"Ben, could you grab the door for us, please?" Mrs. Jones asked.

Ben groaned and slowly wove around the living room furniture toward the hulking figures. No sooner had he opened the door than all three Gurges shoved their way past him and inside the house. Gator, amazingly, was wearing a breezy, yellow sundress, and instead of her customary pigtails, her hair, stringy and thin, drizzled down her back in wispy strands. If Daniel didn't know better, he would've guessed someone had actually attempted to style it. She twisted the corners of her mouth up and squinted her eyes. It took Daniel a minute before he realized she was trying to smile. She might have been wearing make-up, but he wasn't sure. Barth, too, was better dressed than normal. A long sleeve white shirt, buttoned up to his chin, saved the world from the assault of his Horror of Hair. Still, for old time's sake, a few fiery bushels bristled out of the collar like flames. Instead of overalls, Barf sported a ridiculously fancy green ballroom gown, complete with sequins and a corsage.

"Sorry to bother you," Gator mumbled, looking everywhere except at Daniel and Ben.

"Speak up," Barf ordered, bumping Gator forward with her enormous gut.

"Sorry to bother you!" Gator repeated, now shouting. "I brought my popcorn form back for you to look at! I hope this is a good time!"

"That's better," Barf said proudly. She beamed around the room. "Trying to teach my niece here that when you go around drumming up business, you put your best foot forward. You dress like a lady—*burp.*" She stifled a belch. "You show people you're depengable. Depenstaple? Depent … ible?"

"Dependable?" Ben asked hopefully.

"Dependable!" Barf thundered. "Well, aren't you a cutie pie?"

Ben withered under her gaze and backed toward his parents. "Please don't eat me," he murmured under his breath.

"Gator, how come you never told me such handsome men lived in your neighborhood. Quick, put on some more lipstick." She grabbed Gator by the arm and spun her around. From somewhere under her dress strap, Barf whipped out a tube of lipstick and hastily smeared a fresh coat onto Gator's begrudgingly puckered lips. "There, that's better. Now, show them the form and don't take no for an answer."

Alan and Mariah stared on in silent disbelief, clearly uncertain how to handle the intruders.

Gator slowly turned, and Daniel had to bite his lip to keep from laughing. Barf's lipstick application was more than generous. Ben found his seat, muttering something about clown college.

Daniel's biological mother watched the scene unfold with her mouth slightly agape.

Daniel was about to crack a joke, but immediately choked back his comment when he felt a strong check in his spirit. The Three's eyes were on him. He wasn't sure what he was supposed to say, if anything. But he knew kindness and compassion were at least expected. He put a hand on his mother's arm.

"This is Gator Gurge, she's a friend." He looked up at the Gurge clan. "I promise my dad and I, and maybe Ben, will come down to your house tomorrow and order some popcorn."

"What the …?" Ben sputtered. "Do you see how the Barf is looking at me?" he added in a hasty whisper.

Daniel waved him into silence. "*Definitely* Ben."

"There, you see?" Barf rattled the house with her booming voice. "A little business-know-how is all you need. Now, march! We've got more houses to invade!" Barf revolved her substantial girth around and used it to push Gator and Barth out the front door and down the steps. "See you tomor—*BELCH!*—row."

Daniel's mother quietly stared at the doorway, her eyes still wide.

Daniel leaned over and touched her arm. "That's probably as good a place to start as any."

"I'll say," Ben said. "The weirdness will prepare you for the rest of the story."

Daniel continued. "A couple years ago, Barth and Gator showed up at the Holy Moses Home for Bleeding Heart Orphans. And adopted me."

"Oh, Daniel!" his mother said, "I'm so sorry!"

"Just wait," he said, giving her hand a reassuring pat. "It gets better."

~ The End ~

www.ingramcontent.com/pod-product-compliance
Lightning Source LLC
Chambersburg PA
CBHW071508110726
47908CB00003B/766